THE
MARKED
a TALENTS *Novel*

THE
MARKED

a **TALENTS** *Novel*

Inara Scott

HYPERION
NEW YORK

First Edition

1 3 5 7 9 10 8 6 4 2

This book is set in Miller Text.

Printed in the United States of America
G475-5664-5-12055

Library of Congress Cataloging-in-Publication Data
Scott, Inara.
The Marked: A Talents novel / Inara Scott.
p. cm. — (Delcroix Academy; bk. 2)
Summary: In her second semester at a boarding school
for teenagers with special powers, Dancia Lewis faces danger
from both inside and outside of Delcroix Academy.
ISBN-13: 978-1-4231-1637-0
ISBN-10: 1-4231-1637-2
[1. Psychic ability—Fiction. 2. Boarding schools—Fiction.
3. Schools—Fiction.] I. Title.
PZ7.S4257Mar 2011
[Fic]—dc22
2010036293

Reinforced binding
Visit www.hyperionteens.com

For Maia

I couldn't ask for a better cheerleader,
friend, lawyer, agent, or sister.
Thank you.

CHAPTER 1

"THE WORLD around us is fraught with danger." Mr. Judan, Chief Recruiter for Delcroix Academy, gestured broadly as he spoke. His voice, low and sonorous, slid through the cold night air. "Scientists can alter and manipulate the DNA that makes us human. Medical technology can be used to develop lifesaving vaccines—or horrifying biological weapons. Our very earth is threatened by years of abuse and neglect. Civilization stands at the edge of chaos, but the students of the Delcroix Academy Program have the potential to lead it back to peace and security."

A breeze rustled the branches of the trees overhead and shook loose a few scattered raindrops. I wiped a trickle of water from my forehead. Eight candidates, including me, stood in a line at Mr. Judan's left, each of us wearing shiny white robes over our dresses and suits. The rest of the Program students and teachers watched from wooden benches that formed a rough semicircle around me and the other candidates. Though we were barely five minutes from the Delcroix campus, the secluded clearing felt miles away. Huge torches flared into the sky, sputtering and hissing as the rain fell on them.

"Graduates of the Program work in laboratories and hospitals, teach at the world's greatest universities, and serve at the highest levels of government. Their exceptional talents are used to resolve military conflicts and develop cures for devastating diseases. Their physical powers can be used in developing nations to build life-giving infrastructure, and in police forces to track down dangerous criminals. Everywhere, they labor in secrecy, quietly using their gifts to protect, defend, and serve.

"As candidates, you have the potential to join this force of operatives. You can change lives with your gifts of communication, your physical prowess, and your incredible interactions with the natural world. But before you can do any of these things, you must be trained." Mr. Judan swept around to face us and fixed us with a steely eye. "Candidates, you stand before us after being tested and watched by your peers. Each of you has been nominated for Initiation. Step forward and offer yourselves to the Program."

By some great gift of alphabetical fate, I was required to go first. I dragged one foot in front of the other, trying not to shudder as thirty pairs of eyes were trained directly on me. "Dancia Lewis presents herself for acceptance into the Program, sir."

Mr. Judan turned back to the crowd. "Who will stand for this candidate?"

"I will stand for her." Cam rose from one of the benches and stepped forward, a candle flickering in his hand. He wore the green robe of the Life Talents. Though it was too dark to make him out clearly, I imagined his deep brown eyes staring confidently at Mr. Judan. Next to him on the bench was Trevor Anderly, Cam's best friend, wearing the red robe that symbolized the Somatic Talents. Anna Peterson sat on his other side, also clad in red. With her dark hair and creamy skin, Cam's ex-girlfriend looked way too much like Snow White for my liking.

"Cameron Sanders, how do you know this candidate?" Mr. Judan stood in the center of the mock stage.

"I was her Recruiter and Watcher," Cam said, staring at me while directing his words to Mr. Judan.

Candidates for the Program were recruited for Delcroix based on their potential Level Three Talents. During their freshman year, they were expected to prove that they had both the talent and the—I don't know, the *goodness*, I suppose, to be worthy of joining the Program. If they did, they were nominated for entry into the Program, usually by their Watcher. Nominations were made in the fall of sophomore year, and if the nominations were accepted by the school board, students were told the truth about the Program and prepared for Initiation.

Cam had been my Watcher, but he had short-circuited the usual process when he told me about the Program back in November. That meant I was the only freshman among the candidates. Just another addition to the long list of ways I didn't quite fit in.

"And do you believe this candidate will have the courage and integrity to do what is right? To sacrifice her own needs for the needs of others?"

Cam nodded. "I believe this candidate will do all these things. I believe this candidate will be an honor to the Governing Council and to Delcroix Academy."

I knew this was the ritual response given for every candidate. Still, when Cam said it about me, it felt different. Goose bumps sprang up along my spine, as the weight of the Initiation suddenly came crashing down on me.

I was committing myself to the Program. My throat squeezed closed. There was no going back now.

I walked the ten steps to Mr. Judan's side. The fire reflected off his black hair with its snowy white wings at the temples, and he smiled his movie-star smile.

"Dancia, once you join the Program, you will forever be part of an organization dedicated to the promotion of peace and stability throughout the world. You will be carefully trained to maximize the potential of your talent, and you will be expected to serve humanity with your great power." He lowered his voice dramatically. "Are you ready to offer yourself to the Program?"

I stole a glance at Cam, because looking at Mr. Judan made my knees feel as if they were about to buckle. Cam nodded encouragingly—a tiny, almost imperceptible movement. He knew I was nervous. Mine wasn't the usual Initiation.

The problem was, I knew more about the Program than any candidate should. The sophomores standing next to me had been taught that the Program was about spreading peace and happiness. Sure, they knew there were bad guys out there—serial killers, kidnappers, bank robbers, all the usual suspects—and they knew that part of the Program's purpose was to fight those bad guys and protect the innocents who might get hurt along the way. But the candidates were also told that graduates of the Program could serve humanity through medicine, art, or even politics. The new students knew about Watchers—the student kind and the professional ones—but they had never seen them in action.

I had. I had watched those professional Watchers come after a friend of mine with guns drawn, and only my talent had saved him.

I understood why Mr. Judan didn't spend a lot of time talking about that side of things. It wasn't like you *had* to be a Watcher if you joined the Program, or even that the Watchers were the most important part of the Program. The Governing Council, which ran the Program, did a whole lot more than oversee the Watchers.

Still, the fact was that I knew about the dark side of the Program, and the rest of the candidates didn't. I told myself I understood why the Watchers went after Jack. They were just doing their jobs. They thought he was a threat. They thought he could hurt people. They didn't care about him or understand him the way I did. But that didn't stop the taste of bile from rising in my throat every time I pictured Jack's face—scared, hunted—as he jumped over my fence and disappeared.

Cam nodded again, more noticeably this time, and his eyes flicked from me to Mr. Judan. I straightened. After Jack ran away, Mr. Judan talked me through all of this. He explained how the Watchers were peacekeepers, and how worried they were that Jack might use the books he had stolen from the Program library to make himself an even bigger threat than he already was. Jack had made choices, Mr. Judan said, and those choices were what had sent him over the fence. Not the Watchers.

"I am ready," I said.

Really? a little voice in my head asked mockingly. *Are you sure about that?*

Mr. Judan frowned, as if he could hear the voice. I silenced it quickly, just in case he really could read my mind. Cam said he was a persuader, not a mind reader, but with the people at Delcroix, you never knew.

5

"Then let us begin the Initiation. Dancia, you have been given a great talent, the talent to manipulate the forces of nature. You can alter gravity with the mere force of your will. Already a strong Level Three, you have the potential to someday move mountains. Do you pledge to use this talent to benefit others?"

I ignored the bit about moving mountains—I assumed that that was an exaggeration—and focused instead on the pledge. They'd given us the pledges weeks ago, before Christmas, and we had been told to study them carefully and be ready to commit ourselves to them without reservation. The first was the easiest. The one thing I'd wanted all my life was to use my talent to help other people. In the past I'd been too scared to try. I had thought the power was out of my control, and that if I used it, people would get hurt. But now I knew I could control it and harness it for good. The Program would teach me how.

"I do."

"As a member of the Program, you will be a part of something larger and more important than any single person. Do you pledge to sacrifice your selfish desires and dedicate yourself to achieving the goals of the Program?"

This was much harder, because while I agreed with the goals of the Program, every time I got a little distance from Delcroix, doubts kept popping up. Like, if the Watchers were so powerful, why had they been scared of Jack? Why hadn't they helped him when he was a little kid getting beaten up by his dad? Why were they ready to kill him, just because they thought someday he *might* be a threat? Most chilling of all, how many people like Jack had they killed along the way?

I couldn't say any of this to Cam. He was intimately involved in the Program, perhaps more so than any other student at Delcroix, and I knew he believed in the Program one hundred percent. In part, it was his conviction that spurred me on.

I struggled in vain to force the words from my mouth. In desperation, I dropped my eyes toward Cam, and this time he smiled at me. Just like that, the answer came, without any thought on my part.

"I do."

"And finally, Dancia, as a member of the Program, you will be a part of a family, a team dedicated to protecting its own. Do you pledge yourself in support of your new family?"

My shoulders relaxed. This was easy. Though I didn't particularly like the idea of being Anna's sister—after all, she was Cam's ex-girlfriend, and I had the impression she was ready to step back into that role at a moment's notice—I *did* like the idea of having a family. I'd always been jealous of kids who had cousins and aunts and uncles to hang out with at holidays and school breaks. My parents died in a car crash when I was three. I had a few relatives on my dad's side, but they didn't think much of me. The only one I really had was Grandma.

Even if the Program wouldn't have been like a real family, I knew from my friendship with Jack the previous semester that the bonds I had formed with people who were like me could run deeper and stronger than anything I'd ever imagined. It was something about having a shared secret, or knowing you were different from everyone else around you. That, more than anything, kept me going when the doubts sprang up.

"I do."

"Earth Talents, rise," Mr. Judan intoned.

Only two members of the crowd rose. I saw Mr. Anderson,

the gardener at Delcroix, and a guy named Barrett, who I guessed was a senior.

Gesturing grandly, Mr. Judan said, "Earth Talents, you have the power to see and understand the forces of nature. You have the extraordinary ability to manipulate the very ground on which we walk, the air we breathe, and the relationship between energy and matter. Those who share your gifts are few and far between. They must be carefully instructed and their gifts nurtured. Do you pledge to welcome this new member to your group? To help her grow in wisdom and in power?"

Barrett stepped forward. He was tall and lanky, with long black hair that he wore loose around his shoulders. Shadows wreathed his face and obscured his eyes, but I could see that he had heavy brows and a beaky nose. He pointed toward the torch at Mr. Judan's left and then to the one on his right. "The Earth Talents receive you into the Program, Dancia, and pledge our assistance and energy to help you in whatever way you may need."

Then he turned his palms to face up, and the flames of the torch shot high into the air—geysers of fire that illuminated the entire circle and the trees around us in a bright yellow glow. All of the candidates gasped, and Barrett nodded in satisfaction.

I froze, my heart racing. We stood there for a moment, watching the fire gushing into the sky, until Mr. Judan nodded and Barrett sat down. I stared at Barrett, awed and humbled. Sure, I could make sinkholes and drop branches on people. But creating flamethrowers? That was totally out of my league.

Then Mr. Judan leaned forward and unhooked the cloak from my neck. "Dancia Lewis, you have pledged yourself in service and selflessness. The Earth Talents have welcomed you, and your sponsor, Cameron Sanders, has stood in testament to his faith in your abilities. This is a height few achieve, and you should be proud to have come so far."

With a dramatic swirl, he turned my cloak inside out and draped it back around my shoulders, the brown fabric marking my Earth Talent now exposed to the air. The white satin was cool and damp, and a chill stole across my shoulders.

Mr. Judan smiled widely. "The Initiation is complete. Welcome to the Program, Dancia."

CHAPTER 2

CAM AND Mr. Fritz cheered. Mr. Fritz had been my ethics teacher last semester, and even though he was prone to playing head games with his classes, I had the feeling he was someone I could trust. Besides, I loved the little puff of white hair on top of his head, and the absentminded way he'd mumble and pace around his classroom, as if he'd forgotten the class was there. The rest of the crowd clapped politely, but not necessarily enthusiastically. Anna picked at her fingernails. Trevor frowned. Then again, Trevor always frowned.

The ceremony continued. We heard all the candidates' talents, and then Mr. Judan would ask someone from their talent group to welcome them. Life Talents, the ones with the green cloaks, were the communicators. They could talk to animals, read minds, or see into the future. The first Life Talent was welcomed into the Program by a junior who called an owl to his arm. It was a beautiful creature with pointy, tufted ears and bright yellow eyes. After landing briefly, the owl hooted, then rose back into the air, the beating of its wings the only sound in the clearing.

Somatic Talents had extraordinary physical powers. The first Somatic Talent was welcomed by a senior who disappeared and then reappeared next to the candidates, with a flourish and a bow.

There were eight candidates in all, and after the Initiations were complete, Mr. Judan launched into another speech about the Program and the ways we could use our talents. Within a few minutes his voice faded to a dull monotone. If you ask me, speeches are always dull, even if they *are* delivered by people with super powers.

In a matter of minutes my mind drifted to Cam, and I lost track of any concerns I might have had about the Watchers, or Jack, or anything else about the Program. Because tonight was the night. After all these weeks of waiting, Cam and I would finally be together.

We'd been in a weird sort of limbo ever since that crazy, fateful weekend when I'd used my powers to help Jack escape the Watchers after he'd stolen two books from the Program library. Jack's theft (*was* it theft, though?—after all, he'd only taken the books to give them to me) had set in motion a cascade of events that started with my asking Cam what was really happening at Delcroix, and ended with Cam kissing me.

This all sounded good, but unfortunately, things didn't go quite so smoothly for us after that. The problem was, until I entered the Program, Cam was technically my Watcher, and according to him, you can't date and watch at the same time. But after tonight, I was no longer a candidate.

We could finally pick up where we'd left off.

Mr. Judan ended the ceremony by reciting some ancient poem about sacrifice and selflessness. We, the former candidates, our shiny cloaks reflecting the torchlight in a soft palette of browns, reds, and greens, filed out first. We walked in the dark, with nothing more than trickles of moonlight through the trees to guide us. I looked around for Cam, but saw that Mr. Judan had pulled him aside to talk, so I walked by myself.

We were halfway back to the school when a red-robed figure stepped from the rear of the line and headed in my direction.

"Congratulations, Dancia. Welcome to the Program."

I winced at the sound of the voice. Hastily, I arranged my face in a polite smile. "Thanks, Trevor."

Despite the fact that he's Cam's best friend, Trevor has always made me nervous. For one, he's got these intense blue eyes that look right through you—literally, I discovered, because Trevor's Level Three Talent is superhuman sight. He can see people on the other sides of walls, or a gun hidden behind a closed door. Add a military-style crew cut and a perpetually grim expression, and you've got one tough-looking character.

Trevor and I didn't talk much.

We fell into step together. The path narrowed, and I slipped on a mixture of mud and fallen pine needles. Trevor grabbed my arm, catching me just before I fell. "Be careful. You could hurt yourself."

"Sorry. My shoes are slippery." I wondered whether I should try to extract my arm from his grip, but the truth was that my fake patent-leather Mary Janes had no traction, and I appreciated the support.

We walked together for a few minutes. It was clear that he had something to say, and the longer he remained quiet, the more nervous I got.

"So . . . what's on your mind?" I asked. "You here to teach me the secret handshake? I kept waiting for it during Initiation."

It was a weak attempt to make him smile. "No," he said. "No handshake. I just wanted to tell you that I'm sorry. This must be pretty overwhelming."

Trevor hadn't liked the fact that Cam told me about the Program early. Knowing it existed put me in danger, and I had the feeling that Trevor considered protecting me to be one of his duties. He'd said as much when he found me and Cam in the Program library back in November.

I stepped around a particularly large puddle. "There's nothing to be sorry about. I'm excited. I can't wait to start training."

"Of course you are. But you need to understand that things are different now that you're in the Program. You'll be held to a different standard."

"What do you mean?" I asked uneasily.

"Strange things tend to happen when you're around. Like your friend Jack disappearing right after a convenient 'natural disaster' that happened on your street. Guns flying out of people's hands. Tires exploding. Telephone poles falling. You'll have to learn control, Dancia. I just want to make sure you understand that."

I didn't know how to respond. Cam and I had tacitly decided not to discuss with anyone else the damage I'd done on my block. Of course, everyone could see it. It was hard to miss a thirty-foot hole in the street and a bunch of telephone poles ripped out of the ground. But Cam was the only one at Delcroix who could sense when someone was using their talent, and he'd told them the only talent he felt at the site was Jack's. He didn't like lying, but we both knew Jack wouldn't be around now if we hadn't helped him escape.

"You think I was responsible for that sinkhole?" I forced a laugh. "Wow. That would be pretty amazing."

Trevor held back a branch for me to walk past. "I think you're a good kid, Dancia. But the Program puts enormous pressure on people. Especially someone with your talent. This happened too fast."

My face began to burn. "What are you trying to say? That I'm not worthy of being in the Program?"

Trevor turned halfway around, his body sideways in the path. The moon was behind him, and a frosty glow encircled his head. "I'm not saying that," he whispered, looking up and down the line. "I'm just saying I wish things had been different."

The back of my throat stung. He had that same stern look he'd had during Initiation, but up close I could see that there was more. His forehead was wrinkled, and I realized that he was worried. Worried about me. Or maybe about the other people in the Program.

The thought made me sick. "You can't turn back time, Trevor. They made their decision. I start Program classes on Monday."

He jerked his head toward the line and dropped his voice lower. Some of Cam's friends—Anna, Molly, and David— were heading toward us. "This isn't a *game*, Dancia. You'll be training and doing exercises with your talent. You lose control and people could get hurt. You crash a car and people could die."

I took a deep breath. This shouldn't have been a surprise. Trevor and Anna had been whispering behind their hands and rolling their eyes in my direction ever since Thanksgiving. Even Cam had stopped trying to fight it. After a series of uncomfortable lunches, I'd come up with excuses not to eat with Cam and his buddies, and he didn't make much of an effort to convince me otherwise. We spent most of our time together at the Residence Hall after classes, or working out in the weight room and running along the trail around the school.

Now I knew why. Trevor and Anna thought I was some kind of time bomb.

"You can think whatever you want, Trevor," I said. "The fact is that Cam told me about the Program and Mr. Judan decided I should be initiated. I'm on your team now, whether you like it or not."

He shook his head. "You're taking this all wrong, Dancia. I just want you to know I'll be keeping an eye out for you."

It took a moment for the words to register, but when they did, my whole body tightened. He was placing me under surveillance again.

"Thanks, but I think I'll be fine on my own."

"But you're not on your own anymore," Trevor said softly. "You're one of us now. Forever."

With that chilling pronouncement ringing in my ears, I spun around, chin high. I'd like to say that I began a controlled march in the other direction, but it was more of an awkward trot. Naturally, within a few strides I hit another patch of mud and skidded unsteadily on one heel, my arms flailing.

"Whoa!" I started to go down, but was caught around the waist by two strong hands. "Trevor, let me g—" I cried, and began to struggle, but when I craned my neck around, instead of grim, icy blue eyes, I saw a pair of reassuring brown ones and that square chin that I always wanted to touch.

"Hey, Dancia, it's me, Cam."

Before I could think about what I was doing, I turned and flung myself straight into his arms.

I imagine he was pretty surprised, but he just pulled me tightly against him.

"What's going on?" he said. "Are you okay?"

What was going on? Trevor thought I was a loose cannon who shouldn't have been let into the Program, and now all I could think about was who I might inadvertently kill on my first day. Mr. Fritz? Cam? What if Trevor was right? I'd certainly done plenty of damage before I came to Delcroix. I'd put three people in the hospital before the age of ten. I put a guy in a coma last summer. I hated to think what I could do once they gave me a little training.

I buried my face in Cam's shoulder. "It's nothing. Nerves, I guess."

He held me away from him to look at me, but in the patchy light of the moon and the scattered flashlights held by the teachers, I doubt he could see much. Thank goodness. The last thing I wanted was for him to see me crying.

Trevor seemed to have disappeared, for which I gave fervent thanks.

"I know it can be intimidating at first," Cam said. "I walked away from Initiation wondering what the heck I was doing there. I can't disappear or see through walls, let alone do the things you can do. But things changed once I got to know everyone."

He put his arm around me, and we started walking again. A quiver passed through me. I let the feeling crowd out the despair of the moment before. My fingers closed around his, and I savored the warmth of his skin against mine.

"What set this off?" he asked. "Was it just the ceremony?"

I couldn't mention Trevor. All he'd said was that he was looking out for me, and that they were all on my side. Hardly a threat.

"I'm just . . . different," I said.

"What do you mean?"

"You know, being a freshman. Using my talent the way I do . . ."

"You *are* going to fit in, Dancia." Cam squeezed my hand gently. "It's too bad the rest of the school comes back tomorrow morning. It would have been good for you to spend some time with the rest of people in the Program. But you know they can't do that. Initiation's one of the only times we all get to be together."

"It would be nice to know everyone's names, at least," I said.

"In a week or two, Anna's mom is having a Welcome Back party for the Program students. You'll get to know everyone then."

My head snapped back. "Anna's mom knows about the Program? I thought we couldn't tell anyone."

I didn't mean to sound accusing, but it was incredibly hard for me not to tell Grandma the truth about Delcroix. I hid my talent from her because I didn't want her to worry about me, but over the years, that had completely backfired, and she had ended up blaming herself for my lack of friends and for the fact that I didn't fit in at school. If I could have told her about Delcroix she might have felt better. At the very least, she'd finally have understood what had been going on all those years.

"That's true. People who know about the Program are always at risk. But Anna's parents were in the Program, too."

I hadn't thought about parents with Level Three Talents having a kid with Level Three Talents. Delcroix seemed like the sort of secret that parents shouldn't know about. Maybe because parents were always dead in fairy tales, and Delcroix

17

still seemed very much like a fairy tale.

"So, party at Anna's house." I tried to muster up some degree of enthusiasm. "Super."

"Hey, don't get too excited." Cam laughed as he pulled me even closer. "You know, they're awfully strict at school about keeping couples apart. The party's our chance to have some time alone."

I'm not sure how I would have responded, because that was when we heard the explosion, and everyone ducked for cover.

CHAPTER 3

IT WAS an earsplitting boom, like the biggest firecracker on the Fourth of July. I had no idea whether bombs sounded like that or not, but it was loud enough that everyone, including Cam, instinctively dropped their heads and covered them with their hands. Most of us stayed that way until all that was left was an echo, then an uncanny stillness.

Cam straightened up a moment later and looked toward the Main Hall.

I heard a voice over my shoulder: Mr. Judan's deep, distinctive voice, laced with anger. "Let's go."

Cam and Mr. Judan started off at a dead run. Most of the other juniors did too, along with the teachers. A few of them must have had Level Three Talents for speed, or maybe invisibility, because one minute they were there, and the next, they were gone. They didn't say much, just grunted at each other, split into groups, and disappeared. Anna whipped off her shoes and started sprinting just behind Cam.

I tried not to panic, but that was hard when everyone was running away like we were under attack. Was this what Cam meant when he said people who knew about the Program were always at risk?

Jack had made fun of me for believing that the gates and locks and security systems at Delcroix were there to keep us safe. He had said they were there so the school could spy on us. But now it looked as if he had been wrong. Someone *was* trying to get into Delcroix. And tonight they'd succeeded.

Mrs. Callias, Hennie's French teacher and a sort of assistant to Mr. Judan, barked, "Stay here, all of you. Let the rest of them go ahead."

The sophomores and some seniors milled around anxiously. Most of the girls were wearing fancy shoes and dresses, and running didn't appear to be an option for them. The sophomore guys seemed unsure if they should listen to Mrs. Callias or run back to school with the others. A few of them started hesitantly in that direction.

"We don't know what's going on over there. It's not safe." Mrs. Callias glared at the boys lurking around the edges of the circle. "This isn't a request."

I waited until she was occupied in arguing with one of the other sophomores, then bolted through the woods. I mean, come on. It wasn't as if I were the kind of person who could stand around and hide while there was a fight going on. Besides, Anna was over there. And Cam. Whatever they could do, I could do too.

My shoes didn't have much traction, but they didn't have heels, either, and I figured running in them was preferable to being barefoot in the dark. So I kept them on, moving cautiously, with a short stride that wouldn't have gotten me far in a cross-country race but at least would keep me from ending up on my butt.

I passed through the woods to the wet, slippery grass of the playing fields. From there I could see the others, distant figures on the horizon, running ahead of me and widening their lead. I tried to pick up my pace and catch up, but they were too far ahead.

By the time I made it back to the school, most of the students, including Cam, Trevor, and Anna, had disappeared. Mr. Judan stood in front of the imposing marble entrance to the Main Hall, arms crossed over his chest.

Lights from the building blazed through the tall windows, illuminating the red brick structure and shining on the wet grass around it. I could see students from the Program searching the classrooms inside. Mr. Fritz paced up and down the front lawn, running his fingers through his wiry hair and mumbling to himself while other students quietly consulted with their teachers.

I found the scene strangely comforting. No evidence of the explosion could be seen, not even wisps of smoke or debris on the ground. There were no masked gunmen on the roof. No Uzis or rifles were trained on us from helicopters in the sky. We were just a bunch of kids and teachers standing around in funny robes.

I breathed deeply in an attempt to recover from my awkward sprint and approached the only person who didn't seem to have something to do.

"Excuse me, Mr. Fritz?"

"What's that?" He spun around, startled, and then gave me a quick smile. "Oh, Dancia. Congratulations, dear. We're thrilled to welcome you to the Program, you know. Absolutely thrilled."

"Thanks." I motioned toward the Main Hall. "Do they know what happened? Was it a bomb?"

"Good heavens, no, it wasn't a bomb. Well, we're not sure precisely what it was. Some large fireworks, or a small explosive, perhaps."

I paused. "A small explosive? Isn't that the same thing as a bomb?"

Mr. Fritz scratched his head. "You know, I hadn't thought about it. I don't believe I know what the precise definition of a bomb is. But in any case, there wasn't much damage. Just a few windows in the Main Hall blown out by the noise. It was probably just a prank."

"A prank?" I laced my fingers together nervously. "In the Main Hall?"

"They had to come in that way to disable the security cameras," he said. "We don't think anything was taken. The students are checking now to be sure." He squinted at the building thoughtfully. "Rather remarkable that they made it past the gates, but not impossible, of course. We were all at Initiation. It is the most unguarded night of the year. We've got a top-notch security system, but there's ways around those things. Any scientist worth her salt knows that every system has flaws."

"But how could they get past the gates without being seen?" I asked.

"I suspect they came over the wall by the hidden drive-way. We keep that area dark so we can use the garage at night without arousing suspicion. But that does make it more diffi-cult to monitor."

I digested this information slowly. With all the talk of shape-shifting and mind reading, let alone watching people speak to owls and shoot fire thirty feet in the air, I'd had it in my head that we were in some kind of magic bubble here at Delcroix. I hadn't thought they had spells on the place, exactly, but when you start dealing with the ability to manip-ulate the forces of gravity, or see through walls, the line between Level Three Talents and magic didn't seem all that clear. It simply hadn't occurred to me that we didn't have perfect security.

That Delcroix was vulnerable.

"Do we have any idea who did it?"

"Hard to say. It was well orchestrated and had to have been someone who knew the school well, knew the schedule, knew where to get in. . . ." There was a pause as Mr. Fritz seemed to muse over what he had said. Then he adjusted his collar nervously. "Never mind all that. Could have been anyone. Perhaps some local troublemakers."

I tensed. Mr. Fritz knew more than he was saying. "Local troublemakers? Who knew the schedule and where to get in? Who were *well orchestrated*? I'm sorry Mr. Fritz," I said, trying to sound amused, "but that doesn't describe anyone in Danville."

As if on cue, Mr. Judan appeared behind Mr. Fritz, staring down at us in all of his blue-eyed dapperness. His purple cloak had been flung back over his shoulders, and he wore a tailored black suit beneath it. I have no idea how he had managed to run so fast in his perfect black loafers yet somehow not let a single drop of mud spatter the tops of his shoes or the hems of his pants.

He was just that way. I bet mud was scared to land on him.

"You're right, Dancia," he said. "The signs actually point to a gang we've dealt with before. Not from Danville, but Seattle. That's all we know."

A thousand questions died on my tongue when I saw the reproving look in his eyes. If anything, that only piqued my interest more.

Cam ran around from the back of the Main Hall, his cloak back on his shoulders, his hair tousled. He was coming from the Res.

"All clear," he said smartly to Mr. Judan. "No sign of entry in or around the Residence Hall. David is with Pete. There is no need to contact outside authorities."

Pete was a guard at Delcroix. Probably a Watcher. David was one of the other juniors. I wasn't sure what his talent was, but figured it had something to do with communication. Mr. Fritz breathed a sigh of relief. Cam glanced in my direction, and our eyes met for one brief second. Crazy as it was amid all the chaos, my cheeks grew warm, and I had to turn away.

"Well done," Mr. Judan said. "We've got the Main Hall secured, and the Bly, too. Whoever did this is long gone."

I hadn't considered the possibility that they'd try to break in to the Bly. That was where the teachers had their rooms, and the students treated it as sacrosanct. No one even dared walk onto the porch.

"I'd like to search the perimeter now, to see if I can determine the point of entry," Cam said. "I'll lose the marks if I wait much longer."

Cam's talent was sensing when someone had used a Level Three Talent. He could feel it when it happened, but more than that, he could actually see it if he was close enough. Generally, he could tell only how many people had used their talents in an area, not who they were. But there *were* a few marks he knew by sight. He knew mine because he'd been my Recruiter. He'd been watching my mark for years trying to figure out who in Danville was using a Level Three Talent.

He knew Jack's because he'd recruited Jack as well.

Then it hit me, and the warm feeling disappeared in an instant. They thought Jack had done this. They were checking for Jack's mark.

CHAPTER 4

I NEVER did see Cam again that night, but I didn't expect to. Mrs. Callias told us to go to bed and not to leave the Res until breakfast. They canceled the little party we were supposed to have after Initiation. Instead of having us get to know our teachers and learn more about the Program, Mrs. Callias gave us our Program class schedules and told us to save any questions for later.

I walked back to my room and lay on top of my blanket for hours, unable to sleep. Every time I started to relax, my mind would replay the events of the evening like a movie being fast-forwarded. First, Mr. Judan would smile down at me, then I'd make my pledges, and flames would shoot into the air. Faster then, Trevor would grab my arm, Cam would hold me tight, and we'd hear the explosion. Finally, I'd be running through the wet grass to get that first view of the Main Hall, lights blazing.

Everything was different now. I had joined the Program, Delcroix had been attacked, and I would have bet money they were hiding the truth about who did it. Not to mention my fear that Jack had been involved. I had always assumed he was long gone. There were too many people here who wanted him dead—or at least watched, for the rest of his life. It was hard to imagine that he'd have been crazy enough to come back.

I got up early and took a long, slow shower—a luxury I rarely had at school. When I got back to my room, I threw my dirty T-shirt and pajama bottoms onto Catherine's side of the closet. Another luxury. This made me happy enough to forget temporarily how freaked out I was by everything that had happened.

I put on my baggiest jeans and the ribbed red sweater Grandma had gotten me for Christmas. There was nothing to be done about my hair, but with the memory of Esther's voice in the back of my mind urging me to embrace my "natural beauty," I left it loose around my shoulders. It was still hard to get used to trying to look good—I'd been doing my best to stay inconspicuous for so long that nothing about it came naturally.

I turned to head down to breakfast and then jumped. A silent, frozen figure stood in the doorway.

Catherine was back.

Her hair was pulled back in a high ponytail, and her eyes had dark circles under them. She must have lost weight over the break, because her cheekbones stood out even more prominently than I recalled. She wore her usual white button-down shirt and navy pants, and held a suitcase behind her.

"Your clothes are on my side," she snapped, stomping into the room.

"Catherine," I exclaimed. "What a lovely surprise!"

"The first bus left the parking lot at seven."

I knew they were running the Silver Bullet every hour over the weekend, but I hadn't expected to see anyone before breakfast. "And you were on it." I tried for a friendly tone, even though we hated each other. "Did you have a nice break?

Get lots of lovely presents for Christmas?"

"I was trapped in a house listening to my parents fight," she said, dropping her suitcase beside her bed. She made a point of kicking my pajamas across the room. "They gave me a bunch of gift cards and told me to buy something new to wear, so I didn't look like a fifteen-year-old nun. So, yeah, it was fantastic."

This was an unprecedented amount of information about Catherine's life. In our four months of rooming together, I had not avoided hearing a few personal tidbits, which centered primarily around money, town cars, and drivers. But Catherine had never *shared* with me, and she never criticized her parents. She seemed to take their lack of interest in her as a point of pride.

I grabbed my clothes up from the floor. I had no idea what to say to Catherine when she wasn't insulting me or trying to make my life miserable. "I guess it's good to be here, then?" I offered.

"Right." She turned to unlock her suitcase, carefully shielding the lock so I couldn't see her combination, and then began to unpack her clothes. They emerged from her bag perfectly folded. There were four white shirts still in plastic bags and two pairs of navy pants that had tags dangling off the sides. This was astonishing to me. I had assumed Catherine dressed in a uniform because she had a lot of button-downs from her last school and didn't want to bother buying new clothes. It hadn't occurred to me that she might prefer to dress this way.

I'd have given anything for the chance to buy new clothes. Grandma and I barely had money to pay the electric bill, so everything I wore came either from the secondhand store or Walmart.

"How'd you get here before me, anyway?" Catherine asked. "I thought they didn't let anyone come back last night."

I shifted uneasily. This was the question I had hoped no one would ask. They tried to disguise our participation in the Program by holding events like Initiation when the other students weren't around. But it fell to us to come up with excuses to explain why we'd been at school. I had thought that because they ran the Silver Bullet at various times on this day, no one would notice when I arrived at school. I should have known that Catherine would notice—and be offended that I had gotten back to the room before she did.

I gave her the story I'd practiced. "They asked a group of us to come back early for some extra classwork. I guess it was for people who are having trouble."

"Grades didn't turn out like you expected?" she asked nastily.

I nodded. Actually, I'd been pretty happy with my B's. But my response seemed to satisfy Catherine. I sent up a silent prayer to Meredith and Virginia, and all the other sophomores, asking them to forgive me for painting them as failures, too.

Before she could quiz me further, there was a knock at the door, and Esther and Hennie walked in together. A few paces from my bed, Hennie tripped over her own foot and tumbled on top of me with a giggle. Laughing, Esther dived onto the bed too, her cloud of hair surrounding us like a black fog.

"What are you two doing here so early?" I said, as I squirmed my way out of the crush of bodies. "I didn't expect to see you until the afternoon."

Esther sat up next to me. "Hennie stayed with me for the last couple of days. We figured you'd be here early, so we got on the first bus. Besides, my parents couldn't wait to get rid of us. I called you last night to work out the details, but you didn't answer your phone."

"I know, I'm sorry. My battery died." I changed the subject as fast as I could. Luckily, they both started talking at the same time about how they had tried to make cookies to bring to school but burned them because they were also messing around on the Internet, and how they talked all night long until Esther's mom came into their room at two in the morning and told them they were leaving at five to catch the bus and that they'd better be ready or she'd leave them in the parking lot, even if it was raining.

Catherine made a sound of disgust and stomped out of the room.

I grinned. "Thanks for arriving right in the nick of time. She's even grumpier than usual."

Hennie stared thoughtfully at the doorway. "She doesn't seem happy."

"She never seems happy, Hennie. Haven't you noticed?"

"Something happened over break." Hennie smoothed her long brown hair around her shoulders. "Something's upset her."

"You got all that from one little snort?" Esther asked.

"She did mention that her parents were fighting a lot," I said. "Before you came in."

It wasn't hard to imagine that in a year or so, Hennie could be reading minds. When Cam told me how Delcroix developed Level Two Talents into Level Three Talents, he'd mentioned that Hennie might develop a mind-reading skill, just as Esther might someday be able to shape-shift. But that was not supposed to happen until they started their Program classes next year. Still, I tried to wipe the thought from my head as Hennie swung her gaze back to me.

She was just over five feet tall and gorgeous—perfect dusky skin, long wavy hair, dark eyes surrounded by the longest lashes you could imagine. But her sweetness was deceptive: when Hennie wanted to know something, she could be relentless. "So, how did you get here before us? We were on the first bus."

Good grief. Had everyone noticed I wasn't on the bus?

I gave her the same explanation I'd given Catherine, but Hennie wasn't buying it. She cocked her head. "You told me you got B's in all your classes. Why would you need extra tutoring?"

I hadn't practiced a response to that question.

I looked around the room, seeking inspiration for my next lie, and noticed my Program class schedule folded up on the desk.

"Physics," I said hurriedly. "They want me to start taking physics. I told them I was worried I wouldn't be able to keep up, so they said I should come back early and get started."

"Physics?" Esther repeated. "But you're already taking chemistry."

The two of them had me cornered. I could feel the slow, hot crawl of a blush traveling up my neck to the sides of my face. "It's for my new focus: science. I'm also going to take a scientific ethics class with Mr. Fritz, and Mr. Anderson is going to teach me biology."

Esther sat back, nonplussed. I'd never shown much of an aptitude for science, so this was understandable. Usually, a person's focus reflected her gift. Like Esther for acting, and Hennie for languages. No one could claim I was a gifted scientist.

"A science focus," she said. "I never would have guessed. Did you pick it, or did they tell you to do it?"

"I picked it. I was tired of not knowing what I wanted to do. I figured I'd always liked the woods a lot, and I'm definitely into the environmental stuff." I gestured at the window, making a vague attempt to convey some interest in the outdoors. "I wanted to study geology and environmental science, but they said I had to start with the basics, like physics and biology."

It was close enough to the truth that I figured I could fool Hennie. I was right. She had a grave expression on her face as she studied me, but then she nodded. "You do have an affinity for the earth," she said. "That's why you love running so much."

I blinked. "I never thought about that. I guess I do feel especially connected to the earth when I run."

"You are completely nuts about the whole running thing," Esther agreed. "You even love to run in the rain."

"Yeah." I grinned, relaxing once it became clear they believed me. "I'm crazy that way."

"But why didn't you tell us you were doing this?" Hennie asked. "I mean, we talked on the phone a hundred times over break, and you never mentioned it."

"I . . . I didn't want to make a big deal about it," I said lamely. "You guys have had your focus all along. I felt stupid for taking this long to figure it out."

Esther made a sound of disgust. "Are you kidding me? You're one of the smartest people I know. Besides, you're supposed to tell us everything. I don't care how dumb you feel." She looked at Hennie for support. "Right, Hennie?"

Hennie nodded. "Right. That's what best friends are for."

"Now, let's talk about important things," Esther announced. "Like, when does Cam get back? Have you talked to him yet?"

I fiddled with the hem of my sweater, not meeting her eyes. Esther was, to put it mildly, obsessed with romance. She had an encyclopedic knowledge of the opposite sex—something she'd gained after a long series of boyfriends—and firmly believed you only got what you wanted if you went after it. "He's around this morning, I think. But probably busy. You know how he gets. I'll see him at dinner, maybe." I turned to Hennie. "Speaking of guys, was Yashir on the bus with you?"

Talking about Yashir was my tried-and-true way of turning the conversation away from me and on to Hennie. This generally satisfied Esther's need for romance. They were the cutest couple ever. Yashir was tall, with fierce dreadlocks and lots of piercings. Next to him, Hennie looked even smaller and more adorable than usual. He'd kissed her for the first time in a stairwell just before Christmas. Esther and I died when we found out. So did Hennie, almost. She'd never had a boyfriend before.

Hennie worried a lot about what her parents would think of Yashir. He wasn't the sort of guy they'd want her to bring home. He wasn't Indian, for one. According to Hennie, her parents pretty much assumed she'd marry an Indian guy. And then there was the fact that his mom was something crazy, like a massage therapist or herbal healer, while Hennie's dad was in international business. Every time I saw him, he was wearing a dark suit. I'd never met a massage therapist, but I was pretty sure they didn't wear suits.

And I was pretty sure Hennie's folks didn't expect boys to come with earrings. Or miniature barbells in their eyebrows.

Hennie sighed dramatically. "No, he wasn't there."

"Even better," I said. "More time to get ready."

"What if he changed his mind over break?" She slowly rose to her feet. "What if he doesn't like me anymore?"

Esther linked arms with Hennie and me. "Get real. He's totally fallen for you. And we're going to make sure it stays that way." She winked at me. "After that, we're getting Cam for Dancia."

"And then?" I asked. "Will we find the pot of gold at the end of the rainbow?"

"Then we find the perfect guy for Esther," Hennie said.

"I can only hope," Esther said fervently.

We started toward the door. "I was about to head to breakfast," I said. "Are you guys coming?"

"Nah. We ate before we left," Esther said.

Hennie nodded in agreement. "I'm going to unpack. Come by when you're done."

"Okay." We shared a three-way hug.

"It's good to be back," Esther said, bouncing off down the hall, Hennie in tow.

I nodded and waved as I turned in the other direction. It was hard not to be jealous when life seemed so easy for them. All Hennie had to think about was whether her parents would like her adorable boyfriend. I had to worry about pledging my life to a secret organization that killed people it didn't like.

Above it all, two thoughts kept swirling around in my head: what would I do if they wanted *me* to kill someone?

And what if it were Jack?

CHAPTER 5

CAM WASN'T at breakfast, so I grabbed the last remaining doughnut and ran back to the Res, where I spent the rest of the day hanging out with Esther and Hennie. By the time dinner rolled around, the three of us were totally caught up, so we didn't protest when Hennie disappeared on the way to the Main Hall, having caught sight of someone tall and dreadlocked. Ten minutes later, she walked into the cafeteria holding hands with Yashir, with a silly grin on her face and flushed cheeks. Yashir seemed pretty happy, too. It wasn't hard to guess how their reunion had gone.

Our table filled slowly as more freshmen came over from the Res. Everyone was happy to be back at school. Allie and I even hugged each other.

Allie was the one I'd dubbed Perfect Girl last semester because of her halo of wavy, golden brown hair, and her obvious past life as a cheerleader. I'd briefly tried to hate her, but it was no use. She was truly as nice as she was cute, a great athlete, and it turned out, a friend of Jack's. Her very perfection still irritated me sometimes, but only when I was feeling particularly petty and frustrated by my own out-of-control head of whitish-blond frizz.

Allie had been devastated when Jack left school without

a word. It felt good to know there was another person who cared about him; sometimes I felt like I was the only one.

Hector and Alessandro came to sit with us, as did most of Esther's team. She was their unofficial captain, and they tended to congregate wherever she was. Over dinner we threw french fries at one another and generally irritated the teachers. It helped take my mind off the fact that I hadn't seen Cam all day.

Allie and I discovered we were both going out for soccer, so we talked about that while Esther cracked everyone up with stories of her ill-fated cross-country career and Coach Yerkinly's reaction when she'd walked past the finish line for each of our races. She'd never managed to work up to running three miles; one was about her limit.

After dinner, we all headed back to the Res. I was talking to Allie over my shoulder as I pulled open the door and nearly bumped into Cam, who was headed the other way.

"Perfect! I was looking for you," he said.

Allie gave me a knowing smile and kept walking. Esther winked as she passed.

"I didn't see you at dinner," I said, when they'd all disappeared into the Res.

"Mr. Judan had a bunch of things he needed me to do."

"Because of last night?"

"Yeah."

I paused. "Do you . . . um . . . think they'll be back?"

"They wouldn't dare," he said confidently. "Especially now that we've got extra Watchers patrolling."

"Do you know who it was?" I spoke carefully. I kept picturing Mr. Fritz's face and the disapproval I'd seen in Mr. Judan's eyes when I'd asked questions the night before. I suspected Cam knew the truth. Not to mention that I was dying

35

to know if he'd seen a talent mark from Jack.

"Not exactly. We think it's a gang from Seattle," he said. "We've had trouble with them before. But they're just regular kids. Nothing to worry about."

I searched his face. He avoided my eyes, and my heart sank. Cam was lying. I could see it in the way he refused to look at me, and hear it in his voice. He was talking too fast and too loud, trying too hard to reassure me.

I tried to tell myself that it was understandable. He was in the middle of an investigation. He could hardly go around blabbing about it to every person he saw. But it still hurt.

"So . . ." I trailed off, unsure what to do next. "Are you going to get something to eat?"

"Nah." He waved a hand. "I'll just eat double in the morning."

"Oh."

"I thought maybe we could go for that walk now."

"Oh!"

It was damp and cold and would probably start raining any minute, but there wasn't a chance in the world that I'd turn him down. We didn't have to be in our rooms until seven thirty, and while we were supposed to stay around the lawn or the buildings during free time, everyone knew that couples made out in the woods. It was much safer than doing it in your room, where it was not only forbidden (doors open and feet on the floor if you were entertaining!), but also patrolled and monitored.

"We don't have to go far. Maybe just up to the practice fields?"

He gave me that slow smile and stepped closer. I was helpless.

"Sure, yes, that sounds great," I stuttered.

"Do you need to get a jacket?"

If I went upstairs, Esther and Hennie would give me hell. "No, I've got my sweatshirt. I'll be okay."

We started out across the grass. Cam took my hand as soon as we ducked outside the circle of light surrounding the Res. A gentle sprinkling of rain began to fall on us as we made our way through the dark.

"Are you done now?" I asked. "With the investigation, I mean. Now that the real Watchers are coming."

He pushed a lock of thick chestnut hair back from his forehead. "You'd think so, wouldn't you? But I don't know. Mr. Judan told me that he still has leads for me to investigate. It sounds crazy, but sometimes I get the feeling I'm the only one Mr. Judan trusts completely."

"That is crazy. Not that you aren't totally trustworthy," I added hastily. "But it isn't right for him to dump so much on you. You *are* still in school."

"I know. It's just—he's done so much for me. I don't want to let him down."

I could tell how exhausted he was, so I bit my tongue and didn't say what I was thinking: *All Mr. Creepy has ever done is use your talent and feed you an occasional Thanksgiving dinner.*

"You shouldn't feel bad, Cam," I said carefully, anger at Mr. Judan flooding through me. "You don't owe him anything. Besides, you work your tail off for him. He should be grateful he has you on his side."

"Thanks, Dancia. I don't know why, but I don't feel right complaining about him to anyone but you."

I glowed with relief at his words. Cam *did* want to tell me things, even sensitive things about Mr. Judan. He was probably just under some vow of secrecy. I couldn't even be sure

Mr. Judan wasn't using persuasion on him to make him do whatever he wanted.

I didn't quite understand how Mr. Judan's talent for persuasion worked. I had asked Cam about it once, because he's a Level Two for persuasion. Cam could use what you already felt or believed and strengthen it, but Mr. Judan could take things you had never thought about before and make you a fanatical believer in them. That was the difference between a Level Two and a Level Three.

Cam also said that Mr. Judan's talent only worked when you were with him, and that he couldn't control your mind permanently. I found that to be a huge relief.

"Hey, just doing my job." I didn't say anything else about Mr. Judan. I figured Cam was too tired and frustrated to hear anything bad about him just then.

Cam stopped and took my hands in his, turning so that we could face each other. Then he wrapped his arms around my waist and pulled me closer; our bodies were touching, and our faces were just inches apart. "So, anyway . . . I didn't actually come out here to talk about Mr. Judan."

I gulped. All thoughts of Delcroix, secrets, and the Program dissolved in an instant. "No?"

"No. You know I'm not your Watcher anymore."

My heart fluttered. "The thought had occurred to me."

"So where do we go from here?"

"Maybe we pick up where we left off?" I said, my breathing suddenly becoming shallow and tight.

He leaned forward. I tipped my head back up to allow our lips to meet.

The kiss was slow, our bodies in perfect sync. We didn't fumble around or bonk noses or do any of the things I was so terrified of. We just stood there, intertwined. It went on forever, that kiss; or maybe there was a series of connected kisses, I don't know. I remember warmth. I remember his hands around my waist. And I remember wanting him never to let me go.

My eyes shot open early on Monday morning, well before the sun was up. I stayed in bed as long as I could, trying to go back to sleep. It was futile. At about a quarter to six I gave up and rolled out of bed. I knew Hennie and Esther would sleep until the last possible minute, but I couldn't stay in the room any longer.

Careful not to wake Catherine, I grabbed my clothes and headed for the bathroom. She was awake by the time I returned, looking bleary-eyed and grumpier than usual. I waited until she headed for the shower to sit at my desk and pull out my new schedule. It showed my afternoon focus classes, separated each day by topic and instructor. The class names—Scientific Ethics, Introduction to Physics, and independent study—gave no hint as to what would really follow.

I headed for the Main Hall as soon as the cafeteria opened. By then, the halls were a chaotic tangle of girls in towels running between rooms and waiting for the showers. I allowed myself a tiny smile as I started down the stairs. Cam and I had spent most of Sunday together, walking around school holding hands and catching up on everything that had happened over winter break. Hennie and Esther went crazy when they saw us. I think Esther was even more excited than I was.

I lingered in the hall by the second floor, where the juniors' rooms were, hoping to get a glimpse of Cam. This was a huge mistake, because it put me within the sights of Anna, who was in the hall near the stairs with her friends Molly and Claire.

"Well," Anna drawled, "if it isn't Dancia the Wonder Girl."

I debated between sticking out my tongue, shoving her down the stairs, and being polite. It was early, and I hadn't had my morning doughnut, so I wasn't ready for a fight. I decided on polite. "Good morning, Anna."

Anna crossed her arms over her chest and walked to the stairs. Molly and Claire had been relatively friendly to me in the past, but this morning they gave me only guarded smiles before their eyes flicked back to Anna.

"So, you're starting classes today," Anna said. "I guess we'll all have to be careful from here on out."

My smile hardened. "I'll take that as a compliment."

Anna sniffed. "I saw Trevor talking to you at Initiation."

Claire shifted uneasily, looking up and down the staircase. "Anna, we probably shouldn't be discussing this in the hall."

"Keep watch, then," Anna said. "It isn't like anyone could sneak up on you."

I paused for half a second to wonder what that meant. Did Claire have a talent for superhearing? Then I gave Anna a bright smile. "You know what, Anna? Trevor *did* talk to me. He told me how he'd be watching out for me."

Anna moved a few inches closer; just enough to seem threatening. "Trevor's too nice for his own good. Just remember that we don't all buy your stories, Dancia. There better not be any more 'accidents' when you're around."

Molly dug her hands deep in her pockets. She was painfully skinny, and when she got nervous she would squeeze her arms against her sides and practically disappear. "Anna, I think you'd better—"

"I'm not saying anything we haven't all thought." Anna leaned toward me. "I for one do not believe you're committed to the Program just because you made all those pledges."

"Fine." I got right in her face for a minute, close enough to look down at her perfect red lips and thick brown hair. She was a few inches shorter than me, which usually made me feel big and awkward next to her, but right now I liked the fact that she had to look up to meet my eyes as I spoke. "You don't trust me. I don't *care*, Anna. I'm a part of the Program now. I've got as much right to be here as you do."

Anna barely paused. "Oh, really? Then I have a question for you, Dancia. If Jack comes back, are you ready to do the right thing and turn him in? Are you loyal to the Program first, or Jack?"

My mouth flapped open at the unexpected question. It took far too long for me to spit out the words. "Jack's gone, and I chose to stay. I'm loyal to the Program, Anna. That's all you need to know."

Anna turned away, casually flipping a lock of hair over her shoulder. "If you say so." She motioned to Claire and Molly, who followed her down the hall. Just as I had started to relax, she turned back around. "By the way, you told Cam about your little fling with Jack, right?"

I froze. What did Anna know about my—whatever it was—with Jack? "I don't know what you're talking about."

"You and Jack, Dancia. We know you were together."

"You've been spying on me?" I looked at her in horror. The only way Anna could know that would be if she'd watched me in my backyard the day I'd kissed Jack. "Is that how you treat your family?"

Anna gave me a cool smile of satisfaction. "All I care about is the Program. You may have fooled some of the people around here, but I'm still watching."

CHAPTER 6

I RAN down the rest of the stairs and flung open the outside door. Suddenly, it occurred to me that Anna might have had no idea what happened between me and Jack. She might just have made a very good guess. And if that was the case, my reaction had proven her right.

I stopped in my tracks and gazed up at the sky in frustration. How could I have been such an idiot? The last thing I wanted was for Cam to find out what had happened with Jack. I'd always told him Jack and I were just friends. If he found out now that we'd kissed, he'd think I'd been lying all along. And worse yet, he might think I had a thing for Jack, and that that was why I wanted to protect him.

I trotted around the side of the Main Hall, knowing I was risking a full-on hair disaster if I stayed out in the rain. It had drizzled steadily through the night, and the Delcroix dragons that guarded the front of the Main Hall were tinged with gray, water dripping down their wings and falling from their open jaws. Thanks to Mr. Anderson's talent for gardening, the grass around the school was green and springy, without a hint of the mud, decaying leaves, and weeds that riddled most of the houses in Danville. A few roses bloomed beside the Bly, which stood to the left of the Main Hall. Unfortunately,

Mr. Anderson couldn't do a thing about the rain.

I ran up the marble steps and loitered for a moment in the front of the hall, surrounded by the trophy cases and stunning works of art that I barely noticed after the first few weeks of school. There was no reason to panic. I hadn't actually admitted anything, and in any case there wasn't much to admit. Jack and I had kissed once, way before Cam and I got together. It wasn't like I'd cheated on Cam. Besides, Anna would have to admit that she'd been spying on me if she wanted to prove anything.

I walked into the cafeteria and scanned the room. My heart fluttered when I saw Cam at a table with Trevor and a couple of other juniors.

I squared my shoulders. I had to get used to hanging out with Trevor. He was Cam's best friend. Besides, he claimed to want to help me. The same was obviously *not* true of Anna, but it was possible that Trevor was on my side.

I had almost screwed up the courage to walk over to their table when Barrett—the tall senior with the Earth Talent—approached. He was well over six feet tall but couldn't have weighed much more than me.

He handed me a chocolate doughnut as he spoke. "'Mornin', D. You ready to start your focus classes?"

I liked him as soon as he opened his mouth. He had a soft, easygoing lilt to his voice, and when he flashed me a smile, his dark eyes twinkled.

I returned the smile. "Wow, thanks for the doughnut— er—Barrett? Have I got your name right?"

He laughed. "Oh, sorry about that. I've been studying abroad, and I forget that no one knows who I am. Barrett Alterir. The mystery guy on your schedule. Hope it's okay if I call you D."

"I figured that was you. And I don't mind."

Barrett pointed to a small alcove off the main room. It held a couple of couches and comfy chairs. The freshmen had been warned to stay away from it because it was exclusively senior territory. "Come sit with us for a minute. They apply a little persuasion to keep the non-Program students from coming too close. It lets us hide in plain sight."

"I thought we weren't supposed to use our talents on other people," I said in surprise. "I mean, unless there's an emergency."

Barrett grinned. "Mr. Judan does it. I guess he can do whatever he wants with his talent. Come on, I'll introduce you around."

I glanced back at Cam and Trevor, but they were deep in conversation. I didn't think they'd seen me come in. With some amount of relief, I nodded at Barrett. "By the way, thanks for the welcome Friday night," I said as we walked. "That was pretty impressive."

Barrett bobbed his head. "I should be thanking you. We haven't had a new Earth Talent since I entered the Program. I've never gotten to do it before."

"Are there really that few of us?"

"There are more at Delhart and Delmun, the other two schools in the States, but I think we're about three or four times as rare as the other types." He motioned for me to walk in front of him as we passed between two tables. "Your Somatic Talents, those are a dime a dozen. The Life Talents, a little less common. But Earth's the top. You'll see. The bummer is that there aren't many good teachers. I had to go to Switzerland to get past the basics."

"Switzerland?"

"Yeah." He grinned again and reeled off something in

44

a harsh, guttural language that sounded at odds with his otherwise soft voice. "You'll have to start learning German so you can go over and study with Fräulein Weinmacher. She's amazing. She knows how to accelerate individual atoms. Very dangerous, but very impressive."

He stopped when we reached the couches. There were three guys and a girl in the tiny space, all sipping coffee and reading messages on their cell phones. I thought cell phones were forbidden in the cafeteria, but I guess the rules were different for seniors.

"This is D., everyone. D., this is Esteban, Tara, Marcus, and Lucas."

"You're training with Barrett?" Tara asked.

Barrett gave me a hug around the shoulders. "She's my new protégée. My legacy in this world."

"Run now, Dancia. While there's still time," Lucas advised.

There was a chorus of friendly exhortations from the others. "Run!" "Run!" "Before it's too late!"

"Seriously, though, you're lucky. Barrett's the best," Tara said when they had quieted down.

Barrett inclined his head modestly. "Thanks, darling. Your check is in the mail."

She blew him a kiss. Tara had hazel eyes and red hair, which she wore in two low pigtails. There was a vibrant energy about her that complemented Barrett's laid-back surfer vibe. I couldn't tell whether they were friends or a couple. It was hard to imagine them together, but then again, who would have picked Yashir for Hennie?

Barrett motioned for me to sit in an old leather armchair. He perched on the edge of the sofa next to Tara.

"So, can you give me a hint about what we'll be doing today?" I asked.

"Hard to say. Mr. Fritz is in charge of developing your talent. I'm just his helper, to be honest. But I'll be teaching you physics. We figured you needed to get in touch with the forces you're playing with."

A happy shiver danced through me. "I told my friends I was focusing on science. That's sort of true, isn't it?"

"Absolutely. You'll just focus on a unique aspect of the sciences."

"It's hard to know what to say about things. It feels weird to hide this from my friends."

Barrett took a sip of Tara's coffee. "We all feel that way. That's why they try to keep the Program as much like the rest of the school as possible. You may have independent studies that you'll have to be away from school for, or field trips with groups of other Program students, but you'll mostly be in the classrooms upstairs or out in the woods around campus."

"Field trips?" I brightened. I'd never been far from Danville. Even a trip to Seattle would have been a big deal for me.

"Field exercises, to be more specific. But you won't start those until next year. This year, Mr. Fritz will keep you pretty close to home."

"Mr. Fritz is cool. He's your focus teacher, Dancia?" Lucas was sprawled on the sofa beside Tara in a position of total relaxation. He ran a lazy hand over his head of short, curly hair.

"Yep—him, Mr. Anderson, and Barrett," I replied.

Tara raised an eyebrow. "I've never heard of anyone having three teachers. What's that about, Barrett?"

"Dancia's starting out with three of us so we can do a little catch-up," Barrett replied.

I glanced back into the cafeteria, my eyes lighting on

Anna, who was now sitting next to Cam with her hand on his shoulder. I thought about what she'd said this morning, and then what Trevor had said on Friday night, when he'd asked me—begged me, practically—to be careful with my talent. If they thought I was dangerous and untrustworthy, it was a safe bet that there were others who felt the same.

My shoulders sank. "It's okay, you don't have to sugarcoat it. They think I might hurt someone, right? So you're like my new Watcher."

Barrett choked on a bite of his doughnut. "*Scheiss*, a Watcher? Are you kidding?"

He looked genuinely appalled, and I said hastily, "I'm sorry, I didn't mean to offend you. I just meant, well, I know I entered the Program too fast, and I figured you . . ."

"D., you're in the Program now. You don't get watched anymore. Besides, the last thing in the world I want to be is a Watcher." He winked at me. "Don't tell you-know-who I said that. He thinks the sun rises and sets on his Watchers."

I smiled nervously. I figured you-know-who was Mr. Judan. I'd never heard anyone make fun of him before.

But of course, Mr. Judan wasn't the only one who was really into the Watchers.

As if on cue, I saw one of the guys at Cam's table motion toward me and Barrett, then saw Cam turn around to look at us. As soon as we made eye contact, he pushed back his chair, got up, and started walking in our direction.

"Oh, lord," Barrett sighed. "Here comes Mr. Watcher himself." He swallowed the last of his doughnut and wiped his hands on his pants. "I wonder what he wants."

It took Cam a few minutes to reach us. New people were coming in every minute, and half of them wanted his attention. He was polite, but kept on a deliberate path toward me and Barrett. As soon as he reached us, he looped his arm around my waist. It was a possessive gesture, and I tingled all the way down to my toes. "Hey, I didn't see you come in," he said.

"Cameron Sanders, what a pleasure to see you," Barrett said cheerfully. "I missed you while I was away."

"Barrett, welcome back," Cam replied.

Barrett motioned toward me. "Didn't realize you and D. here were an item."

"It's Dancia," Cam said firmly. "Not D."

I loved the idea of being "an item," but I couldn't understand why Cam was acting so hostile. Barrett seemed to be looking to me for some response to Cam's correction. "I told him he could call me D.," I admitted.

Cam gestured toward his table. "You should come get some food, Dancia. I saved you a seat."

"Do you mind, Barrett?" I asked.

"Not at all. I'll see you after lunch, D." Barrett wiped a smear of chocolate from his mouth and elbowed Cam in the ribs. "Be good, man."

Cam forced a smile. As soon as Barrett sat down behind us, the smile dropped from his face. He steered me back to the center of the room. "That guy is such an idiot," he muttered.

"He seemed nice," I said hesitantly.

"He doesn't take anything seriously," Cam said. "Talking to him, you'd think everything at Delcroix was a big joke. They all do." He shook his head at the antics in the Senior Corner, Barrett's group laughing uproariously as Lucas tried to fit two doughnuts in his mouth.

"Can you believe that guy is senior class president? Lucas Williams. He could have been a great Watcher, and all he wants to do is train dogs or something." Cam shook his head in disgust.

"If you say so." I pushed aside my confusion; clearly, I'd have to get to know Barrett on my own time. He and Cam must have some kind of history that would explain the way Cam was acting. "Did you know I'm going to have three teachers?"

"Three?" Cam jerked his head around to look back at Barrett. "He's not one of them, is he?"

"He's on my schedule." I dug around in my back pocket and held it out to Cam. "He said they had some catch-up to do."

"Huh." Cam studied the paper with a frown, then shrugged. "Barrett's a strong Level Three, and the only serious Earth Talent we have. I suppose they had to include him. Besides, you could do a lot of damage if you aren't careful. It's good that they're taking your training seriously."

I frowned. "Do you think I might hurt someone?"

"Hurt someone? Of course not." He seemed surprised by my reaction. "I just know how powerful you are. Remember? I saw it with my own eyes."

I smiled reluctantly, and he continued. "It's just good for you to start training right away."

"Do you think I'll need to go to Switzerland?"

"Oh, man, did Barrett tell you that?" Cam stopped. "Look, you'll have to ignore a lot of what Barrett says, Dancia. He's got his own ideas about things. His dad is on the Governing Council, and he gets away with a lot because of it. There are plenty of good teachers here in the States. You'll see. You'll do great here."

His face softened, and the warmth in his eyes made my heart skip. He put his hands on my waist, earning a stern shake of the head from Mrs. Callias, who was on cafeteria duty. PDA was *not* allowed at Delcroix. With a quick, apologetic smile in her direction, Cam dropped his hands, but the feeling lingered. "I'm going to be pretty busy this week, but maybe we can go for a run sometime? And a walk after dinner tonight?"

"Sure, Cam. That sounds great." I shivered happily as we headed for the table, already imagining the stars overhead and the feeling of another long, lingering kiss.

CHAPTER 7

BARRETT COLLECTED me after English. Though I'd been biting my nails all morning in anticipation of my first Program class, he had such a relaxed air about him it was impossible to be too scared. We headed for one of the practice rooms on the third floor. The room had no windows, just groups of chairs in clusters and a long whiteboard on one side with a music staff running across it. The practice rooms were used by the musicians, but were in fact designed to hide the secret library that was concealed in the space behind the wall. I remembered nervously pacing the width of the room with Jack, my shoes squeaking on the waxed linoleum floor.

Had it *really* been just a few months ago? It felt like a lifetime.

When Barrett and I arrived, Mr. Anderson was already in the room, as was Mr. Fritz.

"Welcome, Dancia." Mr. Fritz beamed. "And *guten morgen* to you, Barrett."

Barrett tossed his backpack into the corner of the room. "'Mornin', Mr. Fritz. You got any Kant for us today?"

Mr. Fritz's smile widened. "Of course! How about this to start our day? '*Experience without theory is blind, but theory without experience is mere intellectual play.'"* He turned to the whiteboard and wrote the quote in bright blue ink.

Barrett stroked his chin, contemplating the words. "Interesting."

I groaned and slumped into a chair. "I thought I was done with Kant." We had studied Kant the previous semester in my ethics class. I hated Kant. I never understood anything he said.

Mr. Anderson stepped forward. He was a heavyset man, wearing a pair of khakis that hung low under his belly and a flannel shirt that spread apart at the buttons to reveal a white undershirt beneath. He had a ring of brown hair, with a shiny bald dome on top. "We definitely aren't here to talk about Kant. We should get started with the real lesson."

"Wait—" Barrett held up his hand and turned to Mr. Fritz. "You're saying that you can't just have theory or experience, you need to have both, right? So books aren't enough, but you need to have some book time, or you don't know what you're doing."

"Perfect," Mr. Anderson interrupted, as Mr. Fritz opened his mouth to respond. "Exactly right. Now, can we get started?"

"All right, all right." Mr. Fritz motioned toward a group of chairs set in a circle. We all sat down. I fumbled in my backpack for a notebook and pen.

"As you know, Dancia, there are three types of talents. Earth, Life, and Somatic," Mr. Fritz began. "But you may not know that your talent reveals something about the type of person you are. The Life Talents tend to be focused on just that—life. They are extraordinarily aware of the people and animals around them, how they feel and communicate. Those with Somatic Talents are physical people. Their focus

52

is on the body. By understanding their physical being they are able to leverage it to do extraordinary things. The Earth Talents have a unique bond with the earth and its natural processes. Some of us suspect this is why there are so few Earth Talents these days. Children are removed from the earth. They don't have time to bond with it, and thus they are unable to develop into Level Three Earth Talents."

"I took earth science in eighth grade, but I only got a B," I said. "I don't truly understand what I'm doing. I just do it."

Mr. Anderson shook his head. "Fritz is making this sound more complicated than it is. When I want something to grow, I imagine it growing. I picture the grass getting taller and the roses blooming. It just works. That's all you have to worry about, Dancia."

"Jim, you know that our job is to make sure they get both the theory and the experience," Mr. Fritz said gently. He turned to me. "When Maria Salvoretto began teaching students with extraordinary talents back in the early fifteenth century, she had no idea what she was doing. It took hundreds of years to gain an understanding of what talents are and how they can be cultivated, and centuries more to document those learnings. The books that were written on these subjects, which are now housed around the world in libraries like our own, are invaluable to our ability to turn a Level Two Talent into a Level Three Talent.

"But, if you do not understand how the natural world works, your ability to manipulate it will be limited. You must know the rules in order to break them. So, for example, Mr. Anderson needed to understand *how* things grow—how the roots move through the soil, how the leaves make food for the plant from the sun—before he could fundamentally alter that process. However, once you understand these concepts, you don't have to think about them every time you use your talent. They simply become part of you." He turned to Mr. Anderson. "Isn't that right?"

Mr. Anderson grunted. The sound lay somewhere between agreement and dissent.

Mr. Fritz continued, "Dancia, you've been using your talent in a way we don't fully understand. Students at Delcroix normally spend their freshman year developing their Level Two Talent. Occasionally they will exercise Level Three abilities, but they typically won't know when they do. It is not until they begin training with the Program that they move into Level Three with any consistency. But you were at Level Three before you even arrived. My guess is that you have a particularly strong connection to the earth, and an innate understanding of the forces around you."

He seemed to be looking to me for confirmation. I wasn't sure I could give it to him. I slouched deeper in my chair and buried my chin in the neck of my turtleneck sweater. "Um, I guess that could be true."

"Or perhaps you received some sort of special training when you were young? Many of our students were sent to camps or had other learning opportunities outside of school. This could have helped your early development."

I pictured my roommate Catherine, who had probably been assigned a tutor the day she came out of her mother's womb. Mr. Fritz was nuts if he thought we did that in Danville. "Nope. No extra classes. Not that I remember, anyway."

"Well then, it's as we thought. You're simply a very special, very unusual young lady."

I felt my cheeks getting warm and wanted to hide under the desk. I changed the subject. "Mr. Judan said I'm manipulating the force of gravity. Do you think that's right?"

"What do you think?" Barrett asked.

"I guess so." I paused to consider my words. "When I look around me, it's like there are a whole lot of lines or ribbons and they're pulling on everything I see. I can sort of tug at the ribbons and change the balance, and that's how I do what I do. But I just started seeing the lines a few months ago. When I was little I did things without thinking. I didn't even know I could control my power until—" I stopped.

"Until what?" Barrett asked.

Darn it—why couldn't I keep my mouth shut? Jack had been the one to make me think I could control my talent, but the last thing I wanted to do just then was talk about Jack.

"Until earlier this year, when I really thought about it." I smiled weakly. "I guess all that stuff from my Earth Science class just finally clicked."

"That could be," Mr. Fritz said. "It is interesting that you say you were only able to control your power after you learned to understand the forces of the earth. But it is also possible you always had the ability to take control, and it was simply a matter of time before you exercised that ability."

I nodded, hoping they wouldn't ask more questions. "I bet I wasn't mature enough to handle it before. But I am now."

"Makes sense to me," Mr. Anderson boomed. He shoved his chair back and stood up. "Now, enough talking. What do we do first, Fritz?"

Barrett grinned. "Mr. Anderson doesn't get to train many students."

"Jim, we have a lot of talking to get through today," Mr. Fritz cautioned. "It's going to take a while. But perhaps we should start with an exercise. Theory and experience, right,

Barrett?" Barrett nodded, and Mr. Fritz motioned for us to stand. I rose slowly, my gaze darting among the three men. Without even trying, I found myself gathering energy from the room around me, anticipating what would come next.

"Now, you recently learned that these practice rooms shield our library. We built them with a titanium shell. Do you know what titanium does, Dancia?"

I shook my head.

"It interferes with the conduction of certain forces— including gravity."

"What?" I raised my eyebrows. "Gravity works the same in this room as it does anywhere else. Watch." I dropped my pen on the floor. It fell and rolled under my chair. "See?"

"So now you know exactly how everything works, do you?" Mr. Fritz said mildly. When I didn't respond, he continued, "What I'm telling you is that your powers won't work in this room the way they do elsewhere. The titanium doesn't alter the normal forces of nature. What it does is interfere with the ability of a Level Three Talent to manipulate those forces. It works on the Life and the Somatic Talents as well. We created these rooms so we can teach without worrying about students practicing on each other or blowing things up. They're safe rooms."

I clearly wasn't buying it. He held out his hands. "Give it a try."

"Seriously?"

"Seriously. Move your pen."

I looked at the three of them. Mr. Anderson was scowling, and Mr. Fritz had a gleam in his eye that I did not like. Barrett slouched against the wall, staring down at his beat-up leather sandals. He wouldn't meet my gaze.

"Fine. I will."

Once I focused my attention, I could see the forces I had described earlier. Everything in the room was covered in a web of material, tangled in strings and ribbons of various sizes that stretched far off into space. There were thick strings tugging on the pen, holding it firm from all directions, the biggest and darkest one coming right up through the floor.

I pushed at that big black string with my mind, trying to move it the way I had in the past. If I could throw off the balance between the forces, even just for a second, the pen would go shooting into space.

I poked the black string. Nothing happened.

I poked harder. Still, nothing.

I pushed and jerked.

Nothing.

I started to sweat. After a few minutes of futile effort, I glared at Mr. Fritz. "Okay, I give up. The titanium works."

Mr. Anderson shook his head. "Dirty trick, Fritz."

"Experience *and* theory, Dancia," Barrett whispered.

I whipped around. "What does that mean?"

"Fritz just told you that the mind plays a large part in the development of a person's talent. Then he gave you a concrete example of it," Barrett said.

I stared, speechless. Mr. Anderson hitched up his pants and checked his watch, as if he were embarrassed for me.

"There's no titanium, is there?" I said flatly.

"Sorry, no," Mr. Fritz said.

I slumped back down in my chair. "Is there a point at which you guys *stop* playing tricks on us?"

"I didn't lie," Mr. Fritz said. "I told you titanium interferes with Level Three Talents—and that's true. It interferes when someone believes it does."

"We aren't just trying to mess with you," Barrett said. "It was actually a very important lesson. It shows the power of your mind. You've got to believe in what you're doing, or the power won't work. It's like in sports. Do you play any sports?"

"Cross-country and soccer."

"Ever notice how you can lose a game just because one player is out? Or you miss a shot and can't recover?"

I nodded reluctantly.

"It's all mental. And so is this." He studied me, his usual relaxed manner gone. "Understand?"

"Sure, fine, it's mental. I get it." I bent forward to grab my pen, avoiding his gaze.

"Barrett's right, but he forgot to mention another reason why this lesson was particularly important for us," Mr. Fritz said.

"What's that?" I asked suspiciously.

"We discovered that your talent has limits. Limits imposed by your own mind, perhaps, but limits."

I furrowed my brow in surprise. "Of course my talent has limits."

He shrugged. "We weren't sure."

Luckily, they decided to stop at one humiliating incident per class. After that, we talked about the history of the Governing Council and the Program, and how they were going to grow my talent by teaching me to control it.

This seemed a little backward to me. Mr. Fritz explained that the first few classes of the Program usually focused on building up the student's confidence—apparently most people don't believe they can talk to animals, or shapeshift, or do whatever their extraordinary talent might let them. They need to learn to trust their abilities. But I had no problem believing I could make things happen with my mind—I'd been doing it since I was a kid.

One might think this would have helped in my training, but the powers that be at Delcroix decided I needed limits, not just to prevent me from doing something dangerous, but to make sure I understood that I was in control of my power.

I saw Cam at dinner; he was leaving as I was going in.

"I've got a bunch of homework tonight," he said. "You want to meet in the library?"

I grinned. "I'll see you in the stacks."

Our spot in the stacks was near the hidden door that led to the Program library. It was quiet and private. After dinner, I went back to my room long enough to shove my books into my backpack, shrugging regretfully at Esther when she asked me to study with her. "I'm meeting Cam," I told her. "Sorry."

She frowned. "I didn't even get to hear about your new focus class. How'd it go?"

"It was fine. Just like ethics class, only we talked about science, too."

"Can you come find me when you're back?" she asked. "I need to ask Trevor a question about our English homework, but I don't want to go alone."

I cringed. The last thing I wanted to do during my free time was hang out with Trevor. "I don't know how long I'll be. Can Hennie go with you?"

Esther wrinkled her nose. "Hennie? She's terrified of Trevor. Besides, she's off with Yashir somewhere."

I shifted my weight from one foot to the other and forced myself not to check my watch. "Is there anyone else?"

"Of course! Allie or one of the other girls can go with me. But you'd better save some time for me tomorrow. I need to hear what's going on in your life, you know." She laughed as if she didn't care, but I could see that she was hurt.

I cleared my throat. "Sure, we'll talk tomorrow. I'd better go. You understand, don't you?"

She bowed grandly. "Who am I to stand in the way of true love?"

A wave of guilt passed over me as I hurried down the hall. Esther had been my first friend at Delcroix, and she and Hennie had been like a lifeline for me the previous semester. I knew she was disappointed that nothing had happened with Chris, the first boy she'd had a crush on that semester, while Hennie and I had both ended up with boyfriends.

I hurried down the stairs and booked across the path to the Main Hall. The entrance to the library was on the first floor, through a set of tall wooden doors that reminded me of something in an old English castle. Unlike the classrooms, which had gray linoleum floors, the library had thick Persian carpets and real lamps, and a mix of long tables and individual cubbies for when you really needed to study. I wound through the stacks until I got to a tiny room tucked at the back of a hall. It was deliberately unappealing, with just a couple of study cubes and dim lights and a bunch of dusty old books. Cam appeared a few minutes later, backpack slung over one shoulder, his blue oxford shirt somehow making his shoulders look even broader than usual.

"So, how was your first class?" Cam asked. He threw off his backpack and slid into the chair next to me. "Did you enjoy it?"

"*Enjoy* is a strong word." I explained what Mr. Fritz had done to me. It wasn't until that moment that I realized how disappointed I was in myself for what had happened. It felt as if I'd been betrayed, not by Mr. Fritz, but by my own mind.

"I couldn't even move a *pen*, just because of something Mr. Fritz told me."

Cam laughed. "Dancia, Mr. Fritz has had tons of practice fooling students. Remember, you may have figured out how to use your talent years ago, but you've still got a lot to learn. That's why we have the Program."

I shook my head doubtfully. "Maybe. But it doesn't feel good."

"If it makes you feel any better, he did the same thing to me. I went from being able to feel the talents of everyone in the room to feeling absolutely nothing—it was like the air around me had gone dead. And it was all in my mind."

"That sounds even worse than what he did to me." I cocked my head to one side. "I don't think I ever asked you before—when did you figure out that you could read talent marks?"

He leaned back in his chair. "I started seeing colors and patterns in the air around certain people in fourth grade. It was terrifying. When I told my dad about it, he said only sick people saw pictures in the air. I tried to pretend they weren't there, but they wouldn't go away. I was too scared to talk to my dad about it again—I thought he'd send me to a hospital or something."

"That's a lot for a little kid to worry about," I said softly.

"Yeah, it wasn't pleasant. I did everything I could to make sure my dad would think I was normal. I got into sports and practiced hard, I made lots of friends and joined every club I could think of. I was the most average, well-adjusted kid I could be. And it worked. Eventually, he forgot all about it."

"How did Delcroix find you?"

"Delcroix Recruiters visit schools all the time. They look for kids that stand out, and the ones who try the hardest not to. Sometimes they go undercover as substitute teachers, other times as parents or relatives. The Recruiter that came to my middle school had a talent for invisibility. He went through the office and looked at files and watched the students for days on end. He was invisible, but his mark was pulsing over his head like a neon sign. When he saw me watching him move around, he knew something was up. He called Mr. Judan, and before long, I was telling him everything."

I thought of my own visit from Cam and Mr. Judan. I had been far too scared of my talent to tell them the truth about it. "Did he . . . um . . . *persuade* you to tell him?"

Cam shook his head. "He didn't have to. After all those years of seeing things, I was desperate for someone to tell me I wasn't crazy. Mr. Judan told me I had a special gift that he wanted to help me learn to use. It wasn't exactly a hard sell. He talked to my dad about giving me a special scholarship to start high school early. I lived at Delcroix that summer, and started freshman year in the fall."

"I had no idea."

He leaned forward, staring intently into my eyes. "That's why I understood how you felt, Dancia, that first time I met you. I could tell you'd been through a lot, just like me. And I wanted to help you understand that it didn't have to be that way. You didn't have to be alone."

I leaned over the table and took his hand. "I'm not alone. Not anymore."

CHAPTER 8

SOCCER SEASON began a week after classes resumed. I was hoping Esther and Hennie would join the team, but they refused. Esther said she'd run enough during cross-country to last a lifetime. Admittedly, she was more of a walker than a runner. Hennie wanted to spend more time listening to music with Yashir, though as far as her parents knew, she needed the extra time to study.

Given my exhausting schedule of classes, homework, and spending time with Cam, I was relieved to find that soccer at Delcroix wasn't exactly a serious sport. Unlike Danville High, where only the best made varsity, Delcroix had barely enough players for a full team. The Delcroix team played in a club league with a bunch of other private and alternative schools. We practiced every day, but only for an hour and a half, and sometimes all we did was run the cross-country course around the school. We didn't win very often, but it was still fun.

Things settled into a comfortable routine, though I knew better than to become complacent. Anna was obviously saving her information about Jack to reveal at the worst possible moment. My Program classes were amazing. Physics kicked my butt, yet somehow Barrett managed to make it interesting. Mr. Fritz had been right when he said it was important for me to understand what I was doing. Even though gravity didn't *seem* like a difficult concept (you drop something, it lands on the ground, right?), there were nuances I hadn't gotten before. Like each thing exerting its own gravitational force. It wasn't just the moon and the earth that were pulling on things—every object pulled on every other object, and I had to learn to distinguish the individual forces before I could learn to control them.

Most importantly, I learned that controlling my mind was easier said than done. Before, I'd only disturbed the forces of gravity for a second or two at a time. Now I was being trained to hold the forces out of alignment. This was surprisingly hard. If I got distracted and my concentration wavered, even for just a second, I would drop whatever I was holding, or send whatever I'd been pulling down back into the sky.

Barrett's talent—generating heat by exciting individual particles of matter—required enormous focus. He said there were several other people in the world with talents like his, but they didn't have his control. They could warm up a bowl of soup. Barrett could create a twenty-foot geyser of flame, set a house on fire, or boil someone's blood. Of course, he was far too laid-back to do any of those things, as far as I could tell, but he did have the power. His Swiss teacher made him do all sorts of weird meditation exercises to improve his concentration. Barrett said I could worry about that later. For now, we'd focus on the basics.

Surprisingly, the class I enjoyed most was Mr. Anderson's. He usually had me follow him around and help with whatever he was working on that day. Sometimes we walked in the woods and noted where blackberry brambles were suffocating native Oregon grape plants, or where ivy was crawling up the trunk of a Douglas fir tree. The next week we'd go back with thick leather gloves and a wheelbarrow and pull the offending invaders from the ground. Still other days, we worked in the garden, adding compost to the soil, weeding, or picking vegetables that grew even though it was the middle of winter.

Mr. Anderson talked a lot about photosynthesis, the process of taking light and making it into food. This transformation, he said, was at the root of everything he did. And everything I did, in a way. The earth was constantly changing, Mr. Anderson said, but everything was in balance. You didn't create new things, you just turned one thing into something else. Light and food. Energy and matter. The earth was about relationships, one thing blending into the next. If I didn't understand that, I would never fully understand how an Earth Talent worked.

Despite my best efforts, I hadn't learned any more about what had happened the night of Initiation. I had the feeling that if it were up to Mr. Judan and the others, I never would. Cam showed no interest in talking about it, the other sophomores didn't seem to care, and the juniors—led by Anna—clammed up whenever I asked any questions. I hadn't screwed up the courage to ask Barrett. I had the feeling he might just laugh and blow it off, the way he did most other things people took too seriously.

I asked Cam about it every so often, but he never quite answered, waving his hands vaguely and saying that things were out of his control. Finally, he told me I needed to let it go. It was in the hands of the Watchers now, and there wasn't anything more he could tell me about it.

That started our first fight. We had just finished running the cross-country loop around the school, and despite the chilly air, my T-shirt clung to my back with sweat. I held it out from my stomach and waved it back and forth to cool myself as we walked.

"But why can't I know what the Watchers are doing?" I said. "I'm in the Program now. There aren't supposed to be secrets anymore. Besides, you said it was just a gang of regular kids from Seattle. If that's true, why are the Watchers involved?"

Cam must have been annoyed by my finding a weakness in his story, because he threw his hands in the air and exhaled sharply. "There isn't any big secret. They're still trying to find the people who broke in. You can't expect the Watchers to tell everyone who their suspects are and what information they've gathered."

"I'm not asking for that," I said, wiping my forehead with the hem of my shirt. "I just think it's strange that they'd send Watchers after some local gang. What will they do if they find the people who broke in? They won't kill them, will they?"

"If they aren't dangerous, the Watchers will let the police handle it," Cam said. "It's up to them. You just have to trust them."

"How am I supposed to trust them if no one will say what they're doing?" I asked.

"That's what trust is," Cam said. "They don't *have* to explain everything."

"I guess I'm not good at trust, then," I said, flaring up.

We walked back to school in silence. A few hours later, Cam texted me while I was studying: *Sorry—didn't mean to fight. I'm tired. Too much homework.*

Relieved, I wrote back: *Me, too. I shouldn't keep bugging you. I know you'd tell me if you could. We okay?*

I waited, staring anxiously at the phone until I got his

response. *Of course. Meet me in the stacks, five minutes.*

I grinned, slipped my phone into my backpack, and headed for the library.

After my fight with Cam, I realized direct questions weren't going to get me far. Instead, I started spending more and more time in the Program library. I didn't know exactly what I was looking for, but I had the feeling that there was more to the Governing Council and the Watchers than they were telling me. So I went hunting for information, studying all the history books I could find. Surprisingly, there wasn't much. I thought there would be huge tomes filled with hundreds of pages on the Governing Council. Nope. Just a few scattered books, one of which was about Maria Salvoretto, whom Mr. Fritz had told me about on the first day of class. Maria, I learned, had a gift for foresight, and after having a vision of a school for students with extraordinary powers, she decided to go out and create one.

Maria sounded pretty smart. She didn't tell anyone what she was doing, so her little traveling band didn't get burned at the stake or anything. But everywhere they went, they did good things. They healed people, used their physical gifts to plow fields and build houses and to rid towns of plagues and dangerous animals. All this in a secret way so that no one knew exactly what had happened. After her death, lots of people wanted her to be made a saint.

Apparently, things had gone on like that for hundreds of years, with the talented roaming the world doing good deeds and learning how to cultivate their skills. It wasn't until World War I that things started to change. The talented got organized and became involved in governments and politics. They formed the Governing Council to centralize the operation of the schools and the efforts of the talented across the globe. They realized that with the proper training, some Level Two Talents could be turned into Level Threes.

The numbers of talented grew.

And then, about ten years ago, Mr. Judan began building his army of professional Watchers. Watchers had been around in some form for a long time. Maria "watched" her pupils for a year to avoid developing the talent of someone who couldn't be trusted. Once the Governing Council realized they could turn Level Two Talents into Level Threes, they started watching likely candidates. But Mr. Judan's Watchers were different. The books I found didn't say the Watchers were killing people, but it seemed obvious to me that that was going on. I just didn't understand why things had become so violent.

Most of what I found in the library described talents and how to use them. In one book there was an account from the seventeenth century by a person with a talent very similar to mine, describing how she had learned to move objects in every direction just by playing with the forces around them. There were detailed lesson plans describing how to move a Level Two Talent for persuasion up to a Level Three, and how to teach a shape-shifter to move smoothly from one form to the next. Seeing that helped me understand exactly why they'd been so worried about Jack's stealing books from the library. If Jack had taken any of these books, he, or whoever ended up getting a hold of them, could have become very powerful, very quickly. It was like handing someone a loaded gun.

A really big, magic gun.

Despite my best intentions, I was too consumed with my research and classes to hang out much with Hennie and

Esther. Any free time I had in the evenings I spent with Cam, and my classes were so hard I spent all my study time actually studying. Hennie was joined at the hip to Yashir, so she didn't notice, but I knew Esther wasn't happy that I was never around. Things only got worse after she developed an interest in a sophomore named Matt, who was in her drama class. He asked their teacher for a different partner for a scene from *Romeo and Juliet* after Esther had maneuvered for them to be together. She was crushed. I texted her every chance I got, and we talked on the phone over the weekend. But it wasn't the same, and I could feel the distance growing between us.

CHAPTER 9

I DIDN'T start getting nervous about Valentine's Day until Esther brought it up on our way back from a soccer game. Anna's dad had come to see the game, and he drove Anna and her friends back to school. That left me and six other players on the bus. It was a sunny day, so Hennie and Esther had decided to tag along as spectators. They were, of course, the only ones.

I was exhausted but happy. Allie and I had each scored goals, and Anna, for once, had not. I sat across from Hennie and Esther with my gear on the seat next to me and tried to keep my eyes open. I didn't get nearly enough sleep these days, and I usually ended up taking a nap on the bus ride home. But it was a rare chance to hang out with Esther and Hennie, so I pretended to be alert.

"So, what are you two doing for the big day?" Esther asked me.

I squinted at her through half-opened eyes. "What big day?"

"Valentine's Day. It's next Friday. What are you and Cam doing to celebrate?"

We hit a bump in the road, and I grabbed my bag to keep it from falling off the seat. This allowed me to avoid meeting

70

Esther's eyes. I didn't want to think about what she'd be doing on Valentine's Day.

"I thought maybe I'd get him some chocolate?" I said tentatively.

Esther's mouth dropped open. "Please tell me you're kidding."

I leaned my head against the seat. It had, of course, occurred to me that Valentine's Day was approaching. I could hardly miss it, with pastel candy hearts and yellow marshmallow chicks displayed in every corner of our grocery store. But I'd tried not to pay attention. The last thing I wanted was to be disappointed by whatever Cam did—or didn't do—in honor of the day.

"What's so bad about chocolate? He loves the stuff."

"It's boring," Hennie said, leaning over Esther's lap from her spot by the window. "Everyone buys chocolate. You have to find something different, something unique that shows how well you know him."

"Great. No pressure or anything. What are you doing for Yashir, smarty-pants?"

"I bought him a new nose ring," she said dreamily.

"Oh, yeah," I snorted. "Nothing says romance like an earring you wear in your *nose.*"

Esther laughed, then sobered abruptly and shook a finger at me. "That does not get you off the hook. You need to come up with something good. Are you going out or anything?"

I sighed. "Actually, Anna's having a party. Cam and I just talked about it this morning. He's borrowing a car to drive us out there."

Esther's eyes widened. "That sounds amazing. Will your grandma go for it?"

"I don't know, probably," I said. Grandma, strangely

enough, was always bugging me to spend more time with my friends. I think it was built-up trauma from watching me having no friends for so long. I hadn't exactly told her about Cam, but she knew. Just last week she'd given me one of those sly, knowing smiles and asked if I wanted her to drive us to the movies someday. Embarrassing, but sweet.

"You don't sound happy," Hennie said. "Why not?"

I crossed one leg over the other and hiked up my sweatpants, studying my shins. Purple bruises marked the spots where I'd been kicked during previous games. Today's kicks were still lumps. It took them a few days to turn black and blue. Even with the shin guards, I was always a mess after we played. "It's at Anna's house."

"So?" Esther said.

"So, Anna's sure to do something to ruin it for me. She hates me. She hates me more and more every day."

Okay, probably an exaggeration. Anna had been lying low since school started and, except for a few incidents on the soccer field, hadn't come after me directly. But all I had to do was think about our encounter in the stairwell and I could imagine the hatred directed my way.

"Of course she does," Esther said. "You're going out with her old boyfriend, who watches you with big brown calf eyes wherever you go. You're like a legend at Delcroix. The girl who stole Cam Sanders's heart."

I smiled. "Now, *that* I would love to believe. Seriously, though, she's probably going to booby-trap the house. I'll walk into the bathroom and water will fall on my head, or I'll reach for a chip and a bowl of salsa will drop in my lap. I'm doomed! I might as well stay home."

"Stop that," Esther snapped. "I will not let you get yourself into a lather about this." Subtly, her face elongated, and her eyebrows arched just like the math teacher Mr. Crestine's. He used to be in the Marines and liked to talk tough. "You are going to that party, and you are going to have a good time. Do you understand?"

I drew myself up straight and saluted her. "Yes, sir, Mr. Crestine, sir."

"And you, Miss Khanna: a nose ring? Does that actually sound romantic to you?"

Hennie hung her head and carefully arranged her skirt to cover her knees. This was not part of the act, but simply because she tended to panic if she exposed too much skin. I guess her parents were pretty strict. "Um, no."

"Of course not," Esther boomed. "You'll return that nose ring and buy that boy a drawing pad and pencil, do you hear me? So he can draw YOU!"

"Yes, sir, Mr. Crestine," Hennie agreed.

Allie peeked around from her seat in front of me. Like me, she was wearing her Delcroix soccer sweats, but unlike me, she had her hair in adorable pigtails, with little tendrils of hair curving perfectly around her face. "What are you guys talking about?"

"You want a piece of me?" Esther demanded.

"Good grief, no!" Allie laughed. "You're terrifying."

Esther giggled. "I know. I could have gotten you all doing push-ups if I wanted."

"Not me. I'm way too tired," said Allie as she got up on her knees and turned around in her seat to face us. "So, what's this about Valentine's Day? Dancia got invited to an off-campus party?"

"With Cam," Esther said self-importantly. "But she doesn't want to go. Is she crazy, or what?"

Allie's mouth dropped open, feigning horror. "Doesn't want to go? She *is* crazy."

The bus hugged a tight curve in the road, and Allie squealed as she fell to one side.

"Sit down in back!" the driver hollered.

Allie sank down in her seat, muttering, "I better hear about this party later."

"Fine, fine." I held up my hands in surrender. "I'll go to Anna's party. But what will I do there? It's Anna and a bunch of her friends. They all hate me."

Everyone from the Program had been invited, actually. They had been planning to have it the week after Initiation, but with all the fuss over the break-in they decided to wait until Valentine's Day to make sure it was safe.

"Are you sure you aren't just being paranoid? Why would the rest of them hate you? For instance, Trevor. He likes you, doesn't he?" Hennie said.

"Sorry, but no. I mean, he doesn't hate me, but it's not like we're friends, either."

Talking a lot about Trevor and Anna was not a good idea. There were too many things I simply couldn't explain. I searched for a subtle way to change the topic. "Hey, Esther, do you have anything to eat? I'm starving."

Esther pulled her backpack into her lap and rifled through its contents. She extracted a granola bar, a slightly mashed bag of crackers, and an apple. Esther always traveled with food. She claimed she had low blood sugar. I think she just liked to eat.

"Seriously," she said, as she handed me the granola bar, "why would Trevor be like that? He's a decent guy, and he's Cam's best friend. I think you've just got to get to know him better. Maybe start eating lunch with them. I'd go over there with you, if you want."

"Wait a minute," I said suspiciously. "Is this about me and Trevor or you and Trevor?"

"Well . . ." Esther paused. "He is kind of cute."

"Cute?" I shuddered. "Trevor is *not* cute."

"Handsome?" Hennie offered, starting to smile.

"*Ew*, no!"

"How about striking? Mysterious? Sexy?"

Allie spun around, her knees swiveling into the aisle. "Trevor Anderly? Hot. Definitely hot," she said.

"I need my aisle clear!" the driver yelled.

Allie faced front again.

I clapped my hands over my ears. "I am not listening to this. Esther, please tell me you don't like Trevor."

Esther narrowed her eyes. "Why not? Why should you be the only one to date a junior?"

"I'm not saying you couldn't, I'm just saying . . ."

"What? That I'm not good enough for him?"

"No!" I held up my hand. "He's not good enough for *you*. He's scary, Esther. Haven't you ever noticed that?"

Esther scowled. "No, I haven't. I think he's a smart, good-looking guy. And I've noticed him staring at me, too. So I'm not crazy, all right? And thanks for the support, by the way."

My heart sank. Trevor was probably *watching* Esther, and she thought he liked her. But there was nothing I could do. "I'm sorry, I didn't mean to sound negative. I didn't realize you were serious about him."

Esther shoved the apple and crackers into her backpack. "Yeah, well I am, and feel free to tell me it's a great idea and you're all for it and you're going to help me get him.

Though I'm not sure how you'd do that. It's not like I see you anymore."

I threw a desperate glance at Hennie. I'd known Esther was annoyed that I spent all my free time with Cam, and I was feeling increasingly guilty about it, but I hadn't known things had gotten this bad. "Esther, I'm the last person to give advice about guys. You know that. You're way cuter and funnier than I am, and you've had, like, six different boyfriends. I didn't even know that I shouldn't get Cam chocolate for Valentine's Day."

"Dancia didn't say you shouldn't go for him," Hennie said. "She just has a thing about Trevor. You know she didn't mean any harm."

Esther hugged her backpack to her chest. "You're right," she said a moment later. "I'm overreacting. I'm sorry."

I handed her back the granola bar. "Probably low blood sugar. You should eat something."

She gave me a tiny, sad smile, and started opening the package. "I'm just so frustrated. Lately it feels like nothing I do goes right. Not with boys or friends or *anything*."

Hennie leaned in toward Esther. "What do you mean? Is there something else going on?"

Esther took a vicious bite of her granola bar. "It's just the usual garbage. After Matt blew me off I practically begged one of the groups in my acting class to let me join in their scene for our next project, and they said no. They said they'd already assigned parts and started rehearsing. But I could tell they just didn't want to perform with me onstage."

Hennie put her arm around Esther's shoulders. "Ignore them. They're horrible, jealous monsters."

Esther's chin wobbled. "I just wanted to be in their scene."

Feeling heartbroken, I reached over and joined Hennie

in hugging her. "Esther, we'll be in your scene if you want."

Hennie nodded vigorously.

Esther let out a long-suffering sigh, and then leaned her head against Hennie's shoulder. "That's sweet, but you guys suck at acting. No offense, but I'll pass. I'd like to keep my A."

We laughed, though it was tinged with sadness.

"You know you can't do anything wrong when it comes to us," Hennie said.

"Absolutely." I nodded. "We're behind you, Esther, for whatever you want—even Trevor."

Given her fascination with the subject of boyfriends, I expected Grandma to *want* me to go to the party with Cam. Still, old people and parents were supposed to worry about this sort of thing, so I figured she'd at least be a little concerned about us driving to Anna's together. We were on the way home from school that Friday in our thirty-year-old Volvo. Grandma had been out for a walk that afternoon, so she had on her thick-soled white sneakers and a baby blue tracksuit.

She barely looked at me as she sailed through a red light and said, "Your Cameron will be driving? I suppose that's all right."

I winced as a car blared its horn and swerved to avoid us. "Grandma, you're supposed to stop for the red ones."

She kept her eyes on the road. "That man was speeding. He had no right to honk at me."

I sighed and waited for the interrogation about the party that should have followed. "I won't be home until after ten," I said, half hoping she would tell me I couldn't go. "I don't know exactly when."

"It isn't as though you're a kindergartner. Just be home

by eleven. And no drinking. You drive that car home if any-one's been drinking. You're better than most drivers out there anyway."

Clearly, she assumed *I* wouldn't drink. It was nice to be trusted and all, but shouldn't she be a little worried about me cutting loose?

"Cam has to ride the bus back to school after he drops me off," I said. "They'd notice if he'd had been drinking."

They ran the Silver Bullet at ten and eleven on Friday night. If you left school, you couldn't be late coming back, or you'd be locked out all night long. One of the teachers met the bus when it got to school and checked to make sure everyone was sober. This was supposed to make parents who let their kids out over the weekend feel better.

"Who else will be there?" Grandma asked. "What about your friend Jack? I haven't heard much about him lately."

I sighed. "Jack's gone, Grandma. I told you that a month ago."

She shook her head, and the car swerved a few inches in either direction. A bottle of water fell down at my feet from where Grandma had propped it between the seats. Someday, I promised myself, I would have a car with actual cup hold-ers. "That can't be right. I could have sworn I saw you with him the other day."

"Maybe it was someone who looked like Jack," I said. "Hector's got the same color hair." Sometimes Grandma would imagine things and then talk to me about them as if they were real. I chalked it up to old age.

Grandma sighed. "You're probably right. It's too bad he's gone. You seemed like such good friends."

"I miss him," I admitted. "But it's for the best. Jack always seemed to be getting into trouble at Delcroix."

"Nothing wrong with a little trouble."

I rolled my eyes. "Yeah, you'd be thrilled if I got detention."

"If it were for something you believed in—yes." Grandma sat up straighter so she could see over the steering wheel as she turned in to our driveway. "I don't care what kind of grades they give you at Delcroix. I wanted you to go there so you'd have the chance to learn how to use your gifts, and be confident enough to fight for what you believe in."

"I know, Grandma," I said. This was a speech she had given me a hundred times before. Whether it was standing up to a bully on the playground or arguing with a teacher at school, Grandma always said, some things were worth fighting for. I'd heard that speech since I was a kid, though I couldn't for the life of me imagine what Grandma had ever had to fight about.

"You know that if anything does happen with Jack, or up at that school, you can always tell me about it."

I glanced over at her, caught off guard by her serious tone. She stared at the house, eyes watering, but before I could ask what she meant, she had tucked her keys into her purse, once again her usual absentminded self.

"And if you have sex with that boy," she said, as she opened the car door, "I'll kill him myself."

My eyes flew open. "Jeez, Grandma, I'm not going to have sex with Cam just because we're going to a party!"

She just smiled a little smile and heaved herself out of the car. "Glad to hear it. Now, would you mind putting in a load of laundry? I'm completely out of clean underwear."

CHAPTER 10

TO SAY that I obsessed over Valentine's Day would be an understatement. First, there was the matter of giving a present. What if I did something elaborate and Cam handed me a card? Then again, what if he did something special and I gave him a bar of chocolate?

I ended up buying him a new Mariners hat. We always joked about how gross our baseball hats were because we worked out in them. So I guess that showed how well I knew him. Maybe not as romantic as a drawing pad, but it would have to do.

Then there was the party—and Anna. It was easy enough to avoid her and her suspicious stares when I was at school, but I could hardly do the same when we were at her house. I would have no excuse not to talk to her. And even if it sounded ridiculous, I wasn't entirely sure she *wouldn't* arrange for some disaster to befall me during the party. Yes, I was paranoid. Delcroix Academy did that to you.

February fourteenth brought a steady, cold rain. I spent an extra half hour that morning putting on makeup and trying on clothes, thoroughly annoying Catherine. I ended up borrowing Esther's cashmere sweater, even though I was terrified I'd spill something on it and have to babysit for the rest of my life to replace it, and I took a pair of ballet flats from Allie's roommate Heather, who was the only one on the floor with feet as big as mine.

I met Cam on the stairs on the way to breakfast. Or I guess I should say he was standing on the first-floor landing, one hand on the old wooden banister, waiting for me. He handed me a dozen red roses and a handwritten note on a piece of white paper. I opened the note first. It said, *I'm yours. Love, Cam.* I clutched the roses to my chest and stared with delight at the confident block letters.

"Do you like the roses?" he asked.

I couldn't speak, so I grinned and nodded stupidly as I handed him the hat, which I'd tucked into a shiny gift bag and tied at the top with a white ribbon. After writing half a dozen notes and consigning them all to the trash, I'd given up and simply written his name on the bag.

Cam tore the package open and pulled out the hat. "Hey, exactly what I needed!" He smiled and kissed me, right there in the stairwell.

I wasn't nervous after that.

After dinner, Molly, Claire, Trevor, and I piled into the old Explorer Cam had borrowed from one of the seniors. It had beaded seat covers and the faint odor of wet dog. Everyone seemed to be in a good mood. Molly smiled and wished me happy Valentine's Day, and Claire was downright chatty. Everyone from the Program seemed to breathe easier when there weren't non-Program students around. The strain of keeping the secret affected us all, even if we didn't talk about it.

Anna lived almost an hour from Delcroix, so we had a lot of time in the car. Unlike Grandma, Cam actually paid attention to traffic signals and drove somewhere near the speed limit. He and Trevor talked most of the way down about some simulation thing they were doing the next week that involved battling another group of Program students. They discussed strategies, how to use the talents of the people in their group, and what their weaknesses were.

I guessed it was Watcher training. Or maybe those "field exercises" Barrett had told me about. I still had a hard time imagining Cam—my Cam—as a full-fledged Watcher. So I tried not to listen.

Anna lived in a suburb outside Seattle. There were lots of hills and huge houses that looked like mansions, all right next to each other, each with matching landscapes of neatly trimmed bushes and flower beds around the front. A few of them still had their Christmas lights up.

Anna and her mom met us at the front door. Anna's mom was small, like Anna, with a thin, muscular build. She had the same heart-shaped face as Anna, but there was nothing Bambi-like about Mrs. Peterson. Her movements had a military precision to them, and her face had serious lines around the mouth and eyes. We exchanged a few pleasantries, during which I had the impression she was analyzing me down to my DNA. I was immensely relieved when she moved on to scrutinizing the others.

Cam was his usual charming self, and Anna's mom clearly loved him. She wasn't a huggy sort of person, but she gave him a warm smile, which is more than she gave the rest of us. I suppose she must have gotten to know him when he and Anna went out. After talking to each one of us, she told us she'd promised Anna she would stay in her office during the party, and headed up the stairs.

The mood changed as soon as she left. Anna shuddered dramatically. "She's so embarrassing."

"What do you mean? I like your mom," Cam said.

"Whatever." Anna adjusted a bowl of salsa on an end table. "You're the first ones to arrive. I was just finishing getting the house ready."

"Anything we can do to help?" Cam asked.

"No, don't worry about it. You can have a seat. There's just some soda in the garage that needs to go in the fridge. I'll grab it." She turned toward the kitchen and almost knocked into me. "Oh, Dancia. I didn't see you there." She barely looked at me before turning back to Cam and fluttering her lashes. "You know, if Dancia could grab the soda you could help me pick out some music."

"You don't mind, do you, Dancia?" asked Cam. He was already hungrily eyeing the stereo.

Don't let her get to you, I told myself. It's too early to lose it.

"Of course not," I said pleasantly. "I'd love to help."

"Great. Now, Anna, I'll pick music, but only if you let me play Seattle bands," Cam said with a grin. The two of them headed toward a cabinet in the back of the room.

"I'll show you how to get into the garage," Molly offered.

"Thanks." I gritted my teeth and followed her through the kitchen into the three-car garage. Molly gave me a pitying smile as we grabbed cases of soda. "Anna and Cam have the same taste in music. No one else quite gets it."

"I listen to those bands all the time," I said with a dismissive flick of my wrist.

The truth was that Cam and I hung out in the woods, ran together, studied, held hands, and kissed. But we never listened to music.

Molly raised her eyebrows in surprise. "You do? Which bands do you like best?"

"Grass," I said, thinking of the CD Cam had given to me a few weeks ago. I had stopped listening after the first two songs. They made my head hurt.

We carried our load back to the kitchen, which was easily the size of my entire house. Polished stone countertops encircled the room; an island with a sink and stove was in the center. Molly pulled open the door of an enormous stainless-steel fridge . . . which was completely full of soda.

For a moment, we stared at the packed shelves in awkward silence. Molly slid her hands deep into her pockets.

"I guess Anna forgot that she'd already brought in the soda," I said finally.

"Must have," Molly agreed.

I sighed. It was going to be a long night.

As the night progressed, the music got louder, and the house became packed with all the Program students. I didn't want to follow Cam around like a puppy, so I talked to some of the sophomores and the seniors I knew from hanging out with Barrett. Cam came by a few times, but I waved him off. Everyone wanted to talk to him. It wasn't easy dating the most popular guy in the school.

I was sitting with Esteban when Barrett arrived. Esteban was a Somatic who was impervious to outside temperature. He wore T-shirts and shorts all winter long, even when it snowed. He also had a tendency to bob his head up and down and hum to himself when he was walking through the halls at school. I assumed that this was because he was always thinking deep thoughts. He read a lot of philosophy and loved to talk about it. I enjoyed the conversations, though I was never entirely sure how to respond when he told me something I'd said was, "deep, man, really deep."

After greeting Esteban, Barrett gave me a bear hug. "Hey, what's goin' on, D.? How's my best girl?" Then he looked around with an expression of mock guilt. "Oops, I better not say that too loud. I don't want Mr. Sanders to think I'm poaching."

I whacked him on the sleeve with a grin, thrilled to see him. I hadn't thought Barrett would come, given his feelings about Cam and his crew, but I guessed the party was big enough to transcend such things. "Shut up, you idiot. Cam knows he has nothing to worry about."

He winced theatrically. "Oh, that hurts. Your boy could work me over, is that what you're saying?"

I wasn't entirely sure who *would* win in a fight between Barrett and Cam. Cam was a serious warrior. I'd seen him and Trevor spar, and it was like watching two kung fu masters. Barrett, on the other hand, resembled an out-of-shape monk. I could hardly imagine him raising a finger to defend himself.

Still, Barrett could throw fire thirty feet across a room. That gave him a serious advantage.

"You'd be too lazy to fight back," I said. "You'd have to pacify him with your stunning good looks."

Barrett flung his long hair back over one shoulder and struck a pose. "Do you think it would work?" He was easily a head taller than anyone else in the room, and with Anna's soft party lighting, his gangly profile threw a huge shadow on the wall behind him.

"I'd go with the fire thing, myself," Esteban said.

"Good plan." Barrett peered around the room. "So, besides the crappy music, how's the party?"

I hid a smile. "Fine."

"Where's the boyfriend?"

I pointed to the back of the room. "Over by the music."

"Waiting for you?"

"No."

Barrett nodded decisively. "I had a feeling you might need rescuing." He grabbed my hand and started leading me toward the door.

"Where are we going?"

"Not far. Just out front."

I hesitated. Cam didn't approve of Barrett generally, and never seemed pleased when I hung out in the Senior Corner with Tara and Lucas and the others.

"Come on, just for a few minutes." Barrett put his hands over his ears and feigned being in pain. "Give your ears a break."

The music was awfully loud. And it wasn't as if Cam's not liking Barrett meant I couldn't be friends with him.

I grabbed my jacket off the hook by the front door and followed him outside.

CHAPTER 11

THE COOL air bathed my cheeks as I left the house. I hadn't realized how hot it had gotten in there. As we walked down Anna's long driveway, the music faded to a dull buzz, and I heard the quiet strains of a different song coming from a hulking SUV parked just down the street. Lucas and Cyrus were sitting on the curb beside the car, and Sarabelle and Elliot—a couple I'd only met a few times—were snuggling in each other's arms at the back of the truck. Tara sat sideways in the front seat with the door open, her feet dangling toward the curb, a tiny black dog in her lap. She leaned over to adjust the stereo, and I nodded unconsciously as I recognized the tune.

I paused a few feet from the truck. Barrett walked over and put his arm around Tara.

"Hey, D.," Tara said, greeting me.

"Any food inside?" Cyrus asked.

"Chips and whatnot. Some wrap things," I replied.

There was a chorus of disapproval. "I thought there'd be food," Lucas grumbled. "They had chicken wings last year. And pizza. Are you telling me there's no pizza?"

"I think Anna's on a diet," I said. "She doesn't eat pizza." There were more groans and a few laughs. I basked in the pleasure of being surrounded by people who disliked Anna as much as I did.

Barrett bobbed his head. "I knew we needed to rescue her, Luke," he said with a grin. "She was trapped in there."

"Well, you got her. Can we go now?"

I turned to Barrett. "I thought we were just hanging out. I can't leave."

"Come on," he said in a singsongy voice. "You can't stay here. The music will rot your brain. Not to mention the company."

"Barrett!" I looked back toward the house, feeling guiltier by the second. "You guys go without me."

"There's a spot nearby where we can get a little privacy," he said. "Luke's dog will keep watch for us. You can practice levitating."

I stuck out my jaw. "I am *not* levitating."

We'd started arguing about this a couple of weeks earlier. Since I could manipulate gravity, Barrett thought I should be able to make myself fly. I, meanwhile, wanted nothing to do with levitation. I was terrified of heights. And I knew better than anyone that my focus still needed work. If my attention wavered while I was levitating, I'd fall like a rock. This had happened a number of times with objects I had attempted to manipulate. I was not prepared for it to happen to me.

"You can practice on me," Barrett said. He walked around to the back of the truck and climbed onto the bumper. "I'll jump off here. Just a few feet off the ground. No one will notice."

"I'll drop you if I get distracted," I warned.

"Don't get distracted," he argued. "Focus."

"Easy for you to say, Zen master. I just started training! You've been doing it for years."

Tara eyed me. "I wouldn't mind if you dropped Barrett on his butt, D."

I rolled my eyes. "I know *you'd* like it, but I still don't think it's a good idea."

Barrett climbed down, apparently having accepted the fact that I wasn't going to change my mind. "You're getting better, D. Last week you moved that chair across the room without blinking."

"You are not a chair."

He grabbed a can of soda from the seat beside Tara and popped open the top. "So you'll try harder. It's good to raise the stakes."

"Kids," Esteban broke in, sotto voce, "sorry to interrupt, but is it just me or is there a menacing gang of thugs headed our way?"

Everyone moved away from the car to get a better look. I strained to see the shapes in the darkness. There were at least eight of them, perhaps more, but it was hard to tell, because every time they got close to a streetlight, a tiny figure would step out of formation and touch the lamppost. Then there would be a fizzing sound, and the light would flare brightly, then go dark.

Without being able to see their faces, it was hard to describe what made these people so frightening, other than the fact that one of them had the power to short-circuit streetlights. It must have been the way they moved—in a phalanx, a stocky guy at the front walking purposefully as they headed toward Anna's house. They also weren't talking. That sent the creepy factor up several notches.

"Not just you," Barrett confirmed. "Definitely menacing."

"Should we go in the house?" I whispered. Suddenly, I desperately wanted Cam next to me.

Right next to me.

Or, better still, in front of me.

They were just a few houses away now, and I could see that there was a mix of male and female, at least ten altogether, some with long coats, others with vests, all wearing red bandannas in one style or another—around the forehead like a headband for the girls, at the wrist or neck for the boys.

There was enough light from the remaining streetlamps and Anna's house to illuminate their faces as they got closer. They were all teenagers, I guessed. The guy in front looked a little older, maybe twenty. The others were hard to make out, especially the ones in the back, but they were all grim and silent, and they were staring right at us.

Cam must have heard my prayers. Or maybe, I realized with no small amount of trepidation, he had felt someone using a Level Three Talent. As the phalanx neared, music spilled out of Anna's house. I turned to see Cam behind me, framed by the light in the doorway.

"Trevor!" he snapped to someone behind him when he saw the gang headed in our direction. "Tell Trevor I need him. Fast."

Barrett and the others inched back toward Lucas's car. Without thinking, I moved closer to the house—and Cam. Unfortunately, this left me isolated from the group. Not exactly what you'd want, when facing down a pack of menacing teenagers who were probably packing *something* under those coats and vests. Still, when Barrett motioned to me to move back in their direction, I shook my head helplessly. My legs seemed to have frozen.

Cam paused next to me as he strode toward the street.

"You should go back to the house, Dancia," he said in a low voice.

His softly spoken command gave me a thrill of pleasure even as it hardened my resolve to stay put. If something was going down, I wasn't going to let Cam deal with it by himself. I had a strong suspicion Barrett and the others would be less than helpful in a crisis.

Esteban elbowed Lucas. "I'm thinking this party officially sucks."

"What do they want?" I heard Tara whisper.

"I'm sure they want to be friends," Barrett said.

Someone snickered. I was too horrified to do anything but stare, wide-eyed, at the approaching nightmare.

Cam paused at the edge of the driveway. The gang stopped in front of him.

"Nice night, isn't it?" Cam said evenly.

"Very nice," the leader of the gang agreed. He jerked his head to the side in an apparent signal to his troops, and they fanned out in a wider formation.

"What do you want?" Cam asked.

"I thought I'd introduce myself," the leader said mildly. He had broad shoulders and a thick chest. His round face might have been sweet if it hadn't been for the fact that he radiated a quiet kind of fury just under the surface. He wore a leather bomber jacket; his bandanna was tied around his neck, train-robber style. "The name is Thaddeus."

"Nice to meet you, Thaddeus. Now, there's a party going on here. I think it's best you leave." Cam crossed his arms over his chest.

"So unfriendly," Thaddeus said reproachfully. "You haven't given me a chance to deliver my message."

"What message?"

"Your Watchers have been giving my people a hard time lately. We'd like for it to stop."

I took an involuntary step back. They knew about the Watchers?

"I'm afraid I can't do that for you," Cam said, seemingly unfazed by Thaddeus's demand. "There was a little disturbance up at the school the other day. We tend to take these things seriously."

"That's too bad. I had hoped we might be able to get along."

Cam leaned back on his heels. "It's up to you. Leave now, and we can."

Thaddeus shrugged. "If that's the way you want it." He turned as if to leave, but took only one step before he stopped. "Just one more thing."

"What's that?" Cam asked.

"A message. For your boss."

That was when Thaddeus did exactly what I'd feared. He reached inside the pocket of his leather coat and pulled something out. I had just opened my mouth to scream when I realized it was a brick, not a gun or dagger. Deliberately, he turned toward Lucas's car and hurled the brick at its front window. The sound of shattering glass sent me ducking for cover, my head in my hands. A second later, I looked up just in time to see Trevor running down the driveway toward Cam, with Sam, Kari, and Geneva behind him. Meanwhile, Thaddeus was headed right for Cam.

Meeting the gang leader's charge, Cam launched himself at Thaddeus with a series of blindingly fast movements. I stared in amazement. Cam was into martial arts, but I was unprepared to see him enter the fight with arms and legs flying—he even went from a full backflip to a spinning kick. The display seemed to stun Thaddeus, allowing Cam to get in a satisfying kick to the face. Thaddeus might have been able to hurl bricks forty feet through car windows, but Cam moved twice as fast. When Thaddeus finally did come out swinging, Cam ducked swiftly to avoid a series of punches, then got in an uppercut before dancing out of reach.

It took only those few seconds for the rest of the group to engage themselves in battle. Trevor faced off against a girl with long brown hair in a braid, her bandanna tied around her forehead. She crouched down, hands loosely guarding her face. He swung at her with a clenched fist, but she spun around him like a tiny cyclone, easily avoiding his punches, then bringing alternating feet under his chin with a staccato motion that sent him reeling. He paused for only a moment before coming back toward her with his hands flying.

Kari sparred with a snarling girl dressed all in black, who seemed to dance as she fought. She reminded me of a ballerina, except that every leap ended with an openhanded strike to the face or jab with an elbow. Geneva and a boy who must have shared her talent for acrobatics turned somersaults in the air and swung at each other while they were ten feet off the ground. A moment later, they would land on the ground like cats, lightly springing on the balls of their feet before launching themselves back into the air.

Barrett and his friends didn't join the fight, despite the fact that there were five of them, and that Cam, Trevor, Kari, Sam, and Geneva were outnumbered two to one. The seniors ducked behind the car and watched. Lucas and Esteban had bemused expressions on their faces, while Tara kept shaking her head and wincing.

But it was Barrett whose behavior I couldn't understand.

He stood beside the curb, lips pressed together tightly, hair pushed back, intently assessing the situation. For once, he wasn't smiling or laughing. In fact, he wore an expression I'd never seen on him before. He crossed his arms over his chest, a mixture of frustration and anger written in his eyes. If I didn't know him, I would have found him distinctly intimidating.

Yet he didn't do anything.

For all his speed, Cam couldn't hold out against Thaddeus's fists forever, and he finally took a direct blow to the face. When he struck back with a blind punch, Thaddeus grabbed his arm and twisted him around, then landed three quick strikes in a row to Cam's lower back. Cam grunted and fell back a few paces.

I whipped around to face Barrett. "Do something!" I cried. "Help him!"

"They created this," Barrett said. "It's their fight now."

"What?"

"It was only a matter of time." He shook his head, mouth tight, dark eyes flashing.

I could hardly process what he was saying. Barrett was standing there watching Cam get beat up because he thought Cam and the others had picked this fight? No way. If your team was threatened, you helped. Even if the people in trouble weren't Barrett's friends, we had all taken an oath of loyalty to the Program. As far as I was concerned, this was an attack on the Program. I didn't know why, or who the gang of bandanna-wearing thugs were, but they were after us.

And they were winning.

I stepped forward a few paces.

"Don't do it," Barrett warned. "You'll get hurt. Let the police handle it."

"But—"

"What are you going to do? Let them use you as a punching bag? You honestly think that's going to help?"

I wanted to argue, but Barrett was right. I fought like a six-year-old girl. When I'd practiced on a bag in my self-defense class, I had been lucky to escape the bag's knocking *me* over. If I took on someone who knew what the heck they were doing, I'd have been a bloody lump in a matter of minutes.

"There are other ways to fight," I said.

I faced Thaddeus and deliberately tuned out the rest of the fighting. I didn't know exactly what to do, but I focused my mind in anticipation of figuring it out.

"Stop, Dancia," Barrett's voice snapped over my shoulder. "You aren't ready."

"But—"

"No."

I'd never heard him sound like that, with no room in his voice for compromise or discussion.

"I want to help."

Cam blocked a kick from Thaddeus but staggered under the force of it. I saw blood dripping down Trevor's face.

"I *need* to help."

"You'll be overwhelmed. You don't have the control yet."

"I'll be careful, Barrett."

"People will get hurt. Seriously hurt. There will be questions."

I shuddered. The teachers at Delcroix had told us hundreds of times that we needed to keep the Program secret. Part of what made Delcroix such a powerful force for good was that people didn't know it existed. Unfortunately, my record for secrecy—let alone moderation—wasn't great. In my fight with the Watchers last semester, I'd left a broken windshield, a downed telephone pole, and a giant sinkhole in my wake. Hardly subtle.

More people rushed past me to join the fight. I overheard a low-voiced argument as Anna and her mom came outside. Anna's mom was telling her to go call the police, while Anna wanted to join the fight. Eventually she did as she was told and ran back into the house. Anna's mom headed for the thick of the battle, joining a junior named Olive against a guy whose hands seemed to be everywhere. Maybe he had more than two. It was hard to tell.

Slowly, our odds improved. Meredith was the first sophomore on the street. She joined the fight beside Sam. She wasn't much on the offensive, but because she could sense her opponent's next move, she always held her own. Alisha, another sophomore, made up for in enthusiasm what she lacked in finesse. Anna's mom fought like three people rolled into one. She grabbed the many-handed guy's head and smashed it against her forehead, then turned around and slammed her foot into the back of a girl behind her.

The scariest person out there was the figure who had been blowing out the streetlights. When they got closer I could see it was a girl, small and slight. She didn't attack anyone directly. Instead, she lurked around the edges of the fight, and when one of the Delcroix kids was distracted, she'd grab them from behind. If she could hold them long enough, they'd scream and twitch, fall down, and take a while to get up.

When the vicious ballerina landed a kick to Kari's ribs that knocked her to the ground, Electricity Girl ducked in and grabbed hold of Kari's arm. Kari struggled, then seized up in a ball and shrieked in agony.

Meredith yelled, "She needs five seconds! Watch out, Sam, she's headed your way!"

Sam paused to duck a punch from a guy with a short, spiky Mohawk, then lashed out at the girl behind him. She danced back, just out of reach. I got the impression electricity was all she had in the way of fighting ability.

Not everyone at the party joined the fight. Besides the seniors, several of the sophomores edged nervously onto the sidewalk beside me, gawking at the brawl. It was primarily the Life Talents that hung back. They didn't seem to have the same aptitude for battle as the Somatics.

Luckily, most of the juniors were Somatics. They didn't pause for even a moment before joining the fight. But for all their Somatic power, the Delcroix kids weren't winning. David ran in and pulled Kari to her feet, helping her limp off the street and onto the grass. Geneva came out next. She landed on her shoulder after a brutal aerial assault. David, who seemed to act as a sort of medic, threw her over his back while Anna's mom provided cover from the acrobat Geneva had been fighting.

Cam *had* done some damage to Thaddeus, who was now swaying slightly. Still, Cam had to land four blows to match a single strike from his superstrong opponent. At the same time, clusters kept springing up with one of our people under assault by two of theirs. Blood dripped down Trevor's face, obscuring his vision, and Sam was barely avoiding the girl with the electric hands. Meredith kept shouting warnings to him, and he'd move out of reach seconds before being shocked, but each time he moved slower, and the girl got closer. Finally, she had him in her grip for a second, then two.

I stood there helpless, trying to think of something, *anything*, to do to help. I was about ready to throw myself after Electricity Girl—she was tiny, after all, so there was a chance I could take her—when I noticed a boy standing quietly on the other side of the street, slouching against a blown-out streetlight.

He was tall and lean, hands tucked in the pockets of a long duster-style coat. His bandanna was tied around his forehead, pushing up dark, spiky hair. I squinted, walking to the edge of the curb in an attempt to make out his face.

The dark figure raised his hand, as if in greeting. I stepped into the street, wanting and yet not wanting to see the face. To make out the features I was sure I knew.

The wail of a siren startled me, and I jumped back onto the curb. Thaddeus paused while Cam panted, doubled over on the street. Then Thaddeus held his fingers to his lips and whistled two short blasts. The gang threw a few last blows at whomever was nearest, then began running back the way they had come. They reached the corner and split into several groups, fading into the darkness in packs of two and three.

As if freed from a spell, I ran over to Cam. "Are you okay?"

His breath whistled unsteadily. He straightened slowly, gritting his teeth. "Did you see which way they went?"

"I think they split up."

"Damn." He spat blood onto the street from a cut on his lip.

Trevor joined us a moment later, blood smeared across his cheek and down his shirt. He said only one word, the sound of it falling from his lips like poison: "Irin."

Cam nodded. The rest of the group gathered silently by the driveway. Kari was limping; Geneva was holding her arm against her stomach. No one appeared unscathed except Anna's mom, who was practically bouncing on her toes, fury radiating from her like heat off the pavement in summer.

Lucas jerked open the door of his car, causing the hood to rattle and glass to fall in a shower from the windshield. He crawled inside and extracted the brick. "I guess he was serious about leaving a message."

"What does it say?" Cam called.

Lucas held it up. The words were written in white—lumpy and uneven.

WHO'S WATCHING WHO?

CHAPTER 12

WHILE WE stared at the brick, a man came out of the house across the street and called to Anna's mom. She hissed something in Cam's direction and hurriedly straightened her clothes. Then she waved and walked over to meet the neighbor. The sirens were getting louder, and more lights were coming on in the nearby houses.

Cam walked up to Lucas.

I followed a few paces behind, flanked by Trevor. "Give it to me," he said quietly to Lucas, holding out his hand.

Lucas shrugged. "I'm not sure why I should. It was my car."

"Funny that you didn't lift a finger to protect it," Trevor snapped.

Lucas hefted the brick in his hand. "Maybe we should give it to the police."

"We need to keep it," Cam said. "You know that as well as I do."

"And what do we tell the police?" Tara asked. "That the windshield spontaneously collapsed?"

Barrett hefted a large rock from the landscaping in front of Anna's house. He pushed past the group and planted the rock in Lucas's front seat. Then he took the brick from

Lucas's hand and gave it to Cam. "No need to fight about it. Cam's just doing his job."

Cam narrowed his eyes, as if trying to determine whether Barrett was mocking him. "Thank you," he said. He took the brick and headed for the house. Lucas and the other seniors watched as two police cars pulled up across the street. Red and blue lights flashed on our faces and reflected off the broken glass in the street.

As soon as Cam left, Anna appeared by my side, her Cupid's-bow mouth twisted and tight. "I hope you're happy."

I closed my eyes and took a deep breath, trying to erase the images from a few minutes before. Cam, bruised and bloody. The boy with the long coat and spiky hair. "Surely you can't think *I* had something to do with this."

Anna stepped a few feet closer and leaned in toward me, putting her hands on her hips. "I don't see why not. First you tell them when we have Initiation, then you let them know about the party. It hardly takes a rocket scientist to figure it out."

I straightened and met her stare. "And tell me why, exactly, you think I'm trying to get my *boyfriend* beat up?"

"Because you stood by and watched while everyone else was fighting," she spat. "You aren't loyal to the Program, and you never will be."

My face flushed as shame and anger washed over me. "You have no idea what you're talking about. I *couldn't* fight them. Barrett told me not to."

She was right. I hadn't fought back. But I had assumed Cam would understand. Now the thought occurred to me— what if he didn't?

Anna stuck her fingers into the pockets of her tiny

low-rider jeans, and turned her face to the side in disgust. "You listened to Barrett?"

"He's my teacher. I'm supposed to listen to him."

"I'm not sure what's worse—that you're a traitor, or that you're a coward. We're in the Program to fight, Dancia. Not to hide behind our *teachers*."

I crossed my arms over my chest. Barrett's warning rattled around in my head. He'd said I shouldn't fight because I wasn't ready, and might hurt someone. Wasn't that the same thing Trevor had said, at Initiation, and what I'd always feared about myself—that when I relaxed my hold over my talent, I'd lose control and people would get hurt? The wrong people?

"You and Trevor better get your stories straight," I said. "Last I heard, he thought I wasn't ready to be in the Program. Now you're telling me I should be in there throwing around my talent?"

"When your *friends* are in trouble, you fight," Anna hissed. "Everyone knows that."

I made one last attempt at reasoning with her. "Look, whether I should have fought with them or not is beside the point. I don't even know who those people are—how could I have contacted some random gang from Seattle?"

"Don't pretend you don't know about the Irin," she said scornfully.

"What?" I asked. "Who is that?"

"The Irin, Dancia," she said impatiently. "We all know *he's* one of them now. All you have to do is call him."

I caught my breath. Unable to prevent it, I let my gaze stray for a moment to the spot where I thought I'd seen him. "Who?" I asked, even though I knew the answer.

"Jack." Her eyes bored into mine. "You still care about

him. You're *helping* him. And as soon as I have proof, everyone will know."

The police questioned all of us, moving systematically through the crowd with their little notebooks, writing down everyone's stories. An ambulance arrived a moment after the police, and paramedics looked at Trevor, Cam, and the girls. They told Trevor he might need stitches in his eyebrow because it kept oozing blood, and said Cam probably had some bruised ribs but didn't need to go to the emergency room. They thought Geneva's arm needed to be X-rayed and offered to take her in the ambulance, but she said she wanted to wait for her mom.

The party began to disperse as soon as the police left. Based on our description of the bandannas, the police had said it sounded like a gang from Seattle that had been making a lot of trouble lately, though they couldn't say why they would have picked a fight with us, or what they were doing in a suburb thirty miles from downtown. Everyone agreed that that was the story we'd tell our parents: random gang violence. There was to be no mention of the fact that their leader had hurled a brick forty feet and broken the windshield of a car, or that the gang included a guy who could fight while leaping twenty feet in the air.

After the police were gone, David sat Trevor down on the curb and pressed his fingers against Trevor's cut. Slowly, as we watched, the skin closed up and a nice, healthy pink line appeared. Then David cupped his hands around Geneva's elbow and squeezed. She turned a ghastly color and groaned softly, but when he let go, she moved her arm around and smiled. He did the same to Kari's belly, and she sighed with relief.

David, as I'd suspected, was a healer. He couldn't bring someone back to life, but he could repair minor wounds and broken bones just by laying on his hands. It exhausted him and the person he healed, though, because he combined his own energy and the energy of the injured person to do the healing. He, Trevor, Kari, and Geneva all went inside to lie down afterward, while Anna's mom fixed them some kind of energy drink to help them regain their strength.

As a stream of cars and anxious parents lined up in front of the house, Cam found me sitting on the curb, staring blindly at the bushes on the other side of the street. He offered his hand. I shook my head, not wanting to hurt him, and got to my feet myself, following him into the house while Anna and her mom said good-bye to the others and tried to allay the parents' fears. Cam slouched deep down in Anna's high-backed leather sofa. I could tell he was in pain. He told the paramedic it wasn't serious, but his breath seemed shallow, and he winced whenever he moved too quickly.

"You should ask David to take care of you," I said.

"He's too tired. I'll be fine."

Cam's eyes closed. The neck of his T-shirt was ripped, and there were dark specks of blood across the front. I thought about what Anna had said, and wondered what to do. Cam hadn't acted any differently toward me since the fight, but he hadn't run up and given me a big kiss, either.

I traced the edge of the couch cushion. "I'm sorry I didn't help."

He opened his eyes. "What are you talking about?"

"I feel bad. Because I didn't do anything. I should have helped you."

"No one expects you to. You're just starting out, and, no offense, but you're a lousy hand-to-hand fighter." He smiled, and we intertwined our fingers. "You made the right decision, staying out of it."

"But I could have . . ." I didn't even have to complete my thought. Cam seemed to understand what I meant.

"Are you kidding? It's not a big deal if someone sees Geneva doing her flips, but for you it's different. People can convince themselves they didn't really see a girl thirty feet above the ground. They can't ignore a sinkhole." He gave me a weak smile, then closed his eyes again. "Fighting's my job, Dancia, not yours. At least for now. In a year or so you can kick their butts for me."

"That's not likely," I said. "You were amazing out there. If you hadn't been up against Attila the Hun, you would have killed him."

Cam shrugged, then grimaced. "I've got no real Somatic talent. I figured when I started the Program I would need to work twice as hard to be able to hold my own in a fight." He squeezed my hand gently. "*You* should have gone into the house. I was worried."

Warm honey coated my insides. I slid closer to him, though I was careful not to lean on his injured side. "Did you really think I was going to go inside? Just because you said so?"

He chuckled, then touched his ribs with his free hand. "Man, that hurts. No, I didn't think you would go inside. But I figured it was worth a shot."

Cam had tried to protect me. I choked up. Usually I was the one protecting other people. I mean, Grandma did her best to take care of me, but she was so fragile herself, it felt like I was the one in charge most of the time. Even when I used my power, it was always to defend someone else. It was just something I did, the way I was.

I loved the feeling that someone was watching out for *me*.

I studied the flat plane of Cam's stomach and the tousled hair that tangled around the bloody cuts on his forehead. I reached over and gently pushed back a lock of it.

"This must be painful," I said.

"Don't worry about it."

I noticed he did not move away from my touch.

"Wait here." I ducked into the kitchen and grabbed a paper towel. I ran it under some warm water, then sat beside him again and dabbed at his cuts.

"That's nice," he said, closing his eyes again. "Thanks."

We sat together for a while. I wished I could have just kept my mouth shut, but something compelled me to break the silence. "So . . . does this sort of thing happen to you very often?"

"Not like this."

He did not elaborate. I waited, hopeful, but I had an idea I could wait all night and he'd never tell me exactly what he was thinking.

"You didn't seem surprised that they knew about the Watchers."

"Some people figure it out. We aren't perfect."

I waited again, but he lapsed back into silence. Finally, I screwed up my courage and used the word Anna had flung at me earlier that night. "Were they part of the Irin?"

Cam stiffened. "The Irin? Where did you hear about them?"

Something about the way he said it sent chills through me. "Anna," I said. "Why do you ask?"

"She wasn't supposed to tell you about them."

A tiny shot of pleasure at the annoyance in Cam's voice was quickly eclipsed by the realization that she knew something I didn't. "But I'm in the Program now. You don't have to keep secrets from me anymore."

"It isn't about you. It's the same for all the first-year students in the Program. They want you to focus on developing your talent this year, not getting caught up in the fight."

"The fight?"

"Against the Irin." Cam turned and heaved himself up into a straighter position and stared into my eyes. "You shouldn't know about them yet. Anna shouldn't have said anything."

I gulped at the worry in his voice. "But she did."

"She did." He stared down at his hands.

"Please, Cam," I said. "I need to understand what's going on."

Especially if Jack is one of them.

CHAPTER 13

"PICTURE A group of people with talents like yours and mine," said Cam. "But they don't want to use their talents to do good—they want power and control. And we won't let them have it. So, to get what they want, they figure they have to destroy us. The Governing Council. The schools. The Watchers. Everyone."

I inhaled. "Jeez. No wonder you don't mention it to newbies."

"Yeah. It's not a pleasant thing to explain. You're just getting a handle on the fact that you're joining a secret program for people with supernatural talents. We figure it's a bit much to throw in the We're Also Here to Fight These Epic Bad Guys stuff at the same time."

I digested that for a moment. "I don't mean to sound skeptical, because they were definitely scary, but those kids tonight didn't exactly seem like supervillains. Couldn't you just bring in a few Watchers and take care of them?"

"I wish it were that easy. We can't go around eliminating every cell that comes along. We don't have enough Watchers, for one thing, and even if we did, it would raise questions for the regular cops that we don't want to answer. Besides, it wouldn't do us a whole lot of good. The group you saw tonight is just one of a hundred cells, spread all over the world. Eliminate them, and a new cell will just take their place."

"But this—what did you call it? A cell?—this cell broke into Delcroix. Isn't that a big deal?"

Cam struggled to sit up more and took a wheezy breath. "We don't think this cell was the one that broke in at Initiation. That group was more organized and more dangerous. Pete was shot that night, Dancia. If it hadn't been for David, he'd be dead right now. We didn't tell anyone because we didn't want to panic the new students or get the police involved. The group we fought tonight wasn't even carrying guns. They were just trying to make trouble, not get anyone killed."

"I see. There are other, more dangerous gangs out there. Good to know." I tried to act calm, but Cam's admission about Pete knocked me back a pace. I had been enormously relieved that no one had gotten hurt at Initiation. It made the whole thing seem a lot less scary. Guns and people dying were an entirely different matter. "But they're all part of the same group?" I asked.

Cam leaned his head back against the couch. "They're all part of a network. It's huge and diffuse, and some cells are more closely tied into the center than others. The Seattle cell is what we call a training cell. They don't have much contact with the leadership. They're mostly teenagers, just starting to use their talents. Other cells are much further along."

I slipped off my shoes and tucked my feet under me. "Who's in charge of it all?"

"There's a guy named Gregori who seems to be their leader. He feeds money and weapons to the cells, and they give him their loyalty. But they do whatever they want, most of the time. There are only a few cells that answer to him directly." Cam paused and pushed his hair back from his face. "The Irin aren't like any other enemy you can imagine," he said. "They don't have a rule book or a single strategy. The cells are independent. The only thing that ties them together is their hatred."

I didn't have a hard time believing that. You could feel the hatred in the way Thaddeus had thrown the brick—like he wanted it to be something far worse. Far more deadly.

"How do they find each other?" I asked.

"We don't know for certain. We assume they recruit, like we do, but instead of searching schools for high-performing kids, they head for jails and street corners. They find the kids who are already in trouble and promise to give them power. Kids like . . ."

He didn't have to finish his thought.

I knew he was thinking about Jack, who had been forced to leave Delcroix and was probably still on the run from the Watchers.

Jack, who had spent time living under a bridge, and believed that that justified his stealing and using his power as he liked.

Jack, who probably hated Delcroix and the Watchers more with every breath he took.

I understood that hatred. It broke my heart, because it meant he now hated everything I stood for, but I understood it, too. I even felt a little of it myself. Delcroix had taken away my best friend. How could I not hate it, just a little?

"So they recruit," I said. "Then what? Do they have schools like we do?"

"The Irin don't have formal training programs, because they can't settle down. We make sure of that. They also don't have our history or our libraries. We've spent decades refining teaching techniques for various talents. They make it up as they go along. We believe their training cells are a sort of testing ground. The members of the cell harass our students, do some damage in the community, and practice their talents—all while making sure not to be so dangerous they get themselves killed off by the Watchers. If they can do that, Gregori brings them into his inner circle, and they get trained by his top operatives."

Questions kept coming to me, increasing in number with everything that Cam said, but his skin was getting paler, and I could tell he was in a lot of pain. I would have to stop talking soon. Still, I couldn't keep myself from asking one more thing, as Jack's image hovered in my mind. "When does a cell get dangerous enough to be eliminated?"

Cam leaned forward and put both hands on his knees. Slowly, he pushed himself up to a standing position, though he remained bent, like Grandma first thing in the morning. His face turned white.

I jumped to my feet and held out my hand to steady him. He did not take it. "You should sit back down," I said. "You aren't okay like this."

"We need to get back. The gates close at eleven."

"As if they wouldn't open them for you."

He acknowledged the truth of my words with a nod of the head. "Still. We should go. I promised your grandma I'd have you back by eleven."

"You just don't want to talk anymore," I said.

"I need to brief Mr. Judan." He straightened with a sharp exhalation. "And I'm tired. I don't want to stay here all night."

"Will he be mad that I know?"

"It's too late to worry about that now, isn't it?" Cam put his hand on my shoulder and took a step toward me, his face gray and drawn.

"Is there more?" I asked. "More that you aren't telling me?"

Warm, strong hands found my waist and pulled me close. He touched my face with one hand, shaking his head in wonder. "Dancia, you never give up, do you?"

As was always the case, my brain started to fog up the second he touched me. I struggled to hold on to my thoughts, to keep pushing at something that had seemed vitally important only seconds before, but became wholly irrelevant when Cam's arms were around me.

My words came out in slow motion. "Is that a bad thing?"

"No." He leaned forward, whispering, his breath warm as he gently kissed my neck. "It's who you are."

The kiss caught me by surprise. I stood still, wanting to savor the feeling as long as I could.

He did it again.

I forgot about the Irin. I forgot my own name. Nothing mattered but the touch of his lips on my skin. He kissed my mouth and I wrapped my arms around his neck. I touched his hair, my knees like jelly.

"I guess this wasn't the best Valentine's Day," he said.

I shook my head slightly. "Best Valentine's Day I've ever had."

He lowered his head to kiss me again. It was the longest, deepest kiss yet. I clung to his shoulders to stay upright.

"Ahem."

We sprang apart guiltily. Anna and her mom stood in the doorway. Anna coughed into her hand, her heart-shaped face registering only polite amusement.

Cam chuckled. "Sorry. Just saying good night."

Anna's mom laughed. "I guess you're getting started early, then, since you're driving her home." She gestured toward the stairs. "I'll check on David and the others. Anna, you keep an eye on these two."

I felt the anger rolling off Anna, but she kept her expression carefully neutral. "Sure, Mom. You can count on it."

To my shock and horror, Grandma was waiting up when Cam dropped me off at my house. She had on her pajamas, which is to say, a threadbare terry cloth robe and an embarrassingly short white nightgown, with curlers in her hair and a white chiffon scarf tied over her head.

Very attractive.

She had, thank goodness, removed the baby-doll makeup that usually colored her lips red and her cheeks bright pink. I suspect she had fallen asleep on the couch, because her eyes were puffy and unfocused behind her thick glasses. She threw open the door just as I prepared to melt into Cam's arms for one last good-night kiss.

Cam and I both froze, startled to see her appear like a white-haired gnome. She held up her watch. "Five minutes late," she declared.

Without a second of hesitation, Cam turned on the charm. Sincerity oozed from every inch of him, from his puppy-dog eyes to the tousled hair across his forehead. "I sincerely apologize for my tardiness in returning Dancia. Unfortunately, there was some unexpected excitement at the party tonight, and we had to stay long enough to talk to the police."

"The police?" Grandma's eyes widened.

"Yes. A gang of miscreants threw a rock at someone's

car, and a fight broke out. There was no serious danger to anyone. It was just a fistfight. You're welcome to call Anna's mother to talk to her about it."

"Is that why your face is beat up?" she asked. "Why you can't stand up straight?"

He pressed a hand against his ribs. "I'm afraid so. I didn't appreciate the way they were acting."

Grandma nodded approvingly. "I like a boy who isn't afraid to fight." She inspected me. "Your clothes aren't even wrinkled. Did you stay out of it?"

"Yes." I pushed past her into the house. She and Cam followed. I moved aside a pile of newspapers and leaned against the dining room table, which sat just a few feet away from the door. Our house was so small you could see the whole thing from the front entry: dining room table pressed against the wall to the left of the living room, tiny kitchen through an entryway beyond that.

Grandma scowled at me. "Why's that?"

Cam seemed startled by her words, but I just grimaced. I was used to Grandma's eccentricities. "You know I'm not the best with my hands, Grandma. Do you want me to get pummeled for no good reason?"

"Your hands are fine. You just need more practice."

"You *want* Dancia to fight?" Cam asked, amazed.

"Of course," she snapped, as if that should have been obvious. "I want her to be able to defend herself. She doesn't need to be stupid about it, but she can't let a boy fight all her battles."

"I don't think that will be a problem," Cam said wryly. "I think Dancia can defend herself just fine."

"If you say so," Grandma said as she started toward the kitchen. "Would you like a soda?"

Cam shook his head. "I need to get back to school."

"Well, that's all right, then. Thank you for bringing Dancia home."

Cam and I shuffled around each other awkwardly. I didn't know if we should shake hands or hug, or if Grandma would be mad if we did either. I decided no touching was the best course to follow. "I'll see you on Monday."

Cam reached forward and squeezed my hand. "See you Monday." He inclined his head toward Grandma in a move that was somewhere between a nod and a bow. "Thanks again for letting me take Dancia out."

She looked at him over the top of her glasses. "You'd better get on back to school."

He drove off slowly. Grandma went immediately toward the phone on the wall in the kitchen. "What's that woman's name? I want to hear about what happened."

"You could just ask me," I said.

She stopped and walked back to the living room, sinking down slowly into her favorite chair, her nightgown billowing around her like a huge white parachute. "All right, tell me about it."

I pulled the old blanket off the back of the couch and wrapped it around my shoulders as I sat down. I explained about the rock and the fight, and how Cam wanted me to go back into the house so I'd be safe.

Grandma held out her hand to stop me. "I understand. He's your knight in shining armor. And I'm happy he's willing to defend you. Just don't think that that excuses him for bringing you home late."

"But, Grandma, there was a fight," I protested. "And *police*. Call Anna's mom if you don't believe me. She'll tell you."

She sniffed. "Oh, I'll call her all right. But still, if that boy was so amazing, he could have gotten you home on time. Even with a fight."

I closed my eyes in frustration. When I opened them, I realized she was smiling. Just a little. "I'm going to bed," I grumbled, realizing I'd been had.

She stood, and I gave her a good-night hug. Grandma came up only to my shoulder. When I hugged her, I could rest my chin on the top of her head.

"I'm glad you weren't hurt, dear child," she said softly. "I wouldn't want to have to traipse around Seattle looking for those kids. My uppercut isn't what it once was."

I smiled at the idea of Grandma fighting Thaddeus. Then I imagined the Irin coming to our house, throwing a brick at our car or through our window, and the smile fell away. In an instant, the purpose of the Program became stunningly clear. How many other Grandmas were out there, needing protection? How many babies or little kids? The gang members that attacked us at Anna's house were frightening, and they were only teenagers. If they got trained they'd be even more powerful, and more dangerous. It didn't matter what Cam wasn't telling me about the Irin—what I knew was bad enough.

"We'll deal with them," I promised. "You don't have to worry about a thing."

I headed back to my room, memories of the night swirling through my head. Cam, fighting like a ninja from some kung fu movie. Anna, accusing me of calling in the Irin. Barrett, eyes flashing, telling me I wasn't ready. And the boy in the long coat. The boy I feared I knew.

I grabbed the handles on the bottom drawer of my dresser, jerking it hard when the old, warped wood refused to move. I must have been rougher than usual, because I knocked over the two silver frames I had on top, with their faded photos of me and my mom and dad just before they died. I was standing the pictures back up when I saw the note, carefully folded into a little tent, my name written across the front in narrow, arching black letters.

My heartbeat roared in my ears. I picked up the note with trembling hands and tore it open.

They're still lying. Ask them where the Irin came from. Ask them what happened to Ethan Hannigan. Call me if you want to know the truth.

There was a phone number. I swallowed hard.
Jack had returned.

CHAPTER 14

I JAMMED the letter into my back pocket, then forced myself to grab my pajama bottoms and T-shirt and head for the bathroom. After I'd locked the door and turned on the water in the sink, I took out the letter and stared at it. My palms began to sweat as I gripped the sheet of paper. It felt hot under my fingers, like it might burst into flames if I held it too long.

I don't know how long I looked at that number, but the hot water from the sink fogged up the mirror, and I knew Grandma would be banging on the door soon, asking what was going on. I had to make a decision. I should have destroyed the letter as fast as I could, but my hands refused to move. Finally, I dug my cell phone out of my pocket, selected "new contact," and paused. It seemed dangerous to use Jack's name, so I typed *Ethan Hannigan* instead. I entered the number from Jack's note carefully, erasing and retyping when my trembling fingers missed the keys. If anyone found it, I figured I could say I had a cousin with that name.

When I was finished, I ripped the letter into tiny pieces and flushed it down the toilet. If Anna or her friends were somehow watching my house, I didn't want to keep any evidence that Jack had contacted me. I might already have been in trouble.

Yet I couldn't throw away a chance to talk to Jack. Not after all we'd been through.

I'm the first to admit Jack and I hadn't exactly parted on the best of terms. He had wanted me to come with him, and I had stayed. I chose Cam and Delcroix over Jack, and he knew it. Still, I felt a bond with him that was difficult to explain—a bond that made it hard for me to believe he'd gone and joined the Irin.

And there was the small matter of the kiss we'd shared in my backyard. I tried not to think about it, because I had a boyfriend now. But still. He was the first boy I'd ever kissed. It wasn't as if I could erase it from my memory.

I knew he had been terrified when he left, on the run from a pack of very determined Watchers. But Jack wouldn't have hurt anyone. If the Irin were truly bad, Jack *couldn't* have gotten involved with them.

Could he?

It didn't help my confusion that, even after talking to Cam, things still didn't add up. Why did a group of teenagers hate Delcroix so much? Cam had said there were hundreds of cells, all over the world. Were they all frustrated bad guys who wanted to take over the world?

There had to be more to their story. I wished I could have ignored it, but Jack's note was right—Cam was hiding something.

I shook my head sourly. And I'd thought once I was in the Program there would be no more secrets.

I stared at the phone for a long time. Then, unable to believe what I was doing, I pushed the button.

"It's about time you called."

I jerked to my feet, heart racing at the sound of the familiar voice.

Black hair, silver eyes, smile lurking at the corner of his mouth.

Helping me over the Wall at orientation. Laughing with me during ethics.

Doing chemistry homework together in the commons. Jack.

"Hey," I gulped, trying to sound casual. "What's up?"

He chuckled. "Not much. Have a good night?"

"Parts were good. Where are you?"

"I move around," he said. "I can't say more than that."

I had to force myself to breathe. All I could think of was the Watchers and their guns. "Are you safe?"

I could imagine the little ironic grin as he spoke. "As much as I'll ever be. How about you? What's Button-Down up to these days?"

Despite everything, I had to laugh. Jack was the one who had coined the name Button-Down for the dictator-in-training who shared my room. "Catherine's her usual self. She reinforced the tape dividing our closet just last week. Hennie thinks there's something going on with her parents. She's been particularly mean lately."

Jack snorted. "You can tell the difference?"

"I guess I've actually been feeling sorry for her," I said.

"That *is* strange. Everything else okay? Is it different now that you know their secret?"

The last time I had seen Jack, he had just uncovered the truth about the Program. But I couldn't be sure how much he understood about the Watchers and the Governing Council. So, while I wanted to tell him about everything—Initiation, classes with Mr. Fritz, and Barrett—I knew I couldn't.

Instead, I mentioned the one thing I figured was safe to

complain about. "I think Anna's spying on me. But it's just her, not the other guys."

Jack made a sound of disgust. "Don't be too sure."

"I'm probably just being paranoid."

"You're away from the windows, right? Not in the living room, I hope?"

"I'm in the bathroom."

"Good. Sit on the floor," he instructed. "By the door."

I did as he said, crossing my legs in front of me. "Jack, what's going on?"

"You need to get out," he said.

I closed my eyes and leaned my head against the wall. "We've been through this. I don't *want* to get out. I want to learn from them."

"They're not what you think."

"Neither are the people you're mixed up with," I said.

There was silence.

"What do you know about us?" he asked.

"That you're called the Irin," I said, "and you're dangerous."

"Do you want to know who Ethan was?"

"No."

"He was a student at Delcroix who was too powerful, so they killed him. They claimed he was unstable and committed suicide, but he had a twin sister who refused to believe their lies. That's how the Seattle group got started. She knew what the Watchers were capable of, and she wanted to protect people like her brother. People like me. People who would be dead if they didn't have someone to help them."

I held my hand in front of my eyes, wishing I could wipe away the picture he'd drawn in my mind. "I don't believe you."

"Yes, you do."

I swallowed hard. "I have to go, Jack."

"There are stories like Ethan's all over the world. They say it's all for good, but it's still killing, Dancia. They'll try to make you believe they're right and we're wrong, but the lines aren't that clear. They want power just like we do. We just don't fool ourselves into thinking that we're doing it for some noble purpose."

That was all I could handle. "I'm sorry, Jack. I shouldn't have called. I've got to go."

"Don't let them do this to you," he said. "They'll eat you alive. You'll start to believe them, and then it will be too late."

"Good-bye, Jack," I whispered. "Be careful."

I shut the phone. The screen went blank, but two words stayed lodged in my mind.

Ethan Hannigan.

Why couldn't I have left well enough alone?

I rode the Silver Bullet to school Monday with only a few other freshmen and none of the upperclassmen. Most people stayed at school over the weekends now, even Hennie and Esther. With spring break only a few weeks away, everyone had exams coming up and nobody wanted to waste time traveling. The only ones who went home were freshman who lived in or around Seattle.

Well, freshmen from Seattle and Catherine, to be precise. Catherine's parents flew her home to California every weekend. This, despite the fact that they were rarely home themselves.

I walked around school that morning in a daze, seeing Watchers and the Irin in every corner. One of the art classes had put up a new photography exhibit in the front hall over

122

the weekend, and it seemed half the school was crowding in front of the pictures. They were weird and artsy—pictures of old cars, parking lots, and chain-link fences. I didn't understand those pictures any better than I understood anything else at Delcroix, and I couldn't fight the mix of frustration and sadness I felt with every image I saw. I had no idea whom I could trust and who was lying, but I feared the answers were "no one" and "everyone."

I expected Esther to pounce on me as soon as I got to school, but I didn't see her until chemistry. When I arrived at class she was sitting in the back row, pulling homework out of her backpack.

I used to sit in the last row with Jack. We'd started passing notes to each other the first week of school. When he left, Esther moved next to me, which was fun but not nearly as helpful. Esther and I passed notes about boys, our horrible hair, and our teacher's questionable fashion sense. When Jack and I had passed notes, it was actually about class.

Jack loved chemistry. He didn't like to admit it, but he did. I guess that made sense, given that he was an Earth Talent, like me and Barrett. Jack had the power to change states of matter—liquid to gas, solid to liquid. We'd talked once about his turning a person into a gas. He'd said he'd never tried it because he wasn't sure if he could reassemble them in the same exact shape they'd been when he started.

What if he tried it now? What if the Irin made him do it?

Hennie sat in the front of the class, four rows ahead of us, her hair in a long shiny braid down her back. She said if she sat next to us, we would get her into trouble. Still, she wasn't too scared to lean against Yashir, who sat on her left, and whisper while our teacher's back was turned.

I plopped down into the seat next to Esther and opened

my notebook. Mr. Abbas started right in on Boyle's law, his notes projected onto the screen in front of the class. Jack would have been thrilled. He'd started studying Boyle's law back in September.

I stabbed the paper with my pencil and scowled. I *had* to stop thinking about Jack.

Esther sighed and stretched, dropping a note on the floor behind my desk. I waited for a few seconds and then turned around to extract my textbook from my backpack. While doing so, I snagged the note.

Trevor blew me off.

I paused and shot her a quick glance. Her usual smile had been wiped off her face, and her dark eyes radiated despair. She looked just like Greta Garbo, whom she'd been studying in her acting class. Her usually unruly hair fell from her face in smooth waves, and her lips formed a perfect red bow.

What happened? Did you make some kind of move on him?

I threw the note back in her direction.

We dutifully nodded and gave Mr. Abbas our full attention as he faced the room, then hurriedly passed another round of notes as soon as his back was turned.

I saw him in the cafeteria on Saturday, and he kept looking at me. Then in the library he sat across the table from me. We talked for a little while and I was superexcited and then he got a text and that was it. He practically got up midsentence and left me there. I saw him walk out with Anna, so I know it wasn't anything important. In English today he said he had a meeting and was sorry for walking out on me. But I know he was lying! What meeting could he have had with Anna that was so important?!

I raised my hand and answered a question to show Mr. Abbas I was paying attention. I got the answer wrong, but he was one of those teachers who always wanted to build your self-esteem, so he was nice about it. When he turned to Hennie to get the correct answer, I scribbled a response and slid the note back to Esther.

I'm sure he wouldn't have lied to you.

I had a feeling I knew exactly what Trevor's meeting was about, but I still wanted to wring his neck. I didn't want to think he was deliberately trying to hurt her, but it was hard to believe he was oblivious to what she must have thought.

Esther sighed deeply and turned to face me. She seemed close to tears. "I asked him if he wanted to get together after school today," she whispered, "but he said he was busy and probably would be for the next couple of weeks. He's just trying to avoid me. It's obvious."

Mr. Abbas cleared his throat, and we set our pencils back to paper. I wondered what Trevor and Anna talked about over the weekend. I would have bet that Trevor was busy with something to do with the Irin.

As soon as class ended, I jumped up, reached out my hand, and pulled Esther to a standing position. Gently, I shook her by the shoulders, relieved to have something to think about besides my new obsession with the Irin. "Never fear, you *will* love again, darling."

She shook her head. "It doesn't matter. I'll never find anyone to love me back. I've lost my touch. I'm a has-been."

I rolled my eyes at all the drama. "Oh, please, Esther, you're getting carried away, aren't you?"

If she was kidding, she masked it well. Tears pooled in her eyes, and I could see beyond a doubt that it wasn't an act.

She jammed her notebook into her bag. "All I know is that ever since we started school, I've been rejected by every boy I even *think* about liking."

Hennie and Yashir walked up, holding hands and looking particularly cute—tiny Hennie, with her pink turtleneck sweater and matching headband, and gangly Yashir, dreadlocks strewn around his shoulders, hoops dangling from his nose and ears.

Yashir took in Esther's appearance; he paid extra attention to her face. "That's trippy," he observed. "You don't look like yourself. You feelin' okay?"

"She's heartbroken," Hennie said.

"Great," Esther said, pulling a lock of hair free from the strap of her backpack and letting it fall over one shoulder. "The last thing I need is for everyone to know about it."

Yashir squinted. "What shouldn't I know about?"

"It's a girl thing," Hennie said to Yashir. "You wouldn't understand."

Yashir shook his head. "You all make my head spin. See you at lunch, Hennie?" He tugged gently on her braid and touched the tip of her nose.

She nodded, a goofy grin lingering on her face as she watched him walk down the hall.

I grabbed Esther's hand. "You need to shake yourself out

of this. You're blowing it all out of proportion. We're talking about Trevor, remember? The guy who never smiles?"

"I've seen him smile," Esther said, a little of the color returning to her face.

"Maybe once or twice. But not on a regular basis."

"He's wicked smart, and he loves books," she rejoined. "We worked on a project together in our AP English class and got along great. He just looks scary. Deep down, he's a sweet guy."

I stifled a groan. "He isn't the right guy for you, Esther."

"Neither is anyone else, apparently."

"You're just having a dry spell," I said. "There's nothing to be worried about. Right, Hennie?"

It took Hennie a moment to realize we were waiting for a response, because she was still staring at Yashir. Or rather, at the spot where Yashir had been. "Huh?"

"We're talking about Esther's dry spell," I repeated. "I'm saying she's got nothing to worry about. There are tons of guys at Delcroix. She just hasn't met the right one yet."

Hennie fell into step beside us as we started toward the stairwell. The halls were a tangle of people moving between classes, and we had to duck around the edges to keep moving. The high ceilings worked like an echo chamber, and you'd think you were in the middle of some huge auditorium, instead of a hallway in a school of fewer than two hundred students. "Esther, you make people laugh and feel good about themselves," said Hennie. "It's inevitable that some guy is going to fall for you."

"I notice you didn't say anything about how I look," she said, smoothing her hair behind her ears. "Next thing I know you're going to tell me I have a good personality. Like *that's* suppose to make me feel better."

"Don't be ridiculous. You're like a movie star, with those enormous eyes and that gorgeous hair. Besides, aren't you the one who's always telling us how friends grow into boyfriends? You've got tons of guy friends. I'm sure someday one of them will want something more."

"None of this helps," Esther said. "You're just convincing me that I'm right. Everyone sees me as just a friend."

"All I'm saying is that you should let things be for a little while," Hennie continued. "It will all work out. By spring break, everyone will be falling all over themselves to get their chance at you."

Esther didn't respond. She gazed down the hall, lost in thought. Then she stopped suddenly. "I've got it."

"What?" I asked, tugging Hennie closer to me to keep her from whacking one of the seniors with her backpack.

"I need a makeover. New hair, makeup, clothes . . . I'll be reborn as the girl people want to date instead of the girl they want for their best friend."

I started to raise my hand in protest, but she didn't notice.

"You said it yourself, Hennie," she said. "They think I'm a better friend than girlfriend. So I'll have to change their mind about that. The only question is what I want to be. Biker chick? Vamp? Cheerleader? What do you think?"

"I say you just be y—" I began.

She put her hands over her ears. "Don't say it!"

"Yourself," I said.

"That's the problem," she said, deflated. "I don't know who that is anymore."

Hennie and I exchanged a worried glance.

She pulled us toward her and said in a low voice, "It's not natural, the way I can become someone else." She held out a lock of her hair, which had started to curl as she spoke. "See?

It's spooky. Sometimes I think there *is* no real me, and acting is all I can do."

"That's ridiculous," Hennie said, though she eyed the curl nervously, as if Esther held a snake between her palms.

"It's the truth. I act like everyone's best friend, and suddenly that's all I am. Maybe it's time I started using that to my advantage. Who says I shouldn't act like a bombshell?" The curl loosened and fell over her eyes in a sultry wave. "I can do sexy, you know?"

Hennie put her hand on Esther's forearm. "It's just your hair, Esther. Not you. You're upset about Trevor and it's making everything seem crazy. You'll feel better in a week or so. I know it."

"Easy for you to say," she said, digging her hands deep in her pockets as she continued down the hall. Hennie and I hurried to catch up. "You've got a super boyfriend, and so does Dancia. I've got nothing but an uncanny ability to imitate people. Everyone in my acting class says it's an amazing gift and I'm such a genius, but then they turn around and avoid me. I feel like a freak."

Her words were painfully familiar. How many times over the years had I thought that same thing? I put my hand on her shoulder and forced her to come to a stop. "You're not a freak. Your acting *is* a gift. It's part of who you are."

"That's right," Hennie chimed in. "You understand other people well enough to act like them. Lots of people would love to have that ability."

Esther's chin trembled. "They can have it. I'm tired of sticking out. My teacher keeps pushing me to do more, to get deeper into my characters, and it just makes it worse. My focus classes are more depressing every day. It seems like the minute I relax, they're putting some new 'challenge' in front of me, and I'm changing into someone new. I wish they'd just leave me alone and let me be normal for once."

Luckily, Hennie responded to that one, because I had to struggle to keep my mouth shut. The truth seared me— the truth about Esther's gift and the way the teachers were molding and developing it, despite all the pain they were causing. And now *I* was letting her feel that pain, just as Cam had let me feel my pain the semester before.

But I couldn't tell her the truth. I couldn't tell her anything.

"Esther, you know nobody around here is normal," Hennie said. "People think I'm weird because I learn languages so quickly. The other day, I heard An speaking in Mandarin and I actually understood her. And I've only been taking lessons for a few months! My teachers keep talking to me in languages I don't know and asking me to try to figure out what they're saying. Half the time I can actually do it. If you're a freak, then I'm one, too."

I should have been expecting it, but Hennie's admission hit me just as hard as Esther's. They were pushing her, too. Was she Level Three already? Could Cam see her talent marks when he walked down the hall?

"At least you've got a useful gift," Esther said. "All I can do is pretend to be someone I'm not."

Hennie's voice softened. "Well, we know who you are. You're Esther Racowitz. You're funny and charming, and everyone loves you because you're so easy to talk to. We're your best friends, and we believe in you, even if you don't."

"Whatever." Esther pushed her curls back behind her ears. "I've got to get to English. I'll see you guys later." She walked away, oblivious of the interested stares she attracted as she made her way down the hall.

"Was she like this all weekend?" I asked Hennie.

"Not this bad." Hennie watched until Esther disappeared from view, and then whispered, "It is a little weird, don't you think? How she changes when she's acting?"

I didn't know how to respond without lying or making light of Esther's very real problem. I decided I'd have to distract Hennie from the subject—never an easy prospect. To my relief, I noticed Barrett and a group of seniors approaching from the other direction. With a silent apology to Barrett for using him, I made a mental tug on his foot and watched as he kicked in response like a girl in a chorus line. It was a little trick I'd played on him before, so I figured he'd know it was me. The seniors all burst out laughing, and Barrett whirled around, grimacing when he spotted me across the hall.

"D.! Good to see you," he called out. "I hope you brought your shorts for our class today. I heard things could get *hot* this afternoon."

A burst of heat passed under the sole of my foot. I smiled and pretended I hadn't noticed. Tara high-fived me as she passed.

Hennie cocked her head, watching the group go by. "What was that all about? I heard they're predicting cold weather all week."

I shrugged. "I have no idea. Barrett hardly makes sense half the time. I can't believe they actually let him teach a class."

We continued walking. "I almost forgot," Hennie said. "How was the party?"

"Eventful." Relieved that I'd finally managed to get her off the topic of Esther, I briefly described the fight with the "gang from Seattle," carefully retelling the story I'd told Grandma. Of course, I left out any mention of my altercation with Anna or of the note I'd found when I got home.

Hennie shuddered. "You must have been terrified."

"I guess. Mostly, I felt stupid letting Cam and the others do all the fighting while I stood around and did nothing."

Hennie wrinkled her perfect button nose. "So you should have thrown yourself in front of someone's fist even though you knew you'd just end up getting hurt? That's crazy."

"Maybe." My lips twisted into a smile. "My grandma wouldn't think I was crazy, though. She wants me to be able to defend myself. She said I need more practice."

"Practice fighting?" Hennie shook her head in wonder. "I can't imagine how much trouble I'd be in if I got in a fight. My parents would never forgive me."

"You know, my grandpa died when Grandma was young, and then my mom and dad died, too. She probably just wants me to be able to take care of myself, in case something happens to her."

I'd never thought much about it before, but Grandma had always encouraged me to do things on my own, even things a kid shouldn't do. Like driving the car when I was thirteen, or learning to shop and cook when I was in elementary school.

"So, what are you going to do about it? Weren't you in a self-defense class last semester?"

"Yeah. It didn't stick." I had a sudden brainstorm. "I should ask Cam to tutor me!"

"Oh, good idea. I'm sure you'll get a lot of practicing done with him." Hennie rolled her eyes.

I hit her playfully as we started down the stairs. "Seriously, it *would* be nice to be a little tougher."

"So you can be like Anna?" Hennie inclined her head toward Anna, who was at the bottom of the stairwell, speaking to Trevor and Molly. Her ponytail swung back and forth as she talked, her hands waving.

"How'd you guess?"

Just the sight of Anna was enough to wipe the smile off my face. She must have felt my presence, because she stopped talking and tipped her head in my direction. Trevor and Molly leaned in as she whispered something, and all three gazed up at us. Then they turned their backs deliberately and moved down the hall.

Hennie gasped. "Wow, that was harsh." She pulled me to one side, dodging traffic and stumbling on the edge of her shoe. "Did something happen with Anna this weekend?"

I laughed nervously, not meeting her eyes. "Apart from the usual 'she hates me with a fiery passion' stuff?"

"Dancia, they just treated you like you've got the plague! Something happened at the party. Something you're not telling me."

I bit my lip, "It was nothing new. Anna kept throwing herself at Cam, but that's just par for the course."

"Throwing herself at him how?" Hennie asked. "Short skirt and cleavage? Karaoke?"

"She tried to make it seem like he still liked her and he and I had nothing in common. They played music together, and she sent me on errands for soda. It wasn't a big deal."

"What did Cam do?"

"He's oblivious. Anna is one of his best friends, and they're both way into music. I'm sure it seemed normal for him to spend the night next to the stereo."

"So, he deserted you?" she said, narrowing her gaze.

"No! Well, sort of. A little. But not completely. And he made up for it at the end of the night."

"You're sure? How'd he make up for it?"

I reveled in the memory of that long, lovely kiss. "He made out with me right in front of Anna."

Hennie glowed with delight. "Well that does make up for it. She must have *hated* that." The bell rang, and we hurried down the rest of the stairs. We paused when we reached the bottom, as Hennie's class was to the right and mine to the left. "I'm still not sure that explains why Trevor and Molly were so rude."

I shrugged off her concern. "Don't worry about them. The important thing is that Cam and I are doing great. He was so sweet after the party and supercool with Grandma, even though she gave him a hard time."

Hennie wasn't convinced, but I seemed to have partly mollified her. "If things get worse with Anna, you've got to tell me about it. You know that, right?"

I nodded. "Of course."

I hurried to my English class, the sour taste of guilt in my mouth, but stopped when I saw Trevor heading my way. I debated whether I should say something or not, and quickly decided I couldn't let it go. I marched over to him, my mind filled with the vision of Esther's eye's pooling with tears.

"I need to talk to you," I said.

He sighed. "We can hardly talk about this here at school. I must say, for your sake, I hope Anna is wrong. If you're in contact with him—"

I held up my hand. Later, I would worry about what he and Anna thought about me. Right now, my anger was more important. "Not about that. About Esther."

"Esther?" His eyes widened. "What about her?"

"Stay away from her. That's what."

"I don't know what you're talking about," he said.

He turned to walk past me, but I planted myself in front

of him. "I'm talking about your performance in the library this weekend. What was that all about? One minute you're talking to her and the next you blow her off?"

"I got a call from Mr. Judan," Trevor said. "He wanted to meet with all of us. It isn't like I had a choice. I don't see what the big deal is, anyway."

"She thinks you *like her*," I said, poking him in the chest with one finger. "She knows you're watching her, and she thinks it's for an entirely different reason than the real one."

Trevor shifted his backpack over his shoulder and shuffled his feet. "I didn't mean—"

"I don't care what you meant," I said. "She's my friend, and you're hurting her feelings. Either figure out how to be discreet or find someone else to be her Watcher. Got it?"

With that, I turned and marched away, leaving him in stunned, openmouthed silence.

It had been a miserable day, and I had a feeling things were only going to get worse. But for one brief moment, I couldn't help smiling.

CHAPTER 15

AFTER LUNCH, I headed for my focus class with Barrett and Mr. Fritz. I hadn't seen Cam. I figured he was holed up with Mr. Judan, planning nasty things to do to the Irin. It was actually a relief not to have run into him. I was afraid my guilt about contacting Jack would be visible on my face.

Mr. Fritz greeted me at the door. "You can set down your backpack and grab your jacket, Dancia. We're headed to the woods today."

I was surprised. After the big fight at Anna's house, I figured we'd be spending this session processing the event, maybe even debating philosophical questions that would leave my brain aching. I had actually been looking forward to it. I'd been thinking about Ethan Hannigan, Jack, and the Irin all day. I could have used something to distract me.

I grabbed my sweatshirt and followed him down the hall. Though I was still irritated with Barrett for not getting involved at Anna's house, it was impossible to have too much righteous anger now that I'd talked to Jack. Everything about the Irin seemed hopelessly complicated, and what Barrett had said right before the fight—"they created this"—was strangely in line with what Jack had said about the Watchers killing Ethan Hannigan.

In any case, Barrett was uncharacteristically serious. He walked with more purpose than usual, striding forward impatiently, his long, long legs eating up the distance.

No one spoke until we reached a secluded spot in the woods. Giant Doug firs loomed over our heads, while the bare branches of the maple trees shuddered in the breeze. The ground was soft and springy, littered with broken sticks, fallen leaves, and the decayed remnants of ferns. On one side of the clearing, the earth sloped sharply away, and you could see from the tops of the trees that we were on the edge of a ravine. The woods around Delcroix were like that. Even though you didn't get much altitude change overall, there were unexpected ridges and slopes around every corner.

I had often wondered if that was due to Program students practicing their talents. Maybe someone had a talent for digging trenches, or moving soil. Or blowing things up.

Mr. Anderson stood at the far side of the clearing, arms resting on top of his belly, his jaw set.

"Let's get this over with," he said.

That's when I started to get nervous. He wasn't looking at me, in spite of my repeated attempts to catch his eye.

"What's going on?" I asked, trying to keep a smile on my face. "They can still hear me scream from here, you know." Barrett, Mr. Fritz, and Mr. Anderson formed a rough triangle, with me in the center. I spun around. "Is this some kind of game, Mr. Fritz? One of your little tests, perhaps?"

"More of an activity than a test," Mr. Fritz said.

Barrett and Mr. Anderson each took a step closer. My heart started to race. I was pinned among the three of them. Surrounded. I tried to back up.

"Sorry, but you aren't going anywhere," Barrett said. "Not until we have our lesson."

"You're starting to freak me out," I said, glancing at him. "What's the lesson?"

"We aren't quite sure yet," Mr. Fritz said. "We'll have to see when we're done."

I dropped my sweatshirt on the ground. "Fine. Do I take you on one at a time, or all at once?"

Mr. Anderson raised both hands. "All at once."

I gaped openmouthed at Mr. Fritz. "Seriously?"

He had barely nodded when Barrett launched the first shot. Heat entered my body through my toes and rippled up my legs. My heart began thumping in an unsteady rhythm. I held out my hands, and, as I watched, my skin flushed a dark pink. Tiny wisps of smoke trailed from my fingers.

It was beautiful but distinctly uncomfortable, like I'd been left to bake in the sun on the hottest day of the year. My face throbbed, and the air that came in through my nose singed my throat and lungs.

"I know you aren't ready for this," Mr. Fritz said regretfully. "But we didn't have a choice. We had to move forward."

I wanted to ask why, what had changed, but the heat in my blood made it impossible to think. I inhaled more deeply, trying to ignore the sensations running through my body. "What am I supposed to do?"

"Fight back. That's what you wanted, isn't it?"

I tried to make sense of what was happening. Why had they all turned against me?

Mr. Fritz seemed to understand. "You're struggling; I thought you might. I'll be honest with you: this isn't going to be easy."

"Thanks for the encouraging words," I panted.

With every breath, I was getting hotter. Barrett wasn't

letting up. I forced myself to squint in his direction. I had to locate the strings around him to pluck the one that would send him crashing to the ground. A smoky haze ran through the clearing, obscuring my vision, but I finally made out the dim image of the dark lines that were my only hope of survival.

I forced the information into my clouded brain. Prickles of fire sent my fingers twitching. I lashed out frantically, tugging the cord that held Barrett to the earth. He fell backward and landed on the ground, flat-backed and limp.

I thought I might have seriously hurt him, because he stayed still and the heat began to fade. I started to take a step toward him, terrified to look at what I'd done, when I felt a tug at the front of my foot and almost lost my balance. I looked down and realized that a thin length of ivy had wrapped itself around my shoe. I shook it off, thinking I'd somehow stepped into it, when another one started to crawl toward me from the edge of the clearing.

I whipped around to face Mr. Anderson and saw that he was muttering to himself, pacing and running his fingers through the ring of hair that encircled the crown of his head. All around me, plants were stirring, reaching, and growing. Vines, like tiny fingers, stretched and moved along the grass. The ivy I had shaken off rose up like the periscope of a submarine, surveyed the clearing until it found me, then began moving in my direction.

I gasped. "Mr. Fritz, call it off! Whatever point you're making, I give up. You're right."

He shook his head. "Sorry, Dancia. I can't do that. You fight until the end."

The end? As in, the end of my life? Barrett still wasn't moving, but the heat had resumed, so I figured he must be okay. The ivy crawled up and over the top of my shoe. A blackberry bramble scraped the back of my calf, its thorns digging into my ankle. Why, oh, why had I worn a skirt today? I moved a few feet away, but they kept coming, wrapping themselves around my legs and holding me fast.

Barrett lifted himself up onto his elbows. I breathed a sigh of relief even as I felt a wave of anger. He was smiling. Or rather, smirking. "Giving up so soon? I thought you'd at least make us work for it."

"This isn't fair," I said. "You haven't told me the rules. I don't know what we're fighting for. I don't know how to win!"

"There are no rules," Mr. Fritz said.

"I don't know how you can win, but I know how you're going to lose," Barrett said.

"Stop being so mean!" I cried.

Pain stabbed my ankle. While I'd been watching Barrett, a bramble had tightened around it. I didn't know how to unwind it without the thorns digging in deeper, so I focused on stopping Mr. Anderson himself. He was bigger than Barrett, his tie to the earth stronger. Throwing Barrett to the ground hadn't made much of a difference, so I decided to go the opposite route with Mr. Anderson, and make him fly. I'd never tried it before, but I didn't have a choice.

I took a deep breath and visualized myself brushing piles of debris and clutter from my mind, leaving behind a clean and empty slate. The irony of that moment was breathtaking; I was using techniques Barrett had taught me only a few weeks before, in order to prepare my mind to fight. I raised my hands, momentarily distracted by the white smoke curling around my fingertips. My skin was a darker red now, as if I'd had a bad sunburn. The heat made it difficult to concentrate, but I clung to the image of my empty mind. When my control felt strong enough, I poured all my attention into the black cords that surrounded Mr. Anderson, from ground to sky. Gently, I pulled on the top one and held it there, straining to keep my energy focused.

He let out an exclamation when first one foot, then the other lost contact with the ground. I moved the cord gently up and down, and Mr. Anderson did the same, jerking it like a yo-yo. Triumph swelled within me when I felt the bramble around my ankle relax. Carefully, I bent over to unwrap the now-still vine, but as I looked down, the steady heat in my body pulsed with a startling intensity. The pain was so strong I staggered back, losing my grip on Mr. Anderson's cord. He swore violently as he dropped to the ground.

I yanked on Barrett, trying to send him back to the ground, but he barely moved before sending another flash of heat through my body. Through swollen eyes, I watched Mr. Anderson rise to his feet; the blackberry vine I still held in my fingers squirmed and wriggled, its thorns digging into the burned skin of my palm.

It was like Whac-A-Mole at the county fair. Each time I knocked one of the men down, the other popped up to assault me anew.

I felt a rush of fury. They were destroying me, and I was holding back, out of some childish fear of hurting them. I glared at Barrett and abandoned any attempt at moderation. With all the energy I had left, I jerked on his cord. This time, I think I did hurt him, because he grunted and the heat abruptly disappeared. The relief was overwhelming.

"Ready to give up?" I yelled.

"We're just getting started," came the hoarse reply from the limp form on the ground.

I jumped; the soles of my feet burned as if they'd caught

on fire. I danced back and forth to lessen the sting.

"This is worse than I thought," Mr. Fritz said sadly. "Don't you realize they're just toying with you? You'll have to think of something much better if you expect to win."

I continued to hop from foot to foot. "Would you please shut up?"

"Perhaps if you beg them to go easy on you, it will help."

The suggestion shocked me. If Mr. Fritz thought I had no chance, why was I bothering to fight?

"You want me to give up?" I asked. Leaves rustled behind me. I figured Mr. Anderson was back at work, but I couldn't screw up the courage to turn around.

He shrugged. "If you're certain to lose, perhaps that would be the best course."

My shoulders sagged. My feet were on fire, the cuts on my legs were screaming for relief, and my skin throbbed with heat. Mr. Fritz was right. I couldn't do it. I couldn't fight them both. Suddenly, I could barely summon the strength to keep standing, let alone keep fighting.

I lowered my eyes, ashamed of what I was about to do. I pictured myself falling to my knees, surrendering. As I studied the ground, I saw my sweatshirt next to me, a limp gray mass balled up next to my feet. I recalled the defiant way I'd dropped it, my brief moment of confidence before this had all begun.

Confidence.

It's all mental . . .

A voice reverberated in my head. I clung to it, closing my eyes so I could focus on the low echo it left behind. It's all mental—what did that mean? Where had I heard that before? The heat and the stinging in my legs brought a fresh wave of dizziness. My thoughts blurred and faded in and out. Then it came to me. The pen. I pictured the pen I'd dropped on my first day in class with Mr. Fritz, and fury slowly replaced the despair that had almost sent me to my knees.

Mr. Fritz had used that pen to trick me into believing I couldn't use my talents.

He'd used my mind against me.

"You're doing it again, aren't you?" I stared at him, wide-eyed. "Making me believe I can't win."

A small army of brambles hit my feet and snaked up my calf. Sharp needles poked my bare skin in hundreds of places. They were moving fast, coiling around my shin and starting up my knee. Mr. Anderson had taken advantage of my distraction to throw everything he had at me.

Mr. Fritz held a hand over his chest in an expression of pseudosincerity. "I'm looking out for you, Dancia. I don't want you to get hurt."

"The hell you don't!" I spat, anger burning my throat as surely as the fire that Barrett had sent licking through my body. I'd been fooled by Mr. Fritz before. I was *not* going to let him take advantage of me again.

What I wanted was to pick Mr. Anderson and Barrett up like rag dolls and throw them on the ground, but I didn't actually want them to *die*. It was clear, though, that I needed to try something new. I focused my attention on the plants Mr. Anderson was using against me and, my whole body shaking with the effort, compressed the soil with the force of gravity that reached up from below. I spun in a slow circle, holding in my mind all that I saw and focusing on the things I couldn't see—the darkness and energy pulsing below the surface of the earth.

As I watched, the ground actually sank—first six inches,

then eight, then a foot. Mr. Anderson stumbled back as I rose above him. The earth fell away, the plants and soil becoming compacted in a thick black stripe. The vines around my leg tightened, then slackened, becoming limp and flat in my hand. I reached down and ripped a handful off, ignoring the bloody scrapes they left behind. All around the clearing, the plants shuddered and fell flat.

I'd created a dead zone. The power of the earth's core had turned the soil into rock.

The sudden change in the level of the ground sent my attackers reeling. Mr. Fritz wobbled and lost his balance, dropping to his knees. Mr. Anderson waved his arms, fell heavily on his rear end, then slowly pushed himself up to a standing position. Barrett, who was still on the ground from the last time I'd dropped him on his back, rolled over in a half somersault before pushing himself into a cross-legged position.

He placed his hands on his knees. "You don't want to fight me, Dancia. You know I've been holding back. You're scared—and if you aren't, you should be."

"Maybe you're the one who should be scared," I snarled. By this point I'd lost any interest in moderation. I pulled down a young maple tree a few feet behind him. It crashed between two Douglas firs, ripping down branches as it fell. This was a risky move. I didn't know exactly how the tree would fall, but I no longer cared. Barrett's voice was cutting right through to my soul. These people I trusted and depended on had turned on me, and the sting of betrayal was as strong as the heat coursing through my legs.

Barrett blinked, and tiny flames licked the front of my shoes, melting the soles and blackening the leather.

"Give up, Dancia," he said calmly. "You're still a child. You can't control yourself."

"Shut up!" I screamed. He was right, of course, and that only made it worse. A shower of branches fell from the trees around us. I hadn't even realized I'd touched them, but they fell straight down like spears, thrusting into the soil in loose circles around Mr. Anderson, Mr. Fritz, and then Barrett himself. He ducked, pushing aside evergreen boughs and maple branches as they landed on him, wincing when they jabbed his skin.

He held out his hand with the palm facing toward me, and pain shot through me. I staggered back as my clothing started to hiss and smoke. Thus far, Barrett had been saving me from serious injury, but as we ratcheted up the violence, things would change. A rhododendron jerked unevenly and flew into the air, spinning with increasing speed, showering us with flying soil and rocks. Clumps of moss and decaying plants rose and fell in dizzying profusion.

"Dancia, what are you doing?" Mr. Fritz shouted, covering his face and crouching down.

"I'm fighting. Just like you wanted." I tried to think, to clear my mind the way Barrett had taught me, but it was too full. The debris of scattered thoughts, confusion, and anger had turned into mountains, filling my head with demands for attention. The pain wanted me; the black lines and forces wanted me. Mr. Fritz was yelling, and Barrett was smirking. Suddenly I was desperate for it all to be silent, for the earth to return to normal and the branches to stop raining from the trees. But I was no longer in control. The forces around me had been sent into chaos. I heard a massive sound, a ripping and tearing, and realized I had somehow knocked loose the trunk of one of the old fir trees that ringed the clearing. It must have been a hundred feet tall, and it was swaying like a stalk of grass in the wind.

I tried to use what power I had left to stabilize it, to push it up while the instability threatened to drag it down. But I was out of juice. The pain Barrett and Mr. Anderson had inflicted, and the effort of using my talent for so long, had left me exhausted. The crown of the tree dipped lower, and the branches knocked against the trunk of a nearby oak. I pushed against it, crying out in exhaustion when nothing happened. I struggled to stay on my feet, unsure how to keep the black lines that held me upright stable and in balance.

"Dancia, stop!" Mr. Fritz yelled, but I was too far gone.

The last thing I remembered was Mr. Anderson yelling at me to run and the sound of crashing branches.

CHAPTER 16

WHEN I came to, I was lying on the ground. I opened my eyes slowly and saw Mr. Fritz anxiously patting my cheeks.

"Oh, thank goodness. Are you all right? Do you feel dizzy? Can you tell me the day of the week? The year?"

"I think you're supposed to ask the questions one at a time, Mr. Fritz," I said sourly, pushing myself to a seated position. My muscles screamed, as if I'd just finished a marathon, and my skin was tight and warm. I held out my hands and saw that they still glowed faintly pink. My shoes were a total loss, the soles unrecognizable, but my clothes were still intact, just slightly singed.

"She's fine," Mr. Anderson barked. He bent over me, his bulk blocking out the light. "You are fine, aren't you?"

"How the heck should I know?" I assessed the damage to the clearing. An oak tree lay on the ground, fresh dirt falling in clumps from the roots. Branches littered the ground, a number of them embedded in it like stakes. There were three rough circles of sticks surrounding the spaces where Mr. Fritz, Mr. Anderson, and Barrett had been, and a line of rock edged the clearing.

The giant fir tree, however, still stood.

Mr. Anderson said gruffly, "I grew the roots as fast as I

could. That gave it a little extra stability. You hadn't knocked it over, just loosened it."

I placed my hands on my knees and pushed my weight onto my feet. A second later, I teetered to one side. A pair of hands steadied me from behind.

"I should get David," Mr. Anderson said.

"She's exhausted, not sick," Barrett replied, over my head.

Mr. Anderson wiped his forehead, leaving behind a smear of dirt. "How can you say that? Did you see her legs?"

"Her legs aren't the problem. This took everything she had. Besides, David needs energy to heal, and she's got nothing left."

He was right. Though I wanted to run away and never look into their faces again, it was all I could do not to collapse into Barrett's arms.

"D., sit back down. You need to get up your strength before you go anywhere."

I tried to shake him off, my voice trembling. "Let me be. You don't care about me anyway. You enjoyed that."

Barrett released my arms, but then my knees buckled. He caught my limp body and lowered me to the ground. "No, I didn't," he said. "I had to act like that so you'd take it seriously. If you didn't believe I would hurt you, you wouldn't have fought back so hard."

I tucked my knees into my chest and began to rock back and forth, fighting the thickness in my throat. Things had changed in an instant. People I thought were my friends had hurt me; the Program I thought would teach me control had sent me reeling into total chaos. "It wasn't supposed to be like this," I said hoarsely. "I was supposed to join the Program and then everything would make sense."

Barrett touched my shoulder. "That's never going to happen. It's only going to get more complicated. I wish I could tell you something different, but I can't. I'm sorry."

I slumped, my shoulders shaking with the effort of maintaining my fragile control.

"What's wrong with her?" I heard Mr. Anderson whisper over the top of my head.

"She's fine," Barrett said to him. "She's just got a lot to work through."

The quiet concern in their voices sent me over the edge. I buried my face in my knees and soaked my skirt with my tears. Barrett gently patted my back. Frustrated sobs passed through me in waves. I'd failed in the most spectacular way possible. I'd failed Barrett and Mr. Fritz and Cam and Trevor and myself. I had no right to be in the Program. Trevor had been right all along. I was a time bomb that had finally gone off.

Finally, after what felt like a lifetime, the storm started to pass. The shudders that had racked my body quieted, and my shoulders stopped shaking.

I turned my head and rested the side of my face on my skirt. The cold, wet fabric felt soothing against the hot skin of my cheeks. I imagined I was in my backyard and that any minute now Grandma would come out and give me a hug and call me "dear child."

Without raising my head, I said bitterly, "So, what's the next stage for me? Isolation chamber?"

"What do you mean?" Mr. Fritz asked.

I couldn't look at him. Even though I know he did it with good intentions, it still infuriated me that he played so easily with my emotions. "Your little demonstration. It worked perfectly. I mean, except for the part where you almost got killed by a two-hundred-year-old tree falling on you. You should have anticipated that part."

"Dancia, we didn't—"

I sailed past his protest. "Of course you did. You three used your talents to show exactly how much damage I would do if provoked. And it worked perfectly."

"It wasn't like that at all." Mr. Fritz crouched down beside me. "We had no desire to set you up. After what happened this weekend, we realized we couldn't make you keep all your power locked inside. You aren't going to be content to stand on the sidelines forever, and we needed to know what would happen when you let go."

"Right," I scoffed. "This was an activity. Not a demonstration of my lack of control."

"You needed to stretch your wings. We wanted to see what would happen if you were provoked, but not because we don't trust you. We've never had someone like you at Delcroix before. We're fumbling through this right along with you."

"Please, Mr. Fritz," I said wearily. "No more lies. Not now."

"This is the truth," he insisted. "When we started your classes we were scared. I'll admit that. We thought we needed to keep things small and force you to learn control that way. But Friday's incident showed us that that was a mistake. We realized we needed to take you to the next level."

"And that is . . . ?"

"Exercising the full extent of your power. Not by moving around sticks and pens, but by confronting real threats. You needed to do that when you were surrounded by friends, not enemies. That was the point of today's exercise. Not to teach you some lesson about being dangerous."

"So we're friends now." I laughed sourly and wiped my

nose on my sleeve. "Could have fooled me."

"Aren't you glad this happened today and not in front of Anna's house, in the middle of Santiam Lane?" Barrett asked. "We're trying to figure out how to help you, D., and train you. You've got to cut us a little slack if we don't get it right the first time."

"You almost set me on fire," I said to him. "You laughed at me. I'm supposed to cut you slack after that?"

He grinned. "You nearly broke my back, but I guess I did want to try flying. It was pretty cool, actually. We'll have to do it again some time."

I was not in the mood for humor. "I don't understand how you can act like this all doesn't matter. I almost killed you. How can I use my powers if I'm such a danger?"

"We're all dangerous. Some of us a little more than others, I admit, but you didn't do anything we didn't provoke you into doing. In fact, you did everything right." Barrett gestured toward Mr. Anderson, who glowered at us from a few feet away. "You kept us both alive while finding ways to beat us back. We provoked you, D., and you reacted like the powerful person that you are."

"But I got overwhelmed. I didn't know what was happening at the end. If that tree had come down—"

"We'd all be dead," Mr. Anderson said. "But it didn't, and we aren't. You kept it together longer than anyone could have expected. You should be proud of that, not beating yourself up."

Barrett jumped to his feet. "Now you know what you need to learn. You're like a kid learning to walk, D. You're going to fall a few times along the way. You just need to trust us to pick you up after you do."

Mr. Fritz ran his fingers through his wiry hair, removing

a clump of dirt and a leaf as he did. "We're trying to help. It may not feel like it right now, but we are. Someday, you'll be a target, Dancia. I hate to say it, but it's true. People will learn how powerful you are, and they won't want you opposing them."

"You mean the Irin?" I asked.

The three of them exchanged meaningful looks. I thought maybe they would protest, or try to lie, but they didn't even act surprised. I guessed Cam must have told them what we'd talked about after Anna's party.

"Yes," Mr. Fritz said, "the Irin. When that happens, we want you to have the tools to defend yourself."

"We care about you," Barrett added. "We're doing this because we want to help you."

"All of us," Mr. Anderson said gruffly.

I blinked through a renewed haze of tears. I had a troll doll, a human torch, and a mad gardener watching over me. It was a measure of my emotional instability that I found this comforting. "Thanks. I think."

We trudged back to school as soon as my legs would hold me. I hobbled along, leaning on Barrett and Mr. Fritz at first. By the time we hit the practice field, I was walking on my own, albeit slowly and somewhat unsteadily. I was stunned when I checked my watch and found that it was only three o'clock. It seemed much later.

Cam came running out of the school as soon as we were within sight of the Main Hall. His usually gentle features had a wildness about them. As soon as he reached me, he immediately wrapped one of my arms over his shoulders and arranged the other around his waist. "What happened to your shoes?" he demanded.

152

"They . . . um . . . melted."

"Lean on me," he directed. "You shouldn't be walking."

I let him move my body; my arms hung limply. I felt strangely shy around him, unsure how I would, or even if I should, tell him what had happened. "I'm okay. Just tired."

"Are you sure?" He studied me from head to toe. "What about your legs?"

I couldn't hide the bloody gashes that crisscrossed my shins. "It looks worse than it is. They're just scratches."

He tightened his hold around my waist. "You can't fool me, Dancia. I've never felt you fight like that before."

I focused on keeping my footsteps even and steady, ashamed to recall just how bad things had gotten. "You knew we were fighting?"

"Not until you got started. I couldn't miss that. Mr. Judan had to tell me what was going on so I wouldn't run out there after you. It was like the Fourth of July for talent marks. You were lighting up the sky." Cam glared at Barrett. "I've never seen so much energy in one place."

"It's part of her training, Cameron," said Mr. Fritz. "We had to move her along. I didn't want to do it, either, but we all know she needed it."

Move her along. Mr. Fritz had told me they had done this to make me safe and protect me from the Irin. But all it was really about was moving me along, testing me, and making me stronger. I felt a surge of anger, and I wasn't sure whom to direct it at.

"You're done now?" Cam said to Mr. Fritz. It wasn't really a question.

"Yes," Mr. Fritz replied. "Mr. Anderson and I need to let Mr. Judan know what happened. You can take her back to the Residence Hall if you'd like. She ought to lie down for a while. It will take some time to get her strength back."

Although it seemed to happen with alarming frequency these days, I had never gotten used to the concept of people making plans for me as if I weren't there. I waved my free hand in front of Mr. Fritz's face. "Hello! I'm still here, remember?"

Mr. Anderson grunted. "Can you walk?"

"Yes."

"Good. Then you're on your own." He headed off in the direction of the Main Hall.

Mr. Fritz sighed. "Of course, Dancia, I didn't mean to imply that—"

"Whatever. It's fine, I'll walk back with Cam."

Mr. Fritz started to walk away, then turned back to me. "I am proud of you. Don't doubt that for a second."

I looked away, wishing more than anything that I could believe him. "Thanks," I mumbled.

"Are you ready?" Cam asked.

"Sure."

The teachers began to walk toward the Main Hall, and we turned toward the Res. Barrett followed.

"I don't know what you were thinking, pitting all three of you against her," Cam said. His words were directed at Barrett, but he didn't turn around.

"It could have been worse," I said. "They actually went pretty easy on me." Hard as it was to believe, considering how much pain he'd inflicted, I knew Barrett could have done more.

"I wouldn't call it easy," Barrett said, sounding almost like his usual, relaxed self. "I'm exhausted. I won't be able to do more than light a match for a few days."

"You shouldn't have hurt her," Cam said coldly.

"It had to be real." With two long strides, Barrett caught up to us on my side.

"What do you know about real?" Cam muttered. "You've never taken anything seriously in your life."

I tensed, fearing that the antagonism simmering between them was about to come to the surface, but Barrett didn't respond. He simply walked beside me, more hawklike than ever in the gray afternoon light, with his high cheekbones and hook nose.

After what felt like a lifetime, the three of us reached the Res. I held Barrett's arm for support while Cam searched his backpack for his ID.

"You're a mess," Barrett said.

"Thanks," I said wryly.

He pointed to my bare feet. "I guess I owe you a new pair of shoes."

"Nah. I'm just grateful you didn't set the rest of me on fire."

He tilted his head, his long black hair falling in his face. "And I appreciate your not dropping me on my head."

We smiled at each other, the antagonism of the fight forgiven. Cam swiped his ID and yanked open the door with more force than necessary. I took an awkward step away from Barrett, not sure what to do. I didn't want to be rude, but I knew Cam was pissed at him. The last thing I wanted was to be stuck in the middle.

"You should go rest," Barrett advised. "Mr. Fritz is right. You're still pretty green."

"I've got a game today. I can rest on the bus." I made a point of starting toward the door on my own but immediately lost my balance and flailed around before Barrett grabbed my arm and steadied me.

"I'll tell them you can't make it." Cam glared at Barrett for a minute before turning back to me. "You should rest, Dancia."

"There's no reason to be like this, Cam. We both want what's best for her," Barrett said quietly.

Cam barely looked at him. He took my elbow and guided me through the door. "I'll believe that when I see it."

I said good-bye to Barrett, and then the door shut behind us. We climbed the steps to the fourth floor, stopping at each landing so I could catch my breath. When we reached my room, I leaned against the door before opening it, keeping tight hold of Cam's hand. "It's not his fault—they were trying to teach me something."

Cam pressed his forehead against mine and closed his eyes. "I didn't mean to be a jerk. But when I thought about you out there . . ."

I laughed. "It was a training exercise, Cam. They wouldn't really have *hurt* me." He didn't reply, and I swallowed nervously. "Right?"

"Of course not," he said unconvincingly.

I pushed back against his shoulders, forcing him to meet my eyes. "Tell me the truth. What did you think might happen?"

"There was a lot of noise out there," he said. "Sometimes things go wrong in the heat of battle. Barrett's got a strong talent, and no one knows exactly what you're capable of."

I slumped back against the door. "You were right to worry. I almost killed us all. I understand what they were trying to do, but it's all happening so fast. Isn't there some way to let things develop naturally?"

"It always feels this way in your first year," Cam said. "Maybe more so for you than for some, but it's inevitable. If we let things take their natural course, half of the students wouldn't even get to Level Three."

"But it *hurts*."

He stroked my cheek. "I wish there was some other way—but the sooner you begin, the stronger you become. That's why we have to push you. Mr. Judan says that all the time."

Frustration boiled up in me. Between Anna's party, the Irin, and Esther's confession, there had been too many things thrown at me over the past few days. "And you believe everything he says?"

"What?" He drew back, eyes widening.

I'm not sure who was more surprised by what I'd said—me or Cam. I clearly should have stopped there, but the words seemed to flow out of their own volition. "I'm sorry, Cam, but when's the last time you questioned something Mr. Judan said? He isn't a god, you know. He's just a guy, and he could be wrong. Maybe you're pushing people too hard and it isn't worth it. Maybe you could give people a choice before you mess with their lives."

"What are you talking about?"

Somehow, the force of my anger gave me the strength to stand up on my own. I began to tick the points off on my fingers. "The *Program*. You bring us here and then deliberately mess with us just to see how we will react; you watch us and write reports about us, and then make some kind of grand decision about whether we'll be trained; you push us to use our talents before we know what our talents are. And then you stick us in some focus class and set us on fire, all so we can have a chance to 'stretch our wings.'"

I was breathing hard and my legs were beginning to shake, but I refused to give in to my body's weakness. Cam paced a ways up and down the hall. "We do give you a choice," he said. "That's what Initiation is. You took the oath of your own free will. No one forced that on you."

"You really think anyone could say no to the oath?" I asked, shaking my head incredulously. "After all we've learned and who we are at that point, do you really think someone could walk away?"

Cam's lips pressed together in a thin line. "You're tired. You should go lie down."

"I'm not tired. I'm sick of this." I turned my back to him and began viciously punching in the combination to the lock on my door. "I'm sick of all the fighting and secrets and mysteries. I just want someone to tell me the truth."

"Dancia, stop. You aren't yourself right now."

"Of course I'm not! A few minutes ago, my skin almost spontaneously burst into flame while a bunch of plants attacked me in the forest. You try getting up after that and heading back to school like nothing happened."

Cam made a sound of disgust and backed away. "I understand. I'm not going to fight with you like this."

"Fine." I flung open the door. "Fine. Leave me alone, then." I walked into the room and threw myself on the bed.

When I looked back at the door, he was gone.

CHAPTER 17

I DID not move again until I heard a voice calling my name from the doorway.

I rolled over and squinted at the shadowy figure. I must have been sleeping for some time, because the sun had set and my room was dark, except for the light spilling in from the hall. I sat up abruptly when I realized who it was.

"Mr. Judan! I . . . uh . . . I was just . . ."

He flicked on the light at the door; I winced at the sudden brightness. "I'm sorry," he said courteously.

"No problem." I glanced at the clock beside my bed. I'd been sleeping for almost three hours. "I should be getting up anyway. It's almost time for dinner."

With a monumental effort, I shook off the torpor in my limbs and set my feet on the ground. I didn't like the idea of being in bed while Mr. Judan stood in the doorway to my room. It made me feel vulnerable.

"We can have dinner brought to you," he said.

"No, that's okay. I just need a minute to wake up."

"Certainly."

He continued to hover in the doorway. I was reminded of the stories about vampires and how they couldn't enter your room unless invited. "You can come in," I said, with some misgivings.

"Thank you." He walked a few paces into the room, angling his body so he could watch the open doorway while talking to me. He looked horribly out of place, a strange, formal figure in a dark blue suit and tie, amid my dirty laundry and cluttered desk. I focused on clearing my head and sending strength into my legs so I could stand as quickly as possible.

"I spoke to Fritz and Anderson," he said, his intense blue eyes flicking from me to the doorway and back again, lingering on my scraped and battered calves. "They told me about the afternoon's events."

I tucked my legs underneath me. "Things got a little out of control."

"They said you did well."

"They did?" I studied him warily. Mr. Judan was probably manipulating Cam, and wouldn't hesitate to do the same to me. But there was little I could do about it. The title of Chief Recruiter didn't begin to tell the story of Mr. Judan's power. I'd seen his picture in the history books I found in the Program library, with a caption underneath full of glowing praise for his efforts to build his army of Watchers. I'd never heard anyone argue with him, even our principal, Mrs. Solom, and she wasn't exactly a pushover. Principal Solom had steel gray hair that she wore in a tight bun on top of her head, and snapping black eyes, the color of which perfectly matched her blocky, three-inch heels. The heels only brought her to a hair under five feet, but we were all still terrified of her.

It wasn't exactly fair to say that Cam believed everything Mr. Judan said. But Cam felt as if he owed Mr. Judan, and because of that, there was no way he would have contradicted him, especially when it came to the Program.

"A bit destructive, perhaps, but you were pushed. I hope you understand what they were trying to accomplish. The last thing we want is for you to get hurt."

I rolled my shoulders experimentally. They were sore, but not so much that I couldn't move. "I need to learn, Mr. Judan. I know that."

"Perhaps." He picked up a picture of me and Grandma, lightly running his thumb across our faces. "But I'm not sure you understand precisely how critical your education is to the Program. You're very important to us, Dancia."

"Me?"

Mr. Judan set down the picture and fixed me with his eyes. I fought off a wave of panic. He'd never focused on me like that, and the force of his stare was overwhelming. I took conscious breaths, the way Barrett had told me to do when I became overwhelmed.

Light glinted off Mr. Judan's perfectly white teeth. "Yes, you. Of course, you know you're powerful. We've told you that before. But you need to know how important that strength is right now: to Delcroix, and to the world."

I stopped trying to breathe. It was futile. "What do you mean, 'right now'? Did something happen?"

"Cam told me that the two of you talked about the Irin." He waited for me to nod before he continued. "And that you discovered they were responsible for what happened at Initiation."

"But not the group from Seattle," I said, hearing Jack's voice telling me how the Seattle cell had been set up to protect people like him. "Some other cell, right?"

"We believe so. The explosion you heard that night was

actually a powerful burst of sound created by a Level Three Talent. We have reports of a Level Three Talent from the Washington, D.C., cell who has this same ability."

He took a few steps closer, and I instinctively recoiled. "The D.C. cell is one of the most dangerous," he added. "They have a number of powerful agents who we believe work directly with Gregori, the leader of the Irin. This is particularly troublesome because several books were stolen the night of Initiation. They were specific, upper-level texts on training Earth and Somatic Talents. It is likely that those books are now in the hands of the Irin's top operatives."

I rubbed my forearms nervously. "They're just books, though. They can't do any serious damage, right?"

Mr. Judan pulled a slender volume from his coat pocket. "Take a look at this." He opened it to a yellowed page showing a woman standing in front of a river, her hand raised. The river stopped several feet in front of her and rose up in wavy lines, as if it had turned to steam. "This is an account from Maria Salvoretto of a woman with a talent for changing states of matter. Maria describes here how this woman dissolved an entire river and sent it hurtling into the sky. The cold air in the upper atmosphere caused the water vapor to turn to ice, and moments later the entire area was hit with a massive hailstorm. Hundreds were killed, and farms and crops were destroyed for miles."

"I can't believe someone would do that," I whispered.

He snapped the book closed. "They did, and they could again. The books that were stolen on the night of Initiation could provide this sort of instruction to the Irin—instruction they have, until now, been lacking."

States of matter.

Hundreds killed.

Jack.

I lurched to my feet, grabbing the desk for support. "Can we get them back?"

"We tried," he said, leaving no question about the results. "It's too late for that. But the books are only as good as the teachers who interpret them and the practice applied to them. At least, that's what we think. But frankly, this has never happened before."

"What can I do?" I desperately hoped he wouldn't tell me they needed me to go into battle against the Irin.

"We need you to keep training. I know this was a difficult day for you, and there may be more days like it in your future. But you must keep fighting. You could be in a position to make a significant difference in the world. You cannot let your frustration guide you."

I wondered what Mr. Fritz and Mr. Anderson had said about the aftermath of our fight. Did they tell Mr. Judan how upset I'd been? How I'd cried? Would Cam tell him what I'd said? "I won't, Mr. Judan. I just got tired, that's all. I thought I'd failed."

He walked over to me and touched my chin, raising it slightly so I could look into his eyes. They were crystal blue, flecked with shards of silver, sparkling with intensity. "The only way you could fail would be to give up and run away, like your friend Jack."

"J—J—Jack?" I stumbled over the word, imagining my cell phone suddenly flashing and ringing from the corner of my desk. Did Mr. Judan know? Could he tell what I'd done?

"You'll never be like him, Dancia." His eyes bored into me. "We tried to help him, but we were too late. He couldn't handle the gift he'd been given. You're different. You're strong. Don't ever forget that."

My body flushed with heat, fear and guilt mixing together as he stared down, his eyes boring a path right into my soul. Words bubbled up in my head, mine and yet not mine, as if I'd spoken them with a different voice. I *was* different. Jack had been a coward. He ran away because of what he imagined *might* happen. Mr. Judan had tried to teach him, had given him a chance when he was sleeping under bridges and robbing convenience stores, but Jack had let him down.

He'd let me down, too.

The voice was right. Jack had given up on Delcroix, not the other way around.

I sucked in my stomach, tensing my whole body so I could stand up straight. "I won't fail you, Mr. Judan. I promise."

Mr. Judan left a few minutes later, and I sank back onto the bed, my body drained, all hope of eating in the cafeteria destroyed.

I'd been *persuaded*. I'd never felt anything like it, but it was obvious that this was what had happened. I should have been furious, but the worst part was, even now that Mr. Judan was gone, I still believed he was right. The thought of Jack's having access to information that could have been used to kill hundreds of people was chilling. As much as I cared about him, when I pictured the look in his eyes before he left—like that of a cornered animal, panicked and fierce—I knew he would have done anything to stay free of the Watchers. I liked to think he wouldn't have killed people, but I couldn't say that that was impossible.

Catherine came into the room just as I slumped back onto my pillow. She glared at me with her usual hostility, though it was compounded with a distinct layer of confusion. "What's going on? I saw Mr. Judan in the hall, and he said you weren't feeling well and I should get you dinner. Have you been bothering him? He's very busy, you know. You can't go around calling him whenever you feel like it."

I closed my eyes. "He stopped by to talk to me about something. He'd heard I was sick. No big deal."

I knew this would be a *very* big deal to her, and felt a jolt of pure, vindictive pleasure. Mr. Judan was Catherine's idol, and he'd been talking to me, the girl she believed to be a blight on the good name of Delcroix Academy.

Catherine sat at her desk, straightening her already neat papers. "What would he have to talk to *you* about?"

"A . . . project. Something I'm doing in my focus classes."

"With Mr. Judan?" She picked up a silver pen and began to twirl it between her fingers. "Mr. Judan doesn't teach any focus classes. I know, because my dad asked him to do one with me and he said he couldn't. He's too busy."

As much as I wanted to irritate Catherine, I was horrible at inventing lies in the first place, much less keeping track of them. "He isn't my teacher—he's more like an . . . um . . . adviser. Mr. Fritz is the real teacher. Mr. Judan just wanted to make sure I understood my assignment."

The pen twirled faster. "He's your adviser? How does that work? Did you ask for him in particular, or did he choose you?" I could practically see the wheels in her head turning as she tried to think up a way to score the same deal for herself.

"He's not like a personal adviser. He's an adviser for the focus classes that Mr. Fritz teaches."

"Hmm." She assessed me silently for a moment. "Well, you are awfully pale. And he asked me to help you out. So, what should I bring you from the cafeteria? I think it's burritos."

If it hadn't been so alarming, it would have been funny. Catherine must have thought I had some connection with

Mr. Judan, and that if she were nice to me, she might get closer to him. This, I knew, wasn't about Mr. Judan. It was purely to please her father.

The pathetic nature of this plan might have elicited some sympathy in me, had it been anyone else. Catherine was desperate for any scrap of attention she could get from her father, who only called to remind her how important it was that she do whatever Mr. Judan wanted. I was pretty sure her dad was in the Program and wanted to make sure Catherine was headed there, too. Given her uncanny abilities in math, I figured they had nothing to worry about. Someday, she'd probably be able to break enemy codes, or program space-ships to travel at the speed of light. But right now, all she knew was that her dad wanted her to get herself noticed by Mr. Judan in any way she could.

The idea that having Mr. Judan as an adviser would bring Catherine's absentee father back into her life seemed very unlikely. Anyone with a heart would find the fact that she was willing to try incredibly sad.

But then again, this was Catherine we were talking about.

I smiled and leaned back into my pillow. "You know, Catherine, now that you mentioned it, I *am* hungry. Can you get me a chicken burrito with sour cream but no guacamole, extra salsa, a bowl of tortilla chips, and a glass of milk? For dessert I'll take whatever they're serving, but if you have time to run back over and tell me what my choices are, I'd really appreciate it."

She gritted her teeth and smiled. "Perfect. I'll just be a few minutes. You lie down."

I closed my eyes with pleasure. "Will do. Thanks for taking such good care of me."

* * *

After dinner, I slept for a couple more hours, then hobbled down the stairs to the second floor, my muscles still quivering. There were a bunch of guys in the hall, and it took all my strength to stand up straight and walk past them to Cam's room like nothing had happened. Cam was sitting on his bed, his back against the wall, head nodding in time to some particularly jarring thrash music. Trevor sat across from him with a calculus book perched on his knees.

"Hey, Cam." I leaned on the door frame and checked the hall for teachers. It was study hours, and girls weren't allowed in the boys' hall.

Cam leaned over and turned down the music. "What are you doing out of bed?"

I tried to gauge his reaction to seeing me, but it was impossible. His deep brown eyes were cool and distant.

"Any chance we could have a minute alone?" I asked.

Trevor glanced at Cam and then back at me. From his lack of surprise, I guessed that Cam had filled him in on the day's events. He grabbed a pencil and some paper and closed the book. "No problem. I'll go down to David's room."

After Trevor left, Cam pointed to his desk chair. "You should sit down before you pass out."

I noticed he didn't sound particularly concerned about that prospect. I cleared my throat. "I'm sorry, Cam. About what I said. You were right—I wasn't myself."

He shook his head, sending thick chestnut hair into his eyes. "Are you sure of that?"

I closed the door behind me, and even though it was completely against the rules, sat down next to him. He made no move to touch me. "I'm still trying to figure this all out, Cam. Esther's upset, there was the whole thing with the Irin, and now this fight. You understand how frustrating it all is, don't you? Didn't you feel this way your first year in the Program?"

He stood up and walked toward the window. "My first year was different. I didn't have your power; the Irin weren't this active—heck, I didn't even know they existed. You can't expect us to treat you like everyone else."

I inched forward, curling my fingers around the rough fabric of his comforter, the weight of my fears returning at the mention of the Irin. "If I'm going to help you fight them, I need to understand what everyone expects of me. Sometimes I think there's this master plan that nobody will tell me about. Like I'm running through this maze blindfolded, while you guys know where all the exits are."

Cam tapped his fingers on the windowsill. "You don't trust me, do you?"

"No, that's not it," I said. "It isn't about you. It's about them, Mr. Judan, my teachers, the Watchers. You're the only one I *do* trust."

I trusted Cam's heart. That I knew for sure.

I walked over and put my hand on his shoulder. The muscles were tight under his T-shirt, and I let my fingers slide up to his neck. "Please," I said. "Don't let me ruin this. I can't do it without you."

He turned and caught me around the waist. The kiss that followed seemed made of equal parts forgiveness and frustration to start, but slowly changed into something so deep and passionate I was left reeling. When a knock came at the door, I pulled away, my chest heaving with the effort to breathe.

Trevor poked his head inside, his hand over his eyes. "Just a warning. They're doing room checks. Better open the door."

"Thanks," Cam said. I noticed he was breathing hard, too.

"I'd better go back to my room," I said. I rested my head against his chest again for one last minute, clinging to him fiercely. His heart thumped steadily, and his arms turned steely, pulling me tightly against him.

His voice rumbled. "You should go." He unpeeled me and gently pushed me away. "I'll see you in the morning."

I studied his face, hoping to see something in his eyes that would tell me that everything was okay. But it wasn't. And I didn't know if it ever would be again.

CHAPTER 18

MY PROGRAM classes were different after that. We went into the forest every day, and I practiced levitating trees, moving rocks, and bouncing Barrett up and down like a giant yo-yo. It was hard work. The heavier the object, the more energy I had to expend to move it. Still, they wanted me to do more than just knock things down and pick them up. They wanted me to learn to control an object's movement down to the inch, and to be able to hold one thing in place while I moved another.

As if this weren't hard enough, I was also forced to practice moving things from side to side.

In case there is any doubt, this is *not* easy.

See, there's a gravitational pull dragging things down into the earth's core, and there's also the pull of the moon, dragging things up into space. But there are other forces, too. Every object exerts its own pull on every other, and with a lot of work, I was able to use these forces to move things wherever I wanted them. But it all took more energy than I could have imagined.

Things with Cam picked up where they had left off, but there was a new distance between us. We pretended it wasn't there. Sometimes we'd go for a run together or hold hands in the hall, and things would feel like they used to. But then he'd start to tell me something and catch himself, and I could see the wall going up.

Several times, I stared at the name Ethan Hannigan in my phone and considered deleting it. But then I would find my finger hovering over the call button, and I knew I wasn't ready to let go.

Esther got more depressed as the weeks passed. Cam told me that what she was going through was normal. Most candidates felt isolated and unhappy before they were initiated. It was this very sense of discontent that allowed them to access their talents at a higher level, and would ultimately inspire them to commit to the Program and all the pressure it entailed. Quite simply, if they were comfortable and happy in the normal world, they'd never have put up with the stress of being in the Program.

This put a new spin on my own miserable existence. It hadn't occurred to me that they might have *wanted* me to be unhappy as a kid, so that I'd be a better candidate for the Program.

I also started to worry about Hennie. Other than her concern for Esther, Hennie was perfectly happy. Things were great with Yashir, she loved her classes, and she was experiencing her first taste of freedom at Delcroix. If she needed to be unhappy to embrace the Program, when would the bad things start happening to her?

Soccer season ended with a whimper, the week before spring break. I was relieved it was done. Because of my training, I'd missed a lot of games and practices, and I'd had to come up with more and more lies to explain my frequent absences. At first, I'd invented colds and headaches. When it became clear

I needed a better strategy, I told Allie and a few others that I was recovering from mono. My story became pretty elaborate. I invented doctor's visits and researched symptoms on the Internet to make sure it all sounded legitimate.

Cam shook his head and laughed when I told him about it. He said being in the Program meant you had to get good at secrecy and disguise. It was part of the bargain.

All that training and lying left me exhausted. So, while Hennie and some of the other girls complained about spring break and being away from everyone for two weeks, I found myself looking forward to it. Cam was going to D.C. with Mr. Judan, on some official Governing Council business. He couldn't tell me exactly what they were doing, and for once I didn't want to know. Knowing, it seemed, only led to more heartache.

Cam and I took a longer walk than usual the night before break began.

"Will you miss me?" I asked as we slipped out of sight of the Main Hall.

"You have no idea," he said, looping his arm around my waist and letting his fingers brush against my hip.

The air was cool and damp against my skin, and the evergreens shushed as a breeze tickled their branches. "Good. You'd better."

We shared a moment of peaceful silence. At times like this, I could forget about our fight and convince myself we were the perfect couple.

"You'll e-mail me?" I asked. "I can check my account from the library. I want to hear about your trip."

"I'll tell you all about it," he promised. "Maybe someday we'll be doing trips like this together."

The path narrowed, and Cam went in front of me,

reaching behind to take my hand. "When do they start sending you out on missions?" I asked. "When you're a junior?"

"It varies. They don't send everyone out," he said. "Lots of people in the Program don't want to become Watchers. Like Barrett and his friends. They're seniors, but they're not involved in Governing Council business."

"But all of you are," I said. I didn't want to say Anna's and Trevor's names. Though neither of them had bothered me since Valentine's Day, I still didn't feel comfortable talking about them with Cam. I think it was my guilt that made things so hard. How could I complain about Anna or Trevor treating me with suspicion when I'd called Jack right after our fight with the Irin?

Cam nodded. "We are."

As we got deeper in the woods, the trees blocked the dim sunlight, and the rich, earthy smell surrounded us. I tried to picture myself on a mission with Cam. First I pictured him knocking down doors and holding an assault rifle. Then I imagined myself beside him, chasing Thaddeus, or levitating him as he tried to run away. I liked that idea. But then Thaddeus's face turned into Jack's, and I got a sick feeling and had to think about something else.

"Will they let you do any sightseeing while you're in D.C., or is it all work?"

"I don't know. Depends on how quickly we get our job done." He pressed his mouth closed as if he regretted what he'd said, and then continued in a lighter tone, "What are you doing over break? Taking Grandma to the doctor?"

"Probably. She doesn't like to drive on the highway anymore, so she scheduled a bunch of appointments for me to take her to while I'm home."

"I can't believe she lets you drive."

I pulled the edges of my jacket around me. "Hey, I'm fifteen. It's almost legal."

He snorted. "I'm sure your grandma could talk a cop out of giving you a ticket."

"They'd be scared to try," I said.

"You know, I think I need to hang out with Grandma more," Cam said. "I have a feeling she's tougher than both of us put together."

We crested the hill, and the lights of the Res came into view. We stopped for a minute and held each other in the dark.

"Be careful," I told him.

He touched my cheek with the back of his hand. "I will," he said. "I promise."

CHAPTER 19

ESTHER, HENNIE, and I wove through the Delcroix parking lot on Friday with our bags of laundry slung over our shoulders and suitcases trailing behind us, searching for familiar cars amid the chaos. It wasn't the most tender of farewells. Esther was grumpy and had been since morning. Her hair was pulled back in a severe ponytail. She looked very thin and beautiful, her eyes deep and sad. She disappeared into the crowd before we could say good-bye.

Hennie watched her go, her brows knitted together in a worried frown. "I don't know what she's planning, Dancia, but I've got a bad feeling about it. We're going to have to keep a close eye on her when we get back from break."

"What about you?" I elbowed her as we dragged our suitcases over the bumpy gravel. "What are you planning to do?"

I was clearly talking about Yashir, who was headed in our direction. He wore his only pair of pants without holes, presumably to meet Hennie's parents.

Hennie closed her eyes and winced. "I don't know."

"Did you tell him?"

"Tell him that I haven't talked to my parents about him? Of course not!"

"Don't you think it might be obvious when they get here

and start talking about all the boys they've arranged for you to date while you're home?"

Hennie made a strangled sound. "They aren't dates, exactly."

I shifted my laundry bag from one shoulder to the other. "They want to arrange your marriage, Hennie. What else would you call them?"

"Dinner with friends?" she said hopefully. When I raised my eyebrows, she sighed. "Any chance I can just run and pretend like I haven't seen him?"

I eyed her suitcase. "You're not much of a runner, and that's a pretty big bag. I'm thinking it's doubtful."

A moment later, she groaned aloud as she caught sight of her father, grinning and waving from across the parking lot, her mother at his side, tiny and beautiful like her daughter. "Dancia, they're so excited to see me. What am I supposed to say to them?" A second later, she wrinkled her nose. "Oh, no. They're thinking about our neighbor's son, Rashid, I just know it. I bet we're having dinner with him tonight!"

"You need to tell them the truth," I said. Hennie's gift for reading people had been getting stronger lately. Several times in the past week she'd read someone across the room without thinking. She always brushed it off afterward as a "good guess."

She gave me a hug. "I can't. Tell Yashir I'm sorry. Please?" With that she sprinted across the lot. Or rather, given that this was Hennie, she half ran, half tripped through the crowd, dragging her wheeled suitcase behind her.

When I turned around, Yashir was beside me, watching her go.

"She was worried they'd be mad if she didn't come right away," I said lamely. "She asked me to say good-bye."

"She's not going to tell them, is she?" he said. "They're going to make her go out with some guy while she's home, and that will be it for us." The barbell in his eyebrow drooped sadly.

I patted his shoulder awkwardly. "They're old-fashioned. She didn't know what to say. That doesn't mean she's about to break up with you."

A tall woman with a ring in her nose and hair down to her waist called to Yashir. "Is that your mom?" I asked.

He nodded, defeated. "I guess that's it, then."

I shook my head. "Don't give up. Call her tonight."

He hoisted his backpack onto his shoulder. "Have a great break, Dancia."

"You too, Yashir."

I had two major reports due after spring break: one on Renaissance architecture for World Civ, and one on Nathaniel Hawthorne for my English class. This meant that watching TV and vegging out for two weeks was not an option.

I could have gone to Delcroix and used the library there, but I wanted as much distance from the school as I could get. So on Monday morning, Grandma drove me to the Danville library. They didn't have many books, but you could get interlibrary loans in a few days, and they had a couple of computers so I could do research on the Web.

Grandma dropped me off and headed for the grocery store. I requested a few books, printed out a couple of articles from the Internet, and then checked my e-mail. There was a long, pitiful letter from Hennie telling me how guilty she felt for ditching Yashir. Nothing from Esther or Cam.

I stared at the screen for a moment, and then, on impulse, typed *Ethan Hannigan* into the search engine.

Thousands of pages came up. Apparently, Ethan Hannigan wasn't an unusual name. I tried again, this time typing *Ethan Hannigan* and *Delcroix Academy*.

Jackpot. The first page of search results was a series of newspaper articles from the *Danville Chronicle* and the *Seattle Times*. I saw headlines that read, *Teenage Suicide Devastates Neighborhood* and *Family Grieves for Lost Child*, but when I clicked on the links, the articles were "no longer available."

I tried again and again, searching for various combinations of Ethan, suicide, and Delcroix. None of the articles I wanted could be read. Even without access to the articles, it became clear that ten years ago, a boy named Ethan Hannigan, who had attended Delcroix Academy, had committed suicide. I was too nervous to ask the librarian for help finding more information. It was possible that the articles had just expired because they were old, but it seemed just as likely that someone hadn't wanted the information out there. And if they didn't want the information on the Internet, they probably didn't want me looking for it, either. I deleted the search history from the Web browser and restarted the computer.

A week passed. Grandma and I got back into our old routines and I caught up on my sleep. Pretty soon, it was hard even to believe that there was a Delcroix, or people with talents, or an Irin.

On Friday night, as I was finishing the dishes from dinner, Grandma suddenly turned up the sound on the TV. I set down the frying pan I'd been cleaning and went into the living room to see what had her so excited.

The words *Breaking News* scrolled across the bottom of the screen, and a reporter began speaking excitedly into a microphone. "I'm Katie Campbell, reporting live from

Washington, D.C., where we've just received word that police have uncovered the early stages of some kind of plot against the president."

The camera cut away to reporters clustered outside a huge building. The entrance was busy with police cars and people running in every direction. "The details are just beginning to emerge," the reporter continued. "What we know right now is that about four hours ago, police discovered, in this warehouse less than five miles from the Capitol building"—she gestured behind her—"three dead bodies, a cache of guns and ammunition, and detailed maps of the White House."

I sank down on the sofa while the reporter continued chattering. They didn't know much. The police had begun searching the area when nearby residents reported that they had heard what they thought was a series of explosions. No actual damage had been discovered, and the location of the explosions was unknown. Then police were given an anonymous tip to check the warehouse. They found the bodies in there, along with a stack of documents that detailed the conspiracy.

The speculation around the person or group that had foiled the crime and killed the president's would-be attackers was fierce. Was it a Good Samaritan? A disgruntled associate? No one knew, and the police said it was far too early to speculate.

I sat there dumbstruck.

I knew who was responsible. I just wondered if the finger on the trigger had been Cam's.

Every day for the next week, the evening news brought a fresh round of stories about the murdered men and the strange events in the D.C. warehouse. The dead were all in their twenties, unemployed, and college-educated. One had been a math major at Georgetown. Another went to Harvard. The third, Charlie Scholz, had graduated from University of Washington in Seattle. They had been living together in D.C. for a couple of years.

Reporters found people who knew the men and interviewed them endlessly. A neighbor said they were quiet boys who mowed her grass when she was out of town. She couldn't believe they'd done anything wrong. Charlie Scholz's uncle said he'd never trusted his nephew. He told the reporters that when Charlie was little he was always hiding in the basement of his house, doing something secretive.

Most of the weapons had been stolen. Based on the location of the bodies, the police had concluded that the men had been surprised, and that there hadn't been much of a fight. The police didn't find much else, and they never did figure out where the noise had come from. There was an office in the warehouse, but no documents other than the ones covering the White House. I wasn't surprised. The Governing Council would have kept any documents of value.

I tried not to fixate on Cam's role in the whole thing. After all, he wasn't a real Watcher. They would have used Cam to track the bad guys, not kill them.

I checked my e-mail every day but didn't get any messages from him. I figured he was busy. After all, they'd just prevented some huge national disaster. But I still wanted to talk to him and hear what had really happened. The police suspected that more people had been involved, based on the number of guns, the cars they'd recovered around the warehouse, and the multitude of fingerprints around the area. I wished I knew exactly what the men had been planning, and how they had died.

On Sunday night, I threw my clean clothes into my laundry bag and packed up my things for school. Grandma had just settled in for some hour-long news show when my phone rang.

The caller ID said *Ethan Hannigan*. I stared in horror at the screen.

Grandma gestured irritably at me from her easy chair. "Answer it, won't you? I'm trying to hear the television."

Indecision locked my hands at my sides. The phone rang again.

"If you don't answer it, I will," Grandma warned.

I jerked it up to my ear and pushed the button. "Hello?" I whispered.

"It's about time you picked up."

"Hey, Esther," I said, for Grandma's benefit. "What's up?"

Grandma turned back to the television. I started for my bedroom, then turned and went toward the bathroom. As soon as I closed the door behind me I hissed, "Jack, you shouldn't be calling me."

He laughed. "You called me the last time. Why can't I call you?"

I straightened the faded blue-and-white hand towels, lining them up by their embroidery. "That was a mistake. This is dangerous for both of us. Especially right now."

Jack's voice turned grim. "They murdered three people this week, Danny. Three guys who had done nothing more than refuse to be controlled by their Governing Council."

"They were trying to kill the president!"

Jack made a sound of disgust. "You don't believe that, do you?"

I perched on the edge of the bathtub. "They found papers. Maps. Drawings. What else could they be for?"

"It was a setup. Someone planted those papers, to distract everyone from the fact that your Watchers *murdered our men*. Going after the president is just plain stupid. We'd attract hundreds of police and probably get a bunch of our people killed, and it wouldn't do a thing toward our ultimate goal. Think about it. Why would we do that?"

Even though I knew he was one of them now, a chill descended on me at Jack's casual use of the phrase *our men*. "Well, then," I said, "what were all the guns for?"

"We have to have guns. To defend ourselves."

"That's crazy. Who do you think you're defending yourselves from?"

"Your boyfriend, for one."

I sat straight up in shock. Had Jack seen Cam? Was Jack in D.C.? "You leave them alone, and they'll leave you alone," I said, trying to sound calm. "Start hoarding automatic weapons and they're going to pay attention. And what do you mean about Cam, anyway? He's still in school. He isn't a real Watcher."

"He is now."

I closed my eyes, running my fingers through my hair, feeling the ringlets pop apart. "This conversation needs to end. You can't imagine the kind of trouble I'd be in if people thought I was talking to you."

"Did you ask them about Ethan?"

"No. He committed suicide. There's nothing more to say." I paced the two steps from the door of the bathroom to the sink and back.

"You know that's not true. When are you going to admit that they're dangerous?"

"When are you going to admit that you're on the wrong side?" I pulled hard on a curl and yanked out a snarl of hair.

Was Jack telling the truth? Had Cam known the documents were fake?

"Your 'right side' is awfully comfortable with killing people."

"We're trying to make things safer," I said, thinking of all the things I'd heard Mr. Judan say. "You didn't stay long enough to learn what the Program's actually about. It isn't just about the Watchers. It's other things too—doctors, scientists, and diplomats. It's all to make things better."

"If that's the goal, you aren't doing a very good job," Jack replied. "The Watchers just killed people with friends in high places—and they aren't happy. From here on out, things will only get worse."

CHAPTER 20

I SLAMMED the phone shut and shoved it back into my pocket. Nausea roiled in my stomach. I leaned over the sink and closed my eyes, waiting for the feeling to recede. When it didn't, I grabbed a washcloth and wet it, drawing the cool rag over my cheeks and the back of my neck. I studied my face in the mirror; my eyes were sunken and dark, the hair around my face a frizzy mass.

I shouldn't, I thought, have taken his call. He was lying to me. He had to be lying.

As I pulled my hair into a ponytail, I heard voices at the front door. My heart sank. I took a deep breath and threw open the bathroom door, certain I would see a group of Watchers standing outside.

Grandma was blocking the doorway, but she was so short I had no trouble making out the person in front of her. A smile of relief split my face. "Cam! What are you doing here?"

"I came to see you, of course," he said. He was wearing his forest green Delcroix T-shirt, the one with the gold dragon on the front. The light from the setting sun left a rosy glow on his features.

I recalled with horror that I had picked my old Danville Middle sweatshirt and matching sweatpants from the dirty laundry basket that morning, but then I caught Cam's eyes and realized it didn't matter. Energy rippled off him; his body was practically vibrating. He shifted from one foot to the other, and I knew he didn't care what I was wearing.

We shared a quick hug under Grandma's watchful gaze. "Did you just get to town?" I asked.

"A couple of hours ago. I borrowed a car as soon as we got to Delcroix so I could see you. I didn't want to wait until tomorrow."

Grandma pointed at the television. "I don't mean to be rude, but I'm right in the middle of this program. Maybe you two should go in the kitchen."

"Actually, I've got a whole bag full of laundry," Cam said. "I had hoped that Dancia could come with me to the Laundromat while I get it started? If I don't get it done tonight, I'll be wearing dirty clothes all week."

Grandma scowled. "You could do a load here. While you talk."

Cam took firm hold of my hand. "That's very kind of you, but I've got at least three, and it would save a lot of time if I could do them all at once."

She grabbed a tissue from the table and dabbed at the corner of her eye. "You can't do laundry at school?"

"The washers were full. I guess I wasn't the only one who brought a load of dirty clothes back from vacation."

The persuasion oozed from him. It was only his Level Two Talent, but Grandma didn't have the strength to resist. "You'll bring her back in before nine?" she said.

"Of course."

"Well, I suppose I can't fault a boy for wanting to do his laundry."

I flung my arms around her. "Thank you, Grandma!"

We got into the car at the curb. It was a tan Buick. I raised a curious eyebrow. "Does Mr. Judan know you've got this car?"

"He said it was okay. He understands."

We drove away from the curb in silence. At the first stop sign, Cam put the car in park and leaned over to kiss me. I couldn't tell what emotion pulsed through him, but it was almost frightening in its intensity.

Another car pulled up behind us.

"Maybe we should go somewhere more private?" I said.

Cam gunned the motor, and we headed toward town.

"So." I tapped my foot on the floor of the car. "How was your trip?"

"I suppose the news made it to Danville?"

I snorted. "Did you see what Grandma was watching? There's been nothing else on TV all week."

Cam rested his hand on the top of the steering wheel as he slid through a stop sign. "I don't mind the coverage. It's good. We wanted to send a warning anyway."

My throat started to tighten. I cleared it and said, "A warning? What do you mean?"

"For the rest of them. Those three weren't working alone, you know."

"Oh." I turned away and gazed at the houses beside us. I thought about the people inside who had no idea what had really happened in D.C. and wouldn't have believed it if you told them. Sometimes I wished I were one of those people.

A few minutes later, Cam pulled into a dead-end street and parked well away from any houses. He angled his body toward mine and took my hands in his. "I'm sorry I couldn't write," he said. "We were moving around too much. I thought about you all the time."

"Who were you with, exactly? Were there other people from Delcroix?"

"Mr. Judan was there," he said.

I waited, expecting to hear Anna's or Trevor's name, but that was all he said. I didn't want to ask him directly. I didn't want to know that Anna had been with him while I was home with Grandma.

"So . . ." I groped for the right words. "What did you . . ."

"I helped them find the warehouse and track the men. Then they brought me in to find talent marks once they narrowed down the area."

"What were they actually planning to do?"

He tucked a loose strand of hair behind my ear. "Something terrible."

"Like what?" The air in the car was heavy and still.

"Kill someone. Probably the president."

"Did you see the plans?" I had to work hard to keep asking questions, because he was touching my neck now, and the heat in his eyes was melting me down to my core. "The ones for attacking the White House?"

"No. I stayed by the front when they went in."

"So you didn't see them . . . you didn't see the Watchers . . . ?"

"If you're asking if I saw them shoot, the answer is no," Cam said.

"I just wondered if maybe they could have arrested them. Sent them to jail instead of killing them."

Cam kissed my cheek. He spoke between soft brushes of his lips against my skin. "One of those men was a shapeshifter. There's no jail in the world that could hold him. Another one was a computer genius. He needed to get access to a terminal only one time, and then he could open the prison gates. The last one could manipulate sound waves. With a little training, he could blow out the eardrums of every person in a two-mile radius. Jail wasn't an option."

Manipulate sound waves. A connection lit up in my head even as Cam's kisses sent ripples through my body. "He was one of the ones who broke into Delcroix at Initiation."

"It was the same guy. I saw his marks."

"Did he make that noise before they killed him?"

"Please," Cam said, pausing. "Don't ask those things."

I tried to focus on how lovely his hands were, how strong and warm. But I kept hearing Jack's voice, and what he'd said about the men being set up. "You're sure they were planning something, though? I mean, there was no chance they were going to do something else with those guns?"

Cam pulled back. "Like what? Send them to underprivileged children? Open a shooting range?"

I squirmed, amazed at myself for pushing things this far. "I don't know. Maybe they had them for self-defense. It's not illegal to have guns, is it?"

"The guns were stolen semiautomatic weapons that they rigged to be automatic. It *was* illegal to have those guns. We have absolutely no doubt how they would have been used, and it wasn't for show-and-tell. We don't let bad things happen just so we can find out exactly what they were planning. We stop bad things *before* they happen."

"It isn't that I don't believe you," I said. "I just need to understand."

"Fine—but can you understand later?" he asked. "I've been thinking and talking about this for the past two weeks. I hoped maybe I could forget about it for a while."

I took advantage of the space between us to wriggle out of my sweatshirt. "It's just that I haven't seen you, and you didn't write or anything. I've been waiting all week to hear the real story."

Cam's jaw tightened. "You want to know about it? Okay. I'll tell you. It made me sick. That's what you wanted to hear, isn't it?" His voice turned rough, and he cleared his throat.

I winced and touched his leg. "Cam, I'm sorry. I didn't mean to upset you."

"It was me, the Watchers, and Mr. Judan," he continued, ignoring my interruption. "They wanted me to tell them whenever I saw a mark. We traced the men through the city and ended up at that warehouse."

He flexed his hands compulsively on the steering wheel. "We didn't think they'd be expecting us, but you never know for sure. They could have had a talent for foresight, or a gift for hearing, like Claire. Mr. Judan told me to stay at the entrance with a phone. I was supposed to call for backup if something went wrong. There was one shot, and then the explosions. Then two more shots, and it was over."

I shuddered, imagining the moment, incredibly relieved he hadn't been inside the warehouse.

"I thought it would feel good to be a part of something like that," he said. "We protected innocent people. Hundreds of them, maybe more, I don't know. The president, even. But I keep hearing that sound, and thinking about those men. . . . It feels wrong, somehow, knowing I was a part of that. I'm sure they could have found them some other way, but *I* led them there." He punched his chest. "*Me.*"

"Don't beat yourself up," I said. "You did what you thought was right."

He shook his hair from his eyes. "I know. I just thought it would feel different. Better. Easier."

"I don't think it's supposed to be easy. Not something like

that." I shifted in the seat, tucking my legs underneath me so I could face him more fully. The heat of the car and my fear of the Irin fell away under his steady gaze.

"You know what I thought about afterward? When I was confused and didn't know what to feel?"

"What?" I asked.

"You. You're like the other part of me, Dancia. Nothing makes sense when you aren't around."

He squeezed my hand, and I felt a little crackle in my heart, like a leaf or a twig bursting into flame. It wasn't persuasion, or his talent, or anything like that. It was love. Love for and pride in this incredible person who, for some crazy reason, wanted to be with me.

I felt a deep ache in my chest when I realized Cam was struggling—maybe even more than me. He was actually out there fighting for what he believed in, while I sat at home thinking I was brave for asking questions and typing *Ethan Hannigan* into a search engine.

I was staying on the sidelines while Cam was out there living with the reality of Watchers and guns and people no jail could hold.

"I probably sound like an idiot," he said. "I shouldn't have come tonight. I should have waited until I was in a better place."

"That's not what we're about," I said. "If we waited until *I* made sense, we'd never talk at all."

He smiled and leaned an elbow against the steering wheel. "Thanks."

I should have told Cam then about my conversation with Jack. I didn't want to lie, or hide things from him. But I knew I couldn't. Cam was absolutely certain the Irin had been plotting against the president. Which meant one of two things: either Jack was lying, or someone was lying to Cam.

CHAPTER 21

CAM ACTUALLY had brought a few loads of clothes with him, so eventually we had to drive to the Laundromat. While the clothes were drying, we shared a milk shake nearby at Bev's. He slowly started to relax, and we walked around holding hands, laughing as we remembered the first time we'd met at Bev's, when he was trying to persuade me to go to Delcroix and I was trying to hide my talent.

He dropped me off in front of our house. Grandma met me at the door. "Took that long to do a few loads of laundry?"

I didn't even flinch. "Yep."

She chuckled and went back to the TV. I went into the kitchen and grabbed a soda. My head was spinning with thoughts of Cam and the conversation I'd had with Jack.

If Cam didn't know they were setting up the Irin, who did? He'd been outside the building while Mr. Judan and the other Watchers were taking their shots. It could have been any of them.

Without even realizing it, I'd accepted that Jack was telling the truth. Now I just had to figure out what to do next.

Esther had told me and Hennie what she was planning, so it shouldn't have been a big surprise, but I was still shocked to see her on Monday morning, holding court to a small circle of boys by the basement lockers. Her hair fell in long, loose waves down her back. Her eyes were surrounded by the thickest, darkest lashes you'd ever seen, and her lips were a perfect shade of red. She wore a pair of tight jeans and a low scoop-neck top. It was Esther, but Esther like I'd never seen her before.

I thought I'd gotten used to Esther's talent. I'd watched her change personas, subtly altering her face and body. But this was different. This transformation went beyond the shape of her eyebrows or the tone of her voice. This change went through to her core.

"Esther?" I asked in disbelief.

She turned to look at me, placing one hand on her hip. "What's up?"

"I guess I should ask you that question." I gestured from her head to her feet. "I see you went through with it."

She laughed a low, throaty laugh. "I don't know what you mean." She regarded the boys around her. "Do you notice anything different about me?"

They nodded vigorously and she laughed again.

I shifted my backpack on my shoulder. I was wearing my standard baggy jeans and hoodie, and felt drastically underdressed by comparison. "I didn't see you at breakfast," I said. "Hennie and I got here early so we could all eat together. You were supposed to meet us."

I didn't mention that Hennie had also run out of the cafeteria the minute she saw Yashir coming. They had texted over break, but she'd hung out with Rashid, the boy her parents picked out for her, three times, and she was feeling painfully guilty about it.

Esther swept a silky strand of hair behind her. "Guess

I slept late. I need my beauty rest, you know."

"Apparently." I hadn't planned on telling Esther the whole story, of course, but I had wanted to tell her how incredible it had felt to be with Cam this weekend, and how I'd fallen in love with him all over again. The first time, it was because of his looks and the force of his personality. On Sunday, I realized I was in love with his soul.

But right now, Esther clearly wasn't interested in Cam's soul.

A bell rang, and Esther linked arms with one of the guys. "I guess we better go to class." She started walking away, and then, almost as an afterthought, trotted a few steps back toward me. She whispered in my ear, "I'll be looking for Trevor. Let me know if you see him, will you?"

I watched her go with dismay. For the first time, it occurred to me that it could be Trevor, not Esther, who needed the protection.

The visitors started arriving early Tuesday morning, and more trickled in throughout the day. They came in ones and twos, wearing suits and carrying briefcases, talking animatedly to Mr. Judan, or each other, as they entered. There were lots of handshakes and greetings, as their belongings were whisked away by students and taken to the Bly, where they were staying. A collection of stony-faced men and women who I assumed were Watchers lurked silently in the background, wires crawling out of their ears. They had their hands on their hips or casually crossed over their chests. It wasn't hard to imagine weapons concealed under their jackets.

After breakfast, Principal Solom's voice came over the loudspeakers to announce that the strangers were there for a meeting of an international nonprofit organization. Alisha, one of the sophomores in the Program, told me they were actually the members of the Governing Council, probably there to discuss what had happened in D.C.

Barrett grabbed me in the hall on the way to my focus class. "There's someone I want you to meet."

The Bly stood a few hundred yards behind the Main Hall. It looked like something you'd see in a postcard, with its gleaming white paint and wraparound porch, and hundreds of red and pink roses growing up the sides. A tall figure with a shock of white hair met us on the porch.

Barrett bobbed his head and gestured toward me. "Dad, this is Dancia Lewis."

The white-haired man held out his hand for me to shake. "Dancia, I'm Ronald Alterir." Hawklike eyes studied me from a long face. The resemblance to Barrett was striking— though, unlike his son, the older man had the bearing of someone used to giving orders and having them obeyed. "I've heard a lot about you."

"All good, of course," Barrett said, flashing a smile.

"Thank you, Mr. Alterir," I said, stepping back nervously after he released my hand. "It's a pleasure to meet you."

"Please, call me Ronald." A small circle of cushioned chairs sat on one end of the porch. "I have a few minutes before our first meeting. Why don't we sit down?"

"We don't want to bother you," Barrett said. "I know you're busy."

Mr. Alterir—I couldn't think of him as Ronald, no matter what he said—sighed. "I don't mind. It's a welcome distraction. These meetings are always tense after we've had an incident with the Irin."

We each took a chair. Barrett and I sat side by side, while Mr. Alterir positioned himself opposite us. I arranged my knees carefully in front of me, my toes twitching with the effort to keep still. I tried to remember everything Barrett had told me about his dad. I'd heard from Cam and a few others that Mr. Alterir and Mr. Judan didn't get along, but I didn't know why. I figured it had to do with the Watchers.

"Another emergency resolution?" Barrett asked.

"Probably." Mr. Alterir crossed one leg over the other. "Normally, I wouldn't speak so frankly to a student in your position, Dancia. But there's nothing normal about you, is there?"

I wasn't sure whether to take that as a compliment, so I just shrugged.

"She's special," Barrett said, stretching his legs out in front of him. His old sandals seemed particularly decrepit in comparison with his father's expensive loafers. "That's for sure."

"I'm sorry you had to experience that incident with the group from Seattle," said Mr. Alterir. "It's always troubling when our students are threatened."

"I guess you can't control the Irin," I said.

"No, but we can try to minimize the threat they pose. That's what we hope to accomplish on the Council. At least, that's what *I* hope to accomplish."

I didn't know how to take that, either, but I couldn't help wondering if it had something to do with Mr. Judan. "So, you're here to talk about what happened in D.C.?"

"Yes, we usually meet if there's been an incident with the Irin that we find particularly troublesome."

"Are you worried about the president?" I said. "Do you think they were trying to kill him?"

Mr. Alterir spread out his hands. "The documents they discovered in the warehouse were fairly conclusive."

I thought of what Jack had said and picked my words carefully. Even though I had a feeling Mr. Alterir would understand, I didn't want to start out my first visit with him by saying I had been talking to one of the Irin. "But it seems a little odd, doesn't it? I mean, going after the president doesn't seem like a particularly effective strategy if what they really want is to attack the Governing Council."

"The same thing occurred to me," Mr. Alterir said, eyeing me thoughtfully. I squirmed a little under his gaze, sitting up straighter in my chair and arranging my hood behind me. "An attack on the president is out of character for our friend Gregori. He likes to consider himself sophisticated and cunning, but he does not like to attract the attention of the conventional police. A high-profile assassination is not his way."

I leaned forward. "How do you know all those things about him?"

"We are a small community," Mr. Alterir said. "Particularly those with strong talents. You will come to appreciate this as you move higher in our ranks. Gregori and I went to the same school. I knew him well."

My eyes widened. Gregori had always seemed like such a mysterious, shadowy figure that I had almost convinced myself he wasn't real. "And now you fight with the Governing Council about him?" I asked.

Mr. Alterir stood up and walked to the side of the porch. He touched a petal of one of the roses. "Gregori was always unstable, even when I knew him. But I never thought he had the potential to become so dangerous."

"You don't think he's as bad as they say?" I asked.

He snapped off the bloom, holding it up to his nose to smell the heady fragrance. "I have no doubt that Gregori has always had a certain ruthlessness about him. I believe if he wants something, he will do anything in his power to get it."

I noticed he didn't exactly answer the question. I tried a different tack. "If you agree with them about Gregori, what do you end up fighting about?"

He handed me the rose and smiled, as if he saw I was trying to pin him down and he found it amusing. "Every time the Irin strike us, we have a meeting to discuss our response. Lately, that response has been to increase the number of Watchers and their power to act without Council oversight."

I gingerly held the prickly stem between my fingers. Mr. Anderson would be pissed if he knew we'd picked one of his flowers. "You don't agree with that?"

He leaned against the porch and shrugged. "I can't help but notice that someone gains more power every time we do this. And that makes me wonder: is it a coincidence or something more? A good question to ask, don't you think?"

CHAPTER 22

THOSE SOFTLY spoken words rattled around in my head all day. The only one I could think of who benefited from the Watchers' getting stronger was Mr. Judan. After all, he was the head of the Watcher program—if they got more powerful, so did he. But what could Mr. Alterir be suggesting? That Mr. Judan had something to do with the Irin?

Two days later, the Governing Council members finished their meeting and left with their Watcher bodyguards in tow. Barrett told me they voted to create some new group of Watchers to guard the president, with special powers to act in an emergency situation. He didn't seem happy about it, and neither did his dad.

Jack called me again a week after that. I didn't pick up. He left a long message telling me about a new band he'd seen at a club the night before. I had to fight the urge to call him right back. The truth was, I missed him. I pictured him in the classes we'd had together. I thought about him when I was studying. Once, I even found myself comparing the way it felt when he kissed me with the way it felt when I kissed Cam. This made no sense, because I knew Jack and I weren't meant to be together. But a nagging voice in my head kept reminding me that somewhere in the middle of our kiss, when we'd lost track of time and I'd forgotten all my doubts, something had felt right.

Thinking about any of this was absurd, given the fact that Jack had joined the Irin.

From what I could tell, he was hovering around the fringes of the Seattle cell, but not participating yet. He'd hinted at spending time in D.C., but I couldn't believe he'd somehow gotten involved with that cell.

Though I didn't want to accept it, I knew what I had to do. The Irin were our enemy. There wasn't a lot of black and white in my world, but even Jack had said things were going to get worse from here on out. They had guns, and they were angry. Jack might have been on the fringes of their group, but he was still part of it.

It was time to cut off all contact with Jack.

No matter what.

Mr. Judan and Mr. Fritz took a small group of us out for a training exercise the first week in May. Barrett gave me a worried look before we left. He said they didn't usually take sophomores, let alone freshmen, on these sorts of trips. This year they were starting early, and Barrett thought it was a bad idea. He said we needed more training before they let us get into "unscripted fights."

Despite my repeated requests for more details, Barrett wouldn't explain what kind of unscripted fight he was referring to. Naturally, this terrified me. My last unscripted fight had ended in a near-death experience. Though I liked to think I was more in control of my talent now, I didn't know what would happen if I were pushed. Mr. Fritz and Mr. Judan also seemed determined to leave us in the dark. My only consolation was that Cam was coming. Unfortunately, Anna was, too.

There were eight of us; we were loaded into a van on Thursday just after lunch. There were two sophomores, three juniors, and me. I wasn't surprised to see Alisha. If they were picking students based on fighting ability, she'd have been at the top of the list. The other sophomore, Xavier, hadn't been at the party, so I didn't know as much about him. I'd heard that he had some kind of super-tracking ability. As in, a person could walk across a concrete floor without leaving a single mark, but Xavier would know exactly where each of the footsteps had landed. He also happened to be gorgeous, with dark skin, high cheekbones, and an athletic build, though Esther said he was more into music than sports.

Esther had considered Xavier as a possible boyfriend target before her transformation. Since then she'd focused mainly on juniors and seniors, and thanks to her new look and attitude she was burning through them at a furious rate. It seemed like she was hanging out with someone new every weekend. Trevor had started looking at her with a sad, puzzled stare; it seemed like she was deliberately flaunting her conquests in front of him. It was all rather disturbing, so I tried to look the other way and pretend it wasn't happening. As hard as it was to admit, I actually found myself feeling a little sorry for him.

I assumed Trevor would be coming along on the training exercise, so I was surprised to see Molly line up for the van. Leaving aside her tendency to try to make herself disappear whenever there was a conflict, I liked Molly. I wasn't sure why she was being sent on a training exercise, as she wasn't much of a fighter. She was the only junior at Anna's house who hadn't joined the brawl. Maybe she was coming with us to get extra practice.

Mr. Fritz drove while Mr. Judan scratched notes onto a

pad in his lap. I sat next to Cam. He was trying to keep the mood light, but it was a challenge, even for him. Eventually, he stopped making conversation, and we sat in silence.

From the highway, we turned onto a gravel road and headed into the woods. The van driver had to stop twice to unlock sets of metal gates. I guess they were serious about keeping people from stumbling in on our activities. After the second gate, we drove a few more miles, then parked at the end of a driveway, beside a small wooden cabin.

We filed out of the van into sunshine and a warm breeze. We'd had weeks of rain and then a miraculous burst of blue skies and seventy-degree weather, which left everything growing twice as fast as usual. The rhododendrons were blooming all over the woods, light pink and purple, interwoven with yellow Oregon grape and some flowering vines.

We stood in a loose group outside the van as we waited for Mr. Judan to emerge. He finally did, with his usual blinding smile. Mr. Fritz went inside the cabin; I had a moment of panic as he walked away. After talking to Mr. Alterir, I didn't know what to think about Mr. Judan. He'd always freaked me out, but now I got nervous every time he looked at me.

"My dear students," Mr. Judan said, "I want to thank you for accepting the challenge to come out here today and play our little game.

"There is, of course, much we can learn in a classroom. But there is also much we cannot. We brought you here because you are each at a crossroads. Some of you asked to be here so you could demonstrate how your skills have grown this year."

Molly's face turned pink, and she pressed her arms against her sides.

"Others of you have been asking for a challenge, and we are excited to present you with one."

Xavier and Alisha smiled a little when he said that.

I waited for him to say something that might explain why *I* was there, but he simply continued, "We felt all of you needed this experience to move to the next level in your training. Now, I am dividing you into two teams. Anna will be captain of the red team." Anna stepped forward, no hint of a smile on her perfect mouth. "Anna, your team includes Dancia and Xavier. Cameron, you are captain of the blue team. Molly and Alisha will be on your team. Anna and Cameron, we have asked you to be captains because we have faith in your ability to guide your teammates through a safe and productive experience. Remember that you are here to learn, not simply to win."

Anna and Cam nodded, and then stepped forward to shake hands with each other. It seemed like a ritual they had performed in the past, and I had the feeling, as I so often had over the year, that Cam and Anna shared a history I would never fully appreciate.

"Somewhere within a mile radius of the cabin we have hidden a single vial. It looks something like this." Mr. Judan pulled from his pocket a small glass cylinder with a black top, similar to the ones we used in chemistry lab. It was about the length of his pinkie, and not much thicker. "Inside this vial is a deadly poison. Thousands could be killed if a few drops were added to a community's water supply. You must find the vial before the other team and bring it back to the cabin, where it can be safely destroyed. The team to arrive at the cabin with the vial is the winner."

He motioned toward the cabin, where Mr. Fritz was bringing out black vests and handfuls of oversize goggles. He threw them on the ground and then marched back inside. This time, he brought out guns.

My eyes widened. They were giving us guns? For a training exercise?

"You'll each get a gun and ammunition. Your supplies are limited, so use them wisely. You'll have a vest, goggles, and gloves. Each vest has a square in the center of the chest. That is the strike zone. You are to aim for that area only. The paintballs won't cause serious injury, but they can hurt."

"And leave a nasty welt," Cam said.

I tried to look sagely at the pile of weapons. They were *paintball* guns. Of course. The bright blue accents and eight-inch cylinders mounted below long, thin barrels should have clued me in that they weren't *real* guns.

"If you get hit in the strike zone, you're out. You can continue to play if you are hit anywhere else. We are relying on your honor to remove yourself from the game if you take a direct hit." He paused. "Any questions?"

"Can we use our talents?" I asked.

Mr. Judan flashed his white teeth. "Of course."

"Is there a safe zone?" Alisha asked, eyes gleaming. She was practically bouncing with excitement.

"Excellent question." He indicated a line of small red flags. I hadn't noticed them before, but now that I did, I saw that they surrounded the cabin, marking a line about thirty feet from the front porch. "The flags mark the demilitarized zone. You may not use your weapons or approach the other team in any way within that zone."

"Do we have to get our entire team back to the cabin?" Xavier said.

"No. One team member must carry the vial into the cabin. That's all." Mr. Judan looked around the circle of faces. "Any other questions?" We shook our heads. "Good. Take a few minutes to put on your safety equipment and become familiar with your guns. You may also take a compass if you'd like. Around back there's a small area within the DMZ for target practice. After you leave the DMZ, it's all up to you."

I kept my face impassive. I refused to let Anna see that I was actually scared of paintballs. I might have been scared, but I was determined, too. It would be like fighting with Barrett and my teachers, but this time I'd know what to expect. I'd use my talent and show everyone how much I'd progressed. Maybe I would even outplay Anna.

Except . . . I looked at the pile of guns again. We'd had a couple of days of target practice with pellet guns right before spring break, and I had been absolutely dreadful. I hadn't hit the target once. And today people would be moving. What chance did I have of hitting a moving target?

Anna motioned for me and Xavier to follow her a few yards away from the cabin. Cam's team did the same, in the other direction. "Grab your guns and pretend like you're going to do some target practice," Anna whispered. "But listen for my signal. We'll take off as soon as they're distracted. We need to get as much of a head start as possible."

"Anna, I've never used one of those guns before." I glanced uneasily at Cam out of the corner of my eye. He looked calm and sure of himself as he spoke to Molly and Alisha. "It might be a good idea for me to get used to it a little. Before they start shooting at me."

"Which is exactly why I want you to run," she said flatly. "Otherwise, Cam will shoot you before you even get started. I've seen him hit people on the run at two hundred yards. You need to get out of his sight, fast."

She had a point, though I didn't like to think of Cam as being so deadly.

"Where should we go?" Xavier asked.

"We'll stay together long enough to establish a base," Anna said. "We need a thicket—dense trees or brambles—anything that can protect our backs. Then we'll divide the area into quadrants for searching. Make sure you both get a compass and watch it. It's easy to get lost out there."

"What about Xavier's talent?" I asked. I didn't even want to think about how ill-equipped I was to navigate by compass. "Shouldn't he start tracking right away? They must have started from the cabin when they hid the vial. We don't want to miss the start of the trail."

Xavier nodded. "I can see a bunch of signs from here, including a trail that I think Fritz and Judan made together. I could follow that while the other team is practicing. Dancia can watch my back."

Anna grabbed us by the shoulders and pulled us together. "If you two slow down and start following a trail right from the cabin, you're dead meat, understand? I appreciate your suggestion, but you've got to trust me on this. We need to get some distance between ourselves and the others as quickly as possible. You can always come back to the trail later."

Xavier and I looked at each other and then back at Anna. The clearing around the cabin had gone quiet. It killed me to have to listen to Anna, but everything she said made sense. "Okay," I gulped. "I'm with you."

Xavier nodded. "Me too."

We put our outstretched hands into a circle, one palm on top of the next. Anna counted softly, "One, two, break!"

We turned around to face the others.

CHAPTER 23

NOBODY TALKED as we picked out our vests and goggles. Mr. Fritz had brought out gloves as well, and we each pawed through the pile to find a pair that fit. I ended up next to Cam as we gathered our gear. Even though I knew it was just a game, I found myself getting more and more nervous, and having flashbacks to the chaos of falling trees and branches.

When no one was looking, Cam reached out and touched my hand. We didn't say anything, but that moment sustained me as I slipped the silver and black mask over my face. Clear plastic surrounded my eyes and forehead, while a plastic grate protected my mouth and chin but allowed me to breathe. It felt a little like wearing a motorcycle helmet, except that it was open on top and in the back. The vests were slid over each of our heads and tightened down on the sides. I wished I could have laughed about the gear, and how ridiculous everyone looked with their armor on, but the participants seemed to be treating this activity with utter seriousness.

Next, we each grabbed a gun. It was lighter than I expected and surprisingly comfortable in my hands. Anna whispered instructions as we clustered around her, explaining that the cylinder held the rest of our ammunition. She showed us how to load the gun and then said, loud enough for Cam's team to hear, "Can we start practicing now, Mr. Judan?"

He nodded. Everyone put their guns over their shoulders and walked around to where a couple of targets had been set up by the far side of the cabin. There were several extra guns on a picnic table nearby. Cam walked beside Alisha, explaining that she should use one of the extra guns to practice with so she didn't waste her ammunition. I felt a stab of jealousy as I watched them, because I knew Alisha was a great shot. I couldn't help wondering whether Cam was relieved he'd gotten her on his team instead of me.

Then I remembered that I could fling her fifty feet into the air, and decided he'd be crazy if he did.

We waited until Cam's team was occupied with picking out practice weapons; then Anna whispered, "Run!"

I bent low, making sure to keep Xavier at my side. We followed Anna, who darted from tree to tree, then began running in an erratic pattern through the woods. I heard Cam swear, and a few seconds later, a paintball whizzed past my shoulder. Anna had been right. He was ready to take me and Xavier out. Our only chance at escape had been surprise.

Anna's dark brown ponytail bobbed as she ran ahead of us. She turned around every ten or fifteen yards to make sure we were still with her. "Are you watching the time?" she asked me at one point.

"What? No," I said, confused.

"We've got a mile radius," she said. "Watch your pace and try to keep track of how far we've gone."

"Oh!" I glanced at my watch. I was gaining a new appreciation for Anna's skills. "Got it."

"You should watch your compass, too. We're moving west-southwest right now. I'll try to keep us on that heading."

I looped the string of the compass around my wrist so I wouldn't lose it.

Xavier was already breathing hard. "Anna," he panted, "do you think they'll look for it themselves, or will they just follow me? If we get it, they can steal it from us, can't they? There isn't any rule against that."

She slowed her pace for a minute. "Good point. Molly can turn invisible, and she's a great stalker, but she doesn't have any talent for finding things, and she isn't much of a shot. Alisha's a good shot, and super fast, but that won't help them locate the vial. I guess they might sit back and wait for us to find it, then try to take it."

"We won't let that happen," I said. My breath had already fogged up the inside of my mask, and I pushed it up and tried to wipe it clean, but realized I couldn't do that without taking the whole thing off; so I gave up. "Once we find the vial, you or Xavier can run it back to the cabin while I hold them off."

"Are you sure?" Anna asked. "Can you handle more than one at a time?"

I told myself Anna was just being a good captain and assessing the skills of her teammates, not making fun of me.

"No, I'm fine with two or three," I said.

Anna stopped suddenly in front of me, and I almost plowed into her back. "Perfect," she said.

I followed her gaze to a small copse of trees. An old maple must have been hit by lightning a few years ago, because the trunk had been split in half and a limb had crashed to the ground beside it. The branch sat at an angle against the trunk, leaving a sort of pocket underneath it. Brambles and shrubs had grown up around the edges, ringing the pocket so you could hide there—or better protect yourself from attack.

"Dancia, you and Xavier stay here while I check out the area. I'll be back in a few."

"Anna!" I called as she started to disappear back into the greenery.

"What?" She paused, keeping a steady watch all around. "Spit it out. Every second matters."

I wiped the sweat collecting at the top of my forehead, above the edge of the mask. "What if you just went back and drew Cam out instead? Molly and Alisha won't know what to do without him. Meanwhile, Xavier and I can start around the perimeter and see if we can pick up the trail that way. We'll head back for base if we get in trouble or run into Cam."

Anna rocked on the balls of her feet as she considered the idea.

"This isn't a very big area for me to search," Xavier said with a burst of confidence. I guess we were all a little cocky when it came to our talents. "I've been looking for stuff like this since I was a kid."

Anna pushed back a lock of hair. "If Molly finds you, you're screwed," she said flatly. "She'll have a clear shot. You'd never know she was there."

"We'll stay on the move," I said. "If she's a rotten marksman we're safer if we keep running."

Anna considered it, then said, "Fine. Give me a few minutes' head start and you can start looking." Without another word, she melted into the trees.

I sighed with relief. The thought of staying there and waiting to get shot had not appealed to me.

Xavier and I tamped down the ground inside our little shelter and tried not to look at each other. Sweat was running down the sides of his face onto his neck, and he kept repositioning his vest. I remembered that Esther had said he wasn't much of an athlete, despite his build. "Are you going to be okay to keep running?" I asked.

"I guess I'll have to be," he said ruefully. "I needed to start working out anyway."

"Which way should we go first?" I wasn't sure who was supposed to be directing our little partnership, but I hoped it wasn't me. I didn't have a clue where to begin.

"That way," he said, pointing to our right. "I caught sight of a trail when we were running up here. It wasn't Judan's trail, but it was very fresh. Today, probably."

We waited another minute, and then, with a quick nod of agreement, started out.

Xavier set out at a decent pace, jumping over logs and side-stepping brambles and decayed stumps. I maneuvered behind him, periodically glancing between my watch and the compass so I had some idea of where we were headed. I had adjusted to the feeling of the mask on my face, but not the way it interfered with my vision; I had to consciously study the ground to keep from tripping. I was acutely aware that I was supposed to be protecting Xavier, so I kept my eyes on the surrounding forest as well, and tried to stay aware of every possible movement. Molly could turn herself and what-ever she was touching invisible, but she couldn't stop sound or her impact on things around her. If she pushed aside a branch or snapped a twig, I'd have known.

In the distance, someone cried out. It was definitely a girl, and though I couldn't identify the voice, I figured it was Anna. The thought that Xavier and I might be on our own was oddly thrilling; though, for our team's sake, I hoped she hadn't gotten hit.

Xavier kept running and so did I. It was like following a bloodhound on a short leash. I jerked along behind him, glancing over my shoulder every few seconds for moving foliage. A line of sweat formed on the back of Xavier's T-shirt.

A couple of minutes later, he stopped and bent forward to examine the ground. "There was more than one of them," he said, pointing to a spot a few feet in front of us. "Three or four, I think. It's from earlier today—maybe just a few hours ago."

I squinted, but all I could see was a thick bed of pine needles and ferns. One of the ferns was torn, and there were a few indentations in a bald, muddy patch of ground. But that was all. Before I knew it, Xavier was moving again, this time in the direction I thought the cabin was. I checked the compass. We had been headed south, and now were looping back around to the east. But we were taking a meandering path that left me unclear as to where we were exactly.

"Why would they have three or four people hiding the vial?" I whispered.

Xavier kept on the trail. "I don't know," he said. "I'm going to follow it in."

We continued on for a few minutes, and then he paused again to assess the ground. "Now, this one is Fritz's," he said. "But it's heading in a different direction."

"Which way is the group trail headed?"

"Toward the cabin."

"Then we follow Fritz," I said.

Xavier nodded and surveyed the trail for another moment. We were lucky we had stopped, because an instant later I heard the snap of a branch about thirty feet to our right.

"Duck!" I yelled.

Xavier threw himself to the ground and started crawling toward a fallen tree for cover. I fumbled for my gun, trying to keep my body between him and our attacker. A paintball hit a tree beside us with a dull thud. I expected to see a splatter of paint, but there was only a faint orange mark where it hit the trunk. Another came a second later. This one glanced off my collarbone as I spun around, ready to fire. The force was enough to knock me sideways, though it didn't burst or splatter, just bounced off. It felt like I'd been hit by a rock. Catching my breath, I scuttled over to Xavier's hiding place.

He touched my shoulder. "There's no mark," he said quietly.

I winced when he trailed his fingers over the spot the ball had hit. It didn't *feel* like a paintball. I knew Cam had said they could hurt and maybe even leave a welt, but this seemed far more painful than a welt. I couldn't imagine what it would be like if it had caught me squarely in the chest. Or head.

His dark eyes showed concern. "You can stay in the game, though, can't you? It wasn't in the strike zone."

I nodded, trying unsuccessfully to tune out the burning sensation in my shoulder. "I think so. But it hurts like hell."

"From the paintball? I thought they said it would just sting a little."

I adjusted my vest, thinking the straps across my shoulders might be making it worse. It didn't help. "That's a heck of a sting," I said.

"Can you shoot?"

"I could if we were desperate."

Xavier rested his gun on the log. "I'll take this one. You watch for Molly."

I peeked out at the clearing, generating the energy of

my talent and feeling the familiar whoosh of power ripple through me. There had been a time when that power terrified me, but now it was comforting. I knew I was in control.

There was no sign of human life, but I did see something on the other side of the clearing, beside the trunk of an old cedar—maybe it was just the wind, or the fluttering of a leaf. I didn't know for sure, but I nudged Xavier, who nodded and squeezed off four shots in a row, blanketing the area.

If it was Molly, she must have hidden behind the tree, because the paintballs sailed through the air without contact. But we had come close to hitting her. We heard leaves crunching underfoot, and Xavier shot again, only a foot or two from the tree. I saw a branch move, then heard a twig break.

"She's on the run," Xavier whispered. "I can't see her trail, but I can see the actual damage she does. If she moves again, I'll have her."

We waited. My heart raced. Then Xavier muttered, "Gotcha." He shot at chest height, where we would have expected Molly's strike zone to be. This time, I heard a human voice grunt and saw a shimmer of color and the ghostly outline of a person shaking out her hand. She dashed from tree to tree, flickering in and out of her invisible state. Xavier shot at her a few more times, but nothing connected.

"It's my turn," I said.

I squinted through my goggles, making sure to get a good look at her before trying to use my talent. She was flashing, like someone walking past a strobe light, but if I focused hard, I could see her outline well enough. Once I got a visual, it was simple to identify the gravitational forces acting on her and send her flying into the air. Molly appeared in full form a moment later, her face showing blind panic.

Xavier looked at me with respect. He ran his hand over his short hair. "Damn," he whispered. "I didn't know you could do that."

Carefully, I brought her higher up in the air. She started firing at us, but the shots went wild as she shook uncontrollably with fear. I pushed her toward the old cedar she'd hidden behind a few minutes before. Moving a wiggling human being sideways tested my strength, but I managed it. Molly held her hands in front of her face as I shoved her through the wide, spreading branches. Then I let her fall a few feet. She shrieked and caught herself on a branch, dropping her gun and coming to rest about fifteen feet above the ground. Satisfied that I could safely leave her there, I turned to Xavier.

"Back to Mr. Fritz's trail," I said.

Xavier and I started running again. I held my arm against my chest because the pain from its bouncing was starting to make me sick. Xavier moved confidently along the trail. When I heard a noise or thought I saw something, I'd elbow him, and we'd take refuge in a cluster of trees or behind a stump. My experience with the paintball that hit me had raised the stakes a few notches, and my nerves were on edge. I kept turning around, expecting Alisha or Cam to appear.

We followed the trail for another fifteen minutes without further incident, running up and down a few wrong paths before finding a spot under a big fern where the earth had recently been disturbed. I kept watch while Xavier dug around in the dirt. He exclaimed happily when he found the small cylinder of glass.

He held it up in front of me, but I pushed it away. "Just stow it and let's get out of here," I said.

"Where should we go? To the cabin?"

I hesitated. "Not yet. I don't want to get ambushed when

we're only a few feet from the end. I think we should go to the base we found earlier and check for Anna." I pulled out my compass doubtfully. "I guess we go . . . west?"

"I can backtrack us," Xavier said. "We aren't that far. I just wish I wasn't so damned tired already. When we're done with this, I'm not running again for a month."

He sounded so sincere I couldn't help laughing. I sobered abruptly as a wave of pain hit. "Lead on, tough guy," I said. "Let's get this over with."

We started toward the base; I was slow and clumsy, thanks to my hurt shoulder and the growing nausea, and Xavier started gasping for air almost immediately. I guess it shouldn't have been a surprise when we saw Alisha hurtling through the woods, weaving back and forth between the trees. My gun hung against my back, but I didn't bother pulling it out. My whole arm was tingling, and I knew I wouldn't be able to grip anything very well.

We were in a small clearing surrounded by a few spreading vine maples. The small, thin trees provided no cover. The only thing we could hide behind was an overturned log. With a quick nod, we jumped over it and crouched. Mud smeared across my knees and caked my palms.

"Keep watch for Cam," I said. "If he comes I'll try to hold them off while you run for the cabin."

I could feel Xavier's rapid breath hot and fast on my neck as we waited. He popped up and took aim at Alisha, but she was impossible to track. She kept moving from tree to tree, taking aim when she could and sending paintballs slamming into the ground in front of us. I wished I could have just thrown her somewhere, but I was fuzzy and tired because of the pain, and she moved too fast for me to get a grip on the black ribbons that trailed from every side of her.

215

Finally, she got close enough for me to get her in focus. I took her up in the air, but she squeezed off a rapid volley of paintballs, and when I instinctively ducked down and closed my eyes, she dropped to the ground. When I realized she'd fallen, I pushed her back up, but I was scared of hurting her, especially with my control wavering. There was no nearby tree to stick her in, so I let her tumble down, still gripping her gun. She rolled in a somersault onto her shoulder, and that's when we caught a break, because the contact with the ground knocked her mask sideways, and she had to pause to adjust it.

Xavier grabbed the opportunity, and one of his paint-balls caught her in the arm. She darted into the woods, using her good arm to fix her goggles as she ran. At the edge of the clearing, she turned and fired, but she must have been unsteady due to the pain from getting hit; her shot went wild, and she only ended up exposing herself even more fully than before.

Xavier didn't hesitate, this time catching her in the thigh and stomach. She shrieked and fell to the ground. We waited for her to get up, carefully looking around for Cam to emerge from the woods.

Muffled sobs came from Alisha as she writhed on the ground.

"Must be a trick," Xavier muttered. "Leave her there."

I nodded uneasily. "Let's head for the cabin. I don't like this game anymore."

"You sure?"

"Yeah. Alisha and Molly are both out. We've just got to watch for Cam."

The thought that we were finally in the homestretch pro-vided us with a final burst of energy. I could see the green roof, then the clearing and the van parked beside it. We ran side by side, and I was almost ready to declare victory when I heard the pop of a gun.

Cam had found us.

The ball made a little buzzing sound as it passed through the air, and I had just enough time to throw myself in front of Xavier. Unfortunately, that meant taking the shot right in the face. My goggles cracked down the middle, sending hard plastic into my nose. A fresh wave of pain started in my forehead and rippled through the rest of my head.

Another shot came from behind me, this one aimed at Cam.

I dropped to the ground, too tired and hurt to care that I was now a sitting duck. I pried the goggles off my face, noticing dimly that they were dripping with a mixture of blood and sweat, and fought a wave of dizziness as the firefight continued over my head.

"Run, Xavier!" I heard Anna yell. She was behind us somewhere, peppering the area with shots to hold off any enemies.

Xavier didn't need any encouragement. He ran with all he had, and I held my breath as he approached the little red flags that indicated safety. Anna and Cam continued their cross fire. Cam stepped into view when Xavier was a few feet from the line. Anna came out as well, and she and Cam each landed a shot on the other. Cam hit her in the chest, and she got him in the arm, then again on the shin.

I was staring at him, of course, so I saw him react to the pain. He whipped around to his left as the ball hit him on the arm, and then to the right as it caught him in the leg. He grunted, then hopped awkwardly on his right leg as he continued to load and shoot.

Mr. Fritz and Mr. Judan were both there, smiling when Xavier ran across the line, but their smiles faded when it became apparent that something about their game had gone horribly wrong. I heard Xavier telling them about Alisha, who might still have been writhing around on the ground for all we knew. Cam hopped awkwardly toward Anna, who was lying on the ground. I let my head come to rest in the dirt, wondering why the world looked so fuzzy, and whether we got extra credit for winning the game.

CHAPTER 24

THE EXTENT of our injuries became evident as we loaded into the van. Cam couldn't put any weight on his left leg, which had a huge lump on the shin. Anna had taken a hit right in the chest. Luckily, she'd had her vest on, which absorbed some of the blow. She wouldn't have much more than a big bruise. Alisha wasn't so lucky. She had taken a shot to the stomach just below the edge of her vest. Everyone was worried she'd suffered some internal injuries, because she was found exactly where we'd left her, still and white, clutching her stomach.

Xavier was completely unhurt, so he helped the teachers track down Molly, who had remained stuck in the tree. She had a broken hand and hadn't been able to get more than a little way down it.

Other than Alisha, I was probably the worst off. My head was still spinning (Mr. Fritz thought I might have a concussion), my forehead kept dripping blood, and I couldn't move my arm because of the pain in my shoulder. A bump had emerged along my collarbone, and I felt a grinding sensation when I tried to lift my arm. There was wide speculation by the teachers and students that the impact of the ball had broken the bone.

Anna apparently thought her role as team captain meant she had some responsibility for me, because she stuck by my side, helping me off the ground so they could look at my shoulder, and running to get me water and a cool bandanna when I thought I might pass out. She called Xavier over before we left and told us how proud she was of the job we had done. She said our strategy had worked perfectly—she and Cam had spent most of the time running around shooting at each other, which had freed me and Xavier up to find the vial and take care of Molly and Alisha. We couldn't help feeling a little happy that our plan had been so successful even though the game had gotten so brutal.

The balls, of course, weren't ordinary paintballs. Instead of being plastic shells filled with liquid paint, they felt as solid as rocks. You could scrape off the outer layer and use it like a big, round crayon. No one was under any illusion that this was simply a manufacturing flaw.

Xavier mentioned that he'd found tracks in the woods—seemingly left by three or four people he didn't recognize, headed toward the cabin. It didn't take long for someone to mention the Irin. And it was only a few more seconds before someone said, "*Jack.*" He could turn liquids to solids, after all. It wasn't much of a stretch to connect him with what had happened. Cam didn't see any talent marks, but that hardly mattered. They could have changed them anywhere and replaced our paintballs with their modified ones, though it seemed most likely he had done it at the cabin, after they were loaded into the guns, so that we wouldn't notice the difference in weight.

I couldn't believe Jack would have done anything that he knew might hurt me. Then again, I wasn't supposed to be there. Barrett had said in the past that these exercises were just for juniors. How could Jack have known they would bring me along?

My head hurt too much to analyze things further. I crawled into the van, holding my arm tight across my chest so it wouldn't bounce. A mixture of dirt, sweat, and blood left my skin feeling hot and tight. Cam helped me into a seat between him and Anna and then buckled the belt across me. Fury radiated from him in hot waves. I suppose part of his anger was at himself, as it always was when it came to Jack. But most of it was for the Irin. If I hadn't been wearing goggles, Cam might have killed me. As it was, he'd probably given me a serious concussion. I could practically hear the thoughts running through his head. This wasn't a prank, but something far more serious.

We pulled away from the cabin, leaving the gear and the guns in a jumble on the front porch. "Don't worry about those things," Mr. Judan said. "We need to get you all back to school."

I kept falling asleep in the van, my head dropping sideways for just a second before I'd feel Cam squeezing my hand. "Stay with me, Dancia," he'd whisper in my ear. "Stay with me." They said that if I had a concussion I shouldn't go to sleep, and Cam was taking no chances.

Normally, I would have loved the attention, but everything hurt too much to appreciate it. I didn't even have it in me to resent Anna. Not when she'd brought me water and held my hand after I got in the van, and looked at me with honest concern. Sometimes, like at this moment, Anna looked almost angelic, even with a smear of dirt on her forehead and a trail of sweat across her temple.

We were about halfway back to school when I saw a black car hurtle around a corner a mile or so away. It was moving fast, and it looked as if it were in our lane.

"What are you doing? Get back in your own lane," Mr. Fritz said, shaking his head.

At first I assumed the driver had been passing, or was distracted for a moment. I waited, expecting to see them swerve back or to see a tractor that they were passing. But there was nothing.

"Are they . . . ?" Cam's question faded away. There was no need to respond.

He nudged me. "Dancia," he whispered. "Dancia, do something."

I was tired and probably still in shock, so it took me a moment to understand that he wanted me—out of all the people in the car—to save us. Me.

I focused with an effort on the car. Ever since I'd been hit, my vision had been distorted by wavy lines and shadows hovering around the edges, and it only got worse when I squinted to see more clearly. I tried to summon my power, but nothing happened. My body stayed limp. No energy crackled through me the way I had come to expect.

"Jesus," Anna breathed. "Look at the front seat."

I forced my eyes to focus, still trying to draw on the energy around me. The blackness around the edges of my vision only grew larger. "I can't do it," I croaked. "I'm sorry, I—"

"It's him," Cam said.

"Him?" I struggled back to an upright position. The car was headed right for us; I caught sight of black hair and dark sunglasses in the passenger seat. But my eyes couldn't quite focus, and the faces were blurry.

"Jack," Anna said impatiently. "Can't you see him? He's right there, in the front seat."

"Dancia, focus," Mr. Judan said, his voice deep and compelling. "Move that car."

I desperately wanted to do what he said. Every fiber of my being concentrated on moving that car away from us. Up or down, left or right, nothing mattered but that it moved out of the way.

"Move the car," Mr. Judan said again.

Fresh pain stabbed my head, and I cried out. I could see him now, in his red bandanna. He seemed to be looking right at me, though surely that was just a coincidence. How could he look at me so calmly while the driver of his car was trying to run us off the road?

Mr. Fritz swore. "Hold on, everyone!"

They could only have been five or ten feet away when Mr. Fritz jerked the wheel to the right. We swerved, continuing forward at an angle for a few feet before the van tipped sideways into a drainage ditch. I flinched and instinctively threw my good arm over my head. We rolled upside down, seat belts locking to hold us tightly in place, water bottles and backpacks flying. Then, slowly, in a moment of eerie silence, we came to rest.

CHAPTER 25

THANKS TO our seat belts, no one was seriously hurt—at least, not much more so than we were before the crash. Mr. Judan called the school, and they sent a couple of cars to pick us up. The pain in my head and arm kept getting worse, and I threw up twice on the way back. Xavier pulled off his shirt to wipe down the car, while Cam held the bandanna to my forehead. When we returned, they put us in the basement. I sat in a chair, my head lolling, while they put Alisha on the floor, robes from Initiation piled underneath her like a multicolored mattress.

David arrived a few minutes later. He went to Alisha right away. They'd had to carry her inside. The seat belt had tightened across the very spot where the paintball had hit her, and she was barely conscious. He spent a long time with his hands on her belly before stumbling backward, looking almost as pale as she was.

He touched my head next, and the blackness that surrounded me gradually lifted. But the absence of pain in my head just made me more aware of the throbbing in my shoulder.

"I'll have to wait a while before I can do more," he said, his hands trembling as he moved them over my shoulder.

"It's definitely broken, but I can't fix it yet. I haven't got the energy, and neither does Dancia."

I couldn't respond. My eyes were already drooping shut.

Mr. Judan handed me a cup of water and a few pills. "This will help the pain," he said. "Cameron can walk you to your room."

"But everyone will see me," I said dully. I could still taste the bile in my mouth, and all I wanted was to curl up in bed and forget that this day had ever happened. "What will I tell them?"

"Accidents happen, Dancia. We were doing an activity in the woods. You slipped on a steep embankment and took a hard fall. You'll feel much better in the morning."

Great. More lies.

Cam got on one side of me, and Anna appeared at the other. I let them support my weight as we wobbled up the stairs and over to the Res.

The momentary goodwill that had existed between me and Anna dissolved bit by bit as we walked. She yanked on my arm a few times as we headed up the stairs, scowling whenever I winced or sighed at a fresh stab of pain.

"Serves you right," she finally muttered, when we reached the top floor of the Res.

Cam eased me onto my bed.

I leaned against the wall, not wanting to lie down with Anna there.

"Leave her alone, Anna," he said.

"I tried to give her the benefit of the doubt," Anna said, positioning herself beside the door with one hand on her hip. "I did what you asked. But this is too much. We could have died out there, Cam. When are you going to see the truth?"

I squinted at her. "If you're suggesting I let us drive into a ditch on purpose, you're insane. I tried to stop the car, but I didn't have the energy. I've got a concussion and a broken collarbone, in case you haven't noticed."

"It was him," she said savagely. "You knew he was there, and you refused to do anything."

"She's been through a lot, Anna. Let's just leave her alone," Cam said. "She's probably right. It was because she was tired. That's why she couldn't help."

Probably right? I sat up in shock. Cam was looking back and forth between me and Anna, vaguely discomfited. He held out his hands apologetically. "You know how mental it all is. Sometimes it's hard to know why something happens. But I'm sure it was because you were too tired."

"When are you going to see the truth?" Anna asked. "She isn't rational about him, and today it almost got us all killed. Not to mention that she's probably been seeing him behind our backs. Who knows how much information she's been giving him? We can't trust her."

"Anna, stop," he warned, slicing the air with one hand.

"You know how close they were before he left," Anna pressed. "I bet you anything they're still in contact. She wasn't even surprised to see him in that car."

"They were friends," Cam said. "But that's over now. Dancia would have told me if it wasn't."

The nausea intensified, though now for an entirely different reason.

"They weren't just friends," Anna spat. "They made out in her backyard last semester. Did she tell you *that*?"

Cam froze. He turned slowly to look at me. "You and Jack?" he asked, shocked. "You told me you were just friends."

The beginnings of panic sent an adrenaline-laced tingle

through me. "It was one kiss," I said. "A long time ago, before you and I ever—"

"See?" Anna broke in triumphantly. "She's been lying to you all this time. What else is she lying about?"

I tried to shake my head, but the movement sent pain coursing through my head and neck. "I never lied. All I ever wanted from Jack was to be friends. The kiss was a mistake. It happened once and I pushed him away. That's why he got so mad at me last semester."

The more I said, more deeply the lines of doubt were etched in Cam's face. "What about now?" he asked, with a quick glance in Anna's direction. "Are you still in touch with him now?"

I didn't answer right away. Anna had her arms crossed over her chest, and she tapped her foot impatiently, waiting for my response. "Well?" she asked.

"I want her out of here," I said. "You've had your fun, Anna. Now, get out of my room."

Anna opened her mouth to protest, but Cam cut her off. He took her arm and guided her to the door. "Anna, she's right. This is between the two of us."

"Fine." She turned back to me, tossing her hair. "And by the way, I'm talking to Mr. Judan right now. I'm telling him everything."

"I see. Then I guess you're telling him how you've been spying on me all semester?" I demanded, trying to push myself a few inches up off the bed.

"I don't want to hear any more of this," Cam said. "Anna, leave. If anyone talks to Mr. Judan, it will be me. Got it?"

Anna scowled at him, but nodded. Then she spun on her heel and slammed the door shut behind her. Cam turned back to me. He hooked his thumbs under his arms. "I don't understand," he said. "What happened?"

Tears pooled in my eyes. "I didn't lie to you, Cam. I just didn't know how to tell you about it. Jack and I were best friends, and one day things got a little out of hand. But that was never what I wanted. All I ever wanted was you."

"I don't care about that. I just want to know the truth. Is he still calling you?" Cam asked tightly. "Is Anna right about that?"

I lowered my eyes. "I've talked to him a couple of times. He told me I should join the Irin. I told him I didn't want anything to do with them and hung up."

"Did he say anything else?"

I hesitated. "He told me about someone named Ethan Hannigan. He said someone in the Program killed Ethan and pretended it was a suicide to cover it up."

"And you believed him?"

"No!" I got to my feet. "Well, not entirely. But Cam, you've got to admit that the Watchers aren't above killing someone they think is dangerous."

He stepped back, bumping against the corner of my desk. "Wait. Are you telling me that all this time you've been listening to Jack saying these things, and *believing* him?"

"You know I would never be disloyal to the Program," I said. "But I wanted to know where Jack was and how he was doing. And then he started telling me about Ethan, and then after D.C. . . ." I trailed off, not wanting to put the final nail in the coffin I seemed to be making for myself.

Cam fixed me with a hard look. "What?"

I dropped my gaze. "He said those papers they found in the warehouse in D.C.—the maps of the White House and stuff—he said those papers were planted there. He said it was a setup."

Cam let his arms drop in disgust. "I saw the guns, Dancia. Did he tell you those were made up, too? And maybe the bodies were made of wax? Did he tell you how we faked the moon landing while we were at it?"

"No, Cam," I said, clenching my fists. "And it isn't that crazy to believe that Jack might be telling the truth. You even told me you felt wrong after D.C."

"What does that mean?" Cam asked. "Now you're on his side? And I'm the bad guy?"

"No!" I cried, feeling Cam slipping away from me. "This isn't about you. It's about this whole crazy place, and the Watchers, and the Governing Council. They lie all the time, Cam. Did you ever consider that they might be lying to you, too?"

We locked eyes for an endless moment. He turned away first, rubbing his hand over his face. "I just don't see why you didn't tell me the truth about Jack. The whole truth."

I no longer understood, either. It seemed like something that had happened a long time ago. "I didn't tell you that Jack and I had"—I forced myself to say the word—"*kissed*, because it didn't have anything to do with us. It was a mistake, and I told him that. And then he was gone, and you and I didn't talk about him."

Cam pushed Catherine's chair, shoving it roughly under her desk. A pencil rolled and fell onto the floor, and I watched it disappear under her bed. There would be hell to pay for that, when she noticed.

"And the phone calls?"

My head throbbed. I touched the lump on my forehead. "Anna scared me. She kept telling me she thought I was a traitor and shouldn't be in the Program. Trevor told me he was watching out for me, but I couldn't imagine he'd be sympathetic if he knew I was talking to Jack."

"If you didn't do anything wrong, you didn't have anything to be afraid of," Cam said.

I grabbed the edge of my dresser for support. "I didn't want you to have to choose between us."

"Because you thought I might take their side? You thought I might try to get you kicked out of the Program?" He looked astonished. "Dancia, I practically got *myself* kicked out so I could tell you the truth last semester. You should know by now how I feel about you."

"I know, and I do, but Anna—"

"Forget it." He threw up his hands in disgust. "This was never really about Anna. This is about you not trusting me, when I never doubted you for a minute."

I stiffened. "That isn't true. You've been hiding things from me all year."

"There's been a few things I haven't been able to tell you, because of the Program, but you ended up finding out about them anyway," he countered.

"Everything? You've told me everything about the Irin?"

He clenched his jaw. "I'm part of something bigger than us. I can't tell you everything we do."

"That's exactly what I mean. When it comes to the Program, I never know if I'm getting the truth from you or not."

"That isn't my choice. It's theirs."

"And you'd do anything they say?"

"Of course not," he scoffed.

"Are you sure? What if they told you I was bad, Cam?" I pressed. "Would you believe them? Would you still trust me after that?"

He crossed his arms over his chest. "When you told me I should stand aside and let Jack go free, I did. When you

230

wanted to talk about the Irin, I told you as much as I knew. I've done everything for you, Dancia. Even when it wasn't what they wanted."

"Wait." I held up my hand. "You didn't let Jack go for my benefit. You did it because you knew it was the right thing to do."

"No. It was the wrong thing to do," he said. "Today proves that beyond a doubt."

I closed my eyes. "The only thing today proves is that Jack has no loyalty to me. If I were working with the Irin, why would they be trying to kill me?"

"I never said you were working with them," he said. "But I don't see why that matters—I doubt Jack's in control of their little group. What they did today took things a step further than their usual antics. I wouldn't be surprised if Gregori himself had something to do with it."

My knees were ready to buckle, so I crossed over to my desk and sat on the corner of it, resting my hands on my knees and rocking a little as the nausea surged and then retreated. The tips of my nails were dark—with blood or dirt, I couldn't tell which. "You told me they were just a training cell. Why would Gregori be involved?"

"Apparently, things in Seattle have changed. Maybe because of what happened in D.C., or maybe because of Jack. I don't know. All I know is, before you came to Delcroix, things like this didn't happen. Now it seems like they're happening all the time."

"And that doesn't strike you as strange?" I asked. "It doesn't make you wonder what else is going on?"

Cam turned his back to me and walked to the other side of the room. "Of course it does," he said roughly. "But it doesn't make me want to call the Irin—or that guy

Thaddeus, and become his new best friend."

Silence surrounded us. My shoulder throbbed, and all I wanted to do was throw myself into his arms and cry out my fear and hurt.

"So, what happens now?" I asked. "Are you going to tell Mr. Judan everything I said?"

Cam stared out the window. "I can't. Not with everyone so upset. I'll tell him that Jack called and tried to get you to join them, but that's it."

"Thanks, I guess." I laced and unlaced my fingers. "And?"

"I need some time to think," he said.

"About me?"

"About everything."

"I'm sorry," I whispered, the tears building up in my throat.

"Me too."

Catherine came in just as Cam was walking out, wearing her usual starched white button-down shirt and navy skirt. She took one look at me and sighed, "Not again."

I hurriedly wiped the tears from my cheeks. "What?"

"You're sick again, aren't you?"

"No." I moved to my bed, careful not to jostle my shoulder. I kept taking deep breaths in an effort to keep myself from crying. It wasn't entirely working.

"What is it, then?"

"Nothing. I hurt my shoulder. No big deal."

"Hmm." She didn't move.

It occurred to me that I probably had a layer of dirt and blood on my face that would belie my words. I started to pull a towel out of my drawer, but I had to pause to steady myself against a new wave of dizziness. I could feel her staring at me. "What are you looking at? I'm going to take a shower, okay? I just stood up too fast."

She opened the drawer, pulled out an old pink towel, and handed it to me. "Did something happen between you and Cam?"

I didn't have the energy to lie. "Yeah."

She nibbled her bottom lip. "That sucks."

"Yeah."

She pulled out her chair and unzipped her backpack.

"Catherine, I bumped into your desk and knocked off a pencil. It rolled under your bed. I'm really sorry," I said hurriedly.

Amazingly enough, she didn't even flinch. "I'll get it later. So, are you breaking up?"

"I don't know. I guess. He said he wanted some time."

"That's never good," Catherine said.

It was hardly the nicest thing to say, but somehow the mere fact that she wasn't being mean sent me over the edge. The tears started flowing, and before I knew it, I was sobbing like a two-year-old.

Catherine's chair scraped on the floor and she pressed a box of tissues into my hand. "You want me to go find Esther?" she asked. "Or Hennie?"

Ever since spring break, things had been weird between me and Esther and Hennie. Esther spent hours on her appearance—straightening her hair, applying makeup, putting together the sexiest outfits she could get away with, then juggling the boys that fell at her feet as a result. Apparently, she couldn't rely entirely on her talent to keep her looks in place all day long. I'd tried to talk to her about it, but she hadn't wanted to be bothered. The only thing she wanted from me was information about Trevor, and when I wouldn't give her any, she'd get mad and stomp away.

Things weren't much better with Hennie, though she and I didn't fight. I just didn't see her very much, because she was spending all her time with Yashir. At least, I assumed she was. Every time I saw her, she was rushing somewhere, usually while listening to music, so I couldn't get her attention. The door to her room was always closed, and she never hung out in the cafeteria after dinner. Sometimes I had the feeling she was deliberately tuning everyone out, though I couldn't for the life of me figure out why.

"No, thanks." I continued to cry, blowing my nose every now and then until I had created a little mountain of Kleenex on the bed next to me.

"If it makes you feel any better, my parents are splitting up," Catherine said.

I turned my body so I could look at her without twisting my shoulder. "As in, they're getting a divorce?"

"Yeah. My dad hasn't been home since Christmas. I thought it was just because he was busy. They told me about it last night. My dad called in on the speakerphone."

"That sucks," I said.

She gave me a tiny smile. "They haven't really lived together for a long time. I suppose I had a fantasy that someday they'd remember how much they loved each other, and everything would work out. But it won't change my life. It's not like breaking up with the cutest guy in school."

A fresh wave of tears came over me, and she slapped her hand over her mouth. "Oh, I'm sorry, I didn't mean . . ."

I laughed weakly. "It's okay. He was always a little out of my league."

"I thought you two were perfect," she said. "Absolutely perfect."

This time, when the tears came, I just let them flow.

CHAPTER 26

OVER THE next week, as the weather warmed, everyone started taking lunch outside and playing Frisbee during free time. It was on one of those emerald-grass-and-cerulean-blue-sky days that Barrett walked me down to the basement of the Main Hall for my focus period. I hadn't spoken to Cam since our fight the week before. Each time we passed each other in the hall, we averted our eyes. Anna ignored me completely. Trevor was so cold I winced when I caught his eye.

Nothing about Delcroix felt right anymore. Without Hennie and Esther, I wandered around aimlessly between classes, alone and unsure of myself. Breaking up with Cam meant I had nothing to look forward to in the evening. No long walks. No stolen kisses. Nothing to get me from one hour to the next.

I found myself constantly looking over my shoulder, wondering whom I could trust and what hidden schemes were going on all around me. I contemplated calling Jack, but that just made me feel like a traitor. If I hadn't known it was futile, I would probably have begged Grandma to let me leave Delcroix and go to Danville High instead.

"Where are we going?" I asked Barrett.

"Art studio," Barrett replied.

I followed him into a familiar room, where I'd taken

ceramics last semester. The Main Hall was set into a hill, so there were long windows on one side looking out over the lawn, and there was lots of natural light.

In one corner of the room stood the pottery wheel. I still had bad memories of the misshapen pots and cups I'd thrown on that wheel. On the other side were easels, several with paintings on them: a landscape on one, a bowl of fruit on another.

"I felt like painting today." Barrett tied a paint-splattered apron around his skinny waist and pointed to an easel with a blank sheet of paper on it. "That's yours over there."

"Mine?" I repeated as he handed me a matching apron. "I'm not very good at art, you know."

"Doesn't matter. Sometimes the only way to relax is to occupy your mind with something completely different."

"Great." I looked sourly at the blank page. "Something new for me to screw up."

Barrett didn't respond. He took a plastic paint tray and filled it with a variety of colors, then began brushing with broad strokes upon the empty canvas. First bright blue, then swirls of yellow.

My shoulder still throbbed when I tried to lift my arm, so I set my tray of paints on the table and picked up a brush, then turned to the easel. Moving awkwardly between the table and the easel, I dabbed red and orange petals on my paper.

Barrett hitched up his faded canvas shorts, which threatened to fall off below his apron, and smiled. "Flowers? You must be in a better mood than you look."

"Ha." I painted a black cloud in the sky. "That's more like it."

"You want to tell me about it?"

I trailed a line of blue paint around my flowers. It actually looked kind of pretty, in a kindergarten sort of way. I pulled that sheet off and decided to start over without the black cloud. "There's not much to tell," I said. "I basically ruined my life. I let everyone down, almost got us all killed, then managed to destroy the most important relationship I'll probably ever have."

"Slow down," Barrett said. He sat down on a table, crossing one leg over the other. "Let's take this one thing at a time. How did you let everyone down?"

"You heard about Jack," I said. "And the van being run off the road."

"That doesn't mean you let anyone down. The way I heard it, you did your best to help but didn't have anything left to give."

"You're just saying that because you like me."

Barrett flashed a smile. "I do like you, that's true. But I'm not the only one who thinks that. You were hurt, D. You can't expect yourself to move a full-size car when you've got a concussion and a broken collarbone."

"They don't care," I said. A single curl kept falling into my face, and I brushed it back impatiently. "They just think that because it was Jack, I didn't even try."

"Who assumes that? Cam?"

I hesitated. "He probably thinks that now. Now that Anna told him about me and Jack, and he knows about the phone calls. . . ." I jabbed at the paper with my paintbrush. "It's hopeless."

"How about you tell me your side of things?" Barrett said softly. "It might help."

I hesitated for only a second before the words came pouring out. I told Barrett everything. I told him how close Jack and I had been last semester, and how I'd pushed him away after he kissed me. I told Barrett how much I missed Jack even now, and how I'd talked to him on the phone when I knew I should have hung up.

"Jack's your friend," Barrett said simply. "You couldn't turn him away. I understand."

"But he's one of the Irin," I said. "I can't be friends with him anymore."

"If I were you, I'd make that decision based on the person he is, not the group you think he's a part of."

I studied the empty page in front of me, Barrett's words ringing in my ears. I decided not to bother with form this time, instead mixing red and blue together on my palette. I pulled a thick brush from the pile of clean ones and began covering the paper with a deep, rich purple. "I just can't believe he was involved in something like turning those paintballs into rocks," I said. "He must have changed. The Jack I knew wouldn't do something like that."

"Are you sure about that?" Barrett asked.

Are you? Honestly, are you?

I set down my brush, defeated. "No, I'm not."

"Just because he wasn't like that when you knew him doesn't mean he isn't like that now. They prey on hate, Dancia, and incubate it. It's part of who they are."

"But why?" I said. "I've never understood why they hate us so much."

Barrett sighed. "They were all students here once—or at least, most of them were. I didn't recognize Thaddeus, but I knew a lot of the others."

I was astonished. "How's that possible?"

"You know they don't let everyone into the Program, right? Even some Level Three Talents aren't brought forward to Initiation."

"Of course. That's why they watch the first year. To figure out who they can bring in," I said.

"Right. So, imagine you've got a bunch of Level Three Talents who aren't brought into the Program. Where do you think they go?"

"They go . . . to regular schools?" I said tentatively. "Or stay at Delcroix but don't find out about the Program?"

"They don't want a bunch of Level Three Talents running around here if they aren't going to be trained. Too much potential for them to discover sensitive information. Mr. Judan finds the parents a new job or gets the kid a scholarship somewhere else, and they move away. Most of the time it works out fine, and they never know what could have been. But sometimes they do find out, and they don't go happily."

I pictured the tan Buick driving down my block, Watchers coming after Jack with guns at the ready. "Like Jack."

Barrett nodded. "Like Jack. The Irin search for people like him, who are alone and scared. We made them, Dancia. Before the schools and all the watching, the Irin were scattered, unorganized, nothing like the force they are now. That's why no one likes to talk about them or where they came from. It's like admitting you caused your own cancer. Everyone wants to sign up to eliminate them, but no one wants to say they created them."

I set down my brush and held my arm against my chest, resting my shoulder. "How do you know all this?"

"I had a friend like Jack—a clairvoyant named Sierra. She figured out about Delcroix when she was a freshman. And like Jack, they didn't trust her. She was . . . unstable. The visions had messed with her brain when she was a kid."

Struck by the sadness in his voice, I turned my full attention on him. "And they kicked her out?"

Barrett hopped off the table and walked over to the window. "Judan sent her back home. He told her parents she was sick and they couldn't care for her here. Her parents thought she was schizophrenic. They arranged for her to see counselors and get drugs, but all it did was make her worse. She killed herself last year."

"Oh, Barrett." I walked over to stand next to him, placing my hand on his arm. He swallowed, and the tendons in his neck tightened with emotion. "I'm so sorry," I said.

"Just before she died, she told me the Irin had contacted her. They told her joining up with them would mean leaving home, being on the run, and being watched. They were open about that. But they also told her if she joined them she'd have a chance to fight back against the ones who were truly dangerous. They kept calling her, sending people after her, and leaving her notes. They told her they were freedom fighters, beating back the Governing Council; but she had visions of them attacking schools and killing innocent students in the Program. It drove her crazy."

I pictured the Irin finding Jack somewhere, cold and alone, ready to hate Delcroix and everything it stood for. He would have believed whatever they told him.

"Barrett, who was Ethan Hannigan?"

He didn't seem surprised that I mentioned that name. "Ethan was a student at Delcroix."

"Did they kill him?"

He didn't blink, just stroked his chin and said steadily, "I don't know."

"You don't know, or you don't want to tell me?"

He shot me a hard look. "Ethan died under suspicious circumstances. I certainly wouldn't put it past the Program to have eliminated him. He had a strong talent for controlling the weather. He was also incredibly smart and ambitious, and they believed he'd do whatever he deemed necessary to advance his own interests. He was headed for something dangerous, as far as the Program was concerned."

"How do you know all this?" The errant curl fell back across my face. Red and blue paint covered my fingers, so this time I pushed it behind my ear with the back of my hand.

"I got some information from Sierra, and my father told me what he knew, which wasn't much."

"So what am I supposed to think about all of this?" I crossed the room to get to the window. The green lawn beckoned to me, and I imagined leaving Delcroix and all its secrets and mystery behind and running away through the woods. But what would I lose if I ran away? Friendship? Love? A chance to do something good, maybe even make up for some of the wrongs that had been done in the past?

"Damned if I know." Barrett ripped the page from his easel. "My father believes in the Council and the Program. He thinks he can make things better if he just keeps fighting."

"And you?" I shook my brush at him. "You'd better not tell me you're running away to join the Irin. That might send me over the edge." My smile faded when I saw his serious expression. "Oh, no, you're not, are you?"

"No, of course not."

I waited for him to elaborate. When he didn't, I said, "But . . . ?"

"Every time our Watchers kill one of their people, the Irin get madder and stronger. I'm just tired of it, that's all."

"So what are you going to do about it?"

"Me? Nothing. I'm just one guy, Dancia. There's nothing I can do."

"You're giving up?" I was astonished. "Barrett, you're a

strong Level Three. Your father is on the Council. If anyone can do something about it, it's you."

Barrett carefully dipped his brush into the red paint and started making long streaks on a new sheet of paper. "Tara and I are going to bum around for a while after graduation. It'll be fun."

"Fun? Barrett, they tried to kill us last week. You're going to walk away from that to have *fun*?"

He stiffened, defensive. "I don't need your criticism, D. No one appointed me savior of the world."

I had to take a deep breath, because the last thing I wanted to do was fight. I forced an apologetic smile. "I'm sorry. You're right. You'd just better make sure I have your phone number. I might need help levitating someone next year."

"I'll be traveling a lot," he said evasively. "I can't promise anything."

I gripped my paintbrush, carefully maintaining my composure. "So, you're ditching me. That's what this all comes to. After all we went through this year, you're just done. Done with the Program *and* with me."

"D., it's not like that."

"But you can't even give me a cell number," I said steadily.

"They're going to want to use you in the Program," he said. "I'm not sure I can be a part of that."

"I understand," I said. "You're running away. You don't like what the Council is doing, so you're taking your talent and all your power and running away."

"That's just it: I don't *want* to use my power for their purposes." He slammed his brush against the easel, leaving the rickety structure shaking. "I've got friends in Europe I've been meaning to visit. It's going to be a good year."

"Right. A vacation. I hope you enjoy it." I grabbed my

brushes and marched over to the sink, turning on the water and rinsing out the paint in the metal basin. Streaks of red, blue, and purple washed down the drain.

I felt Barrett's hand on my shoulder, but didn't turn around.

"I'm not a fighter," he said. "But you are. You're strong enough to be on your own, D. You don't need me anymore. And I hope you keep fighting. Whether I'm here or not."

I ran up the stairs after class, unable to look Barrett in the eye or give him a hug good-bye. I felt betrayed, and I couldn't pretend otherwise. I had always assumed he would be around for me, even when he wasn't at school anymore. It gave me hope when I contemplated life at Delcroix during the coming year. Now that little bit of hope had been taken away, too.

I passed Esther in the hall; she was flirting with some junior I barely knew and I didn't even bother to say hi. She caught up with me a moment later.

"Way to ignore me," she said, pulling out a compact and peering at herself in the tiny mirror as we walked.

"Who's that guy, Esther? I thought you were with David."

"That's Alex. Isn't he cute? He stopped me in the hall to talk to me. He said he's been watching me all week." Her lips tightened. "And you know I'm not serious about David. We were just hanging out together."

I shook my head. "Whatever you say."

"David and I are friends," Esther said. "It isn't like I'm cheating on anyone."

"Of course not," I said sarcastically.

"You're in a foul mood," she observed. "What happened? And where's Cam been lately? I haven't seen him around."

"I don't know. We're taking a break."

"What?" She snapped her mirror closed and grabbed my arm. "Are you serious? When did this happen?"

"A week ago."

Her mouth fell open. "You broke up with Cam a week ago and didn't tell me?"

"We're taking a break," I repeated. "We didn't break up. There's a difference. And how was I supposed to tell you? Every time I look for you you're wrapped around a different guy."

She pulled me to a stop. "It's been a month since spring break and I've dated two guys. You make it sound like I'm some kind of slut."

I immediately felt bad, but I was too upset to reverse myself completely. "Of course you're not a slut. It's just hard to get your attention these days."

Esther adjusted a barrette in her hair. "That's rich, coming from you. How many times have you blown me off this semester because you had to make time for Cam?"

I thrust my hands deep in my pockets and stared down at my old sneakers. It would be the perfect ending to my day if I managed to destroy my friendship with Esther. "I'm sorry. You're right. It's just been a rough week."

Her voice softened. "Can we talk about it?"

"I don't think so. Not right now."

"Then we'll just sit around and make fun of Catherine. How does that sound?"

I smiled reluctantly. "You know, she's actually been okay lately."

Esther stumbled back dramatically. "What? She's been *okay*? Did anything else in your life change in the past few days? Did you grow a third arm or become a saint or something?"

I laughed. "Her parents are splitting up and she's going through a hard time. I don't think she has a lot of other people she can talk to about it."

"Of course not," Esther said. "She's a freak. And she was mean to you for the first eight months of school, so don't expect me to forgive her so quickly."

For a minute, with her hands on her hips and a look of maternal irritation in her eyes, Esther resembled her old, sturdy self.

"I appreciate the loyalty. But seriously, you have to be nice."

"Hmph." She narrowed her eyes. "We'll see. She says one mean thing and I'm back to hating her."

"Deal."

We headed down the marble steps on the way to the Res and were immediately pelted by rain. Esther held her backpack over her head. I started running, and she followed a few paces behind, panting by the time we reached the door.

"You can't be out of breath from a two-hundred-yard run," I said.

"Yes, actually, I can. That's the most I've run since cross-country season ended, you know."

We laughed, and I realized how much I'd missed her. We walked up the stairs arm in arm, and for a moment, it almost made up for everything else in my life being so rotten.

"Can you believe there are only three more weeks of school?" Esther asked as she opened the door to her room.

I collapsed onto her bed. Unlike me, Esther had a fancy matching comforter and pillowcase. I buried myself in the soft material and blocked out all thoughts of Barrett. "I can't," I said. "And the camping trip is next week. Do you think there's any way I can get out of it? Tell them I'm allergic to the great outdoors or something?"

Each year, the freshmen took a four-day trip to the San Juan Islands. It was supposed to provide a little break before the final push to the end of school. We would drive out on Monday and return on Thursday. The team leaders from orientation and a few other juniors came along to lead groups on kayak trips and nature walks. Cam would be there. So would Anna and Trevor.

A few weeks ago, this had sounded like a delicious opportunity for Cam and me to sneak off into the woods together. Now it just sounded depressing. I couldn't help noticing that they were bringing all the juniors from the Program, probably as Watchers. A camping trip would be a great opportunity to stress people. They probably planned to dump us all into the frigid waters of Puget Sound to see how we reacted.

"So what's Alex like?" I asked. "Isn't he on the Model UN team with Hennie?"

"I don't know," Esther confessed. "I've barely talked to him. It was just flattering, you know, that he was interested in me."

"A lot of guys are interested, Esther." I indicated her new look. "Wasn't that the whole point of this?"

"I guess." She stared into the mirror beside the door and then pulled her makeup bag out of her backpack and began touching up the eyeliner at the corner of one eye. "But to tell you the truth, it's getting a little old. I have to focus all the time on my hair and clothes and trying to be cute and flirty. And these guys only got interested in me because of how I look—so what happens if I can't keep it up?"

I couldn't disagree, so I just nodded sympathetically.

Esther gave herself one more long look before turning back to me. "You think I need to give it all up, don't you?"

"Esther, I want you to be happy. If this makes you happy, then I'm all for it."

"Why do I hear the word *but* at the end of that statement?"

I hesitated, trying to think of a way to tell her what she needed to hear without betraying Delcroix. "I think you have a gift. You can become whoever you want. But that means you've got to fight to keep a hold of who *you* are. I think if you aren't careful, the real Esther could get lost under all of this."

Esther nodded sadly. "I hate to say it, but I think you're right. At least now that I've spent all this time being someone else, I have learned one thing about the real Esther: she is *not* a boy magnet."

"She's something much better than a boy magnet," I said softly. "She's my best friend."

Esther sat beside me in her desk chair. A framed picture of her and her mother stood on the windowsill beside her; it showed the old Esther with her round face, frizzy black hair, and huge smile. "Thanks," she said, "but enough about me. Tell me what happened with Cam. Last I heard, he showed up at your house after spring break and made out with you in a car for an hour."

"It wasn't an hour," I said. "And it's hard to explain. We had a fight."

"About what?"

I struggled, as I always did, when trying to figure how much I could say to Esther. "I never told Cam about how Jack and I had hooked up last semester. Somehow, Anna found out and told him. He was pretty upset."

"But you two weren't even going out then. What was he so mad about?"

"He was hurt because I hadn't trusted him enough to tell

him. He said he'd always trusted me and it wasn't right that I didn't do the same."

Esther patted my shoulder gently. As we talked, some of the curl returned to her hair, which she took such pains to straighten these days, and something in her face softened. It was hard to describe exactly what changed, but it made me feel much more comfortable. "I can sort of see his point. Why didn't you tell him?"

"Because of stupid Anna." I pounded my fist into Esther's flowered pillow, imagining it was Anna's face. "She got me all nervous and worried that Cam would be upset if he found out. I should have known better than to listen to her."

Of course, I couldn't explain the significance of Jack—or my fear of being thrown out of the Program. But I didn't have to, because at that moment Hennie came in and threw herself down at my side, her long braid falling over her shoulder and catching me on the chin.

"What happened?" she demanded. "I had a weird feeling. . . . Are you okay?"

"Dancia and Cam broke up," Esther announced.

"No!" Hennie turned to me, shocked. "I can't believe it. He's so into you—and you're crazy about him. How could you possibly break up?"

"He found out that Jack and Dancia were more than just friends last semester," Esther said, before I could respond.

"It was just one kiss," I said, flipping onto my back and throwing the pillow over my face. "Why does everyone want to make it into something more?"

"It wasn't just a kiss for Jack," Hennie said. "He was in love with you."

Esther rubbed her forehead thoughtfully. "Come to think of it, every boy you hang out with seems to end up that way.

You'd better stay away from Alex. And David."

I moved the pillow so she could see me roll my eyes. "Esther, you have a very active imagination."

Hennie arranged her legs under her. She ignored Esther and pinned her eyes on me. "When did it happen?"

"A week ago."

"I can't believe I missed this. And nothing in particular happened today? You're sure?"

I kept my mind focused on Cam. Things with Barrett were too complicated. I didn't want Hennie figuring out how upset I was at the thought that he wouldn't be around for me next year. "It happened on Wednesday. But I did just see him in the hall talking to Anna. Maybe that's what you felt."

Hennie stopped and thought a moment. "Wednesday? Oh, that's what that was! I was so depressed that day, and I had no idea what was going on. Why didn't you tell me?"

"I didn't want to talk about it. Besides, you've been busy with Yashir."

A pained look crossed her face. "No, I haven't been busy with him. I've been *avoiding* him."

"Avoiding Yashir? Why?"

"Because I have to break up with him," Hennie said miserably. "And I can't do it. I need your help. You've broken up with lots of guys, Esther. You've got to tell me how to do it."

Esther came over to the bed and climbed onto it, worming her way between the two of us. "Wait a minute," she said to Hennie, "you still like him, don't you?"

Hennie nodded sadly.

"And I know he still likes you," Esther said, "so I hardly think there's any reason to break up. Unless . . . wait, did your parents say you had to?"

"My parents don't even know about him," Hennie said.

"That's the whole problem. They think I'm going to marry Rashid. I know that sounds crazy to you, but my mom got married when she was sixteen, and our families are so close she thinks it's the perfect match. Now every time I see Yashir I can hear him thinking about how much he likes me and how worried he is that I'm going to break up with him for some boy my parents like. But then, over spring break, all I heard was how much my father liked Rashid, and how impressed his family would be that I'm going to Delcroix and doing so well at school." She pulled her knees against her chest. I'd never seen her so upset. "And my teachers are all thinking how important it is for me to focus on my talent. I don't even know what they mean by that, but I think there's some special program they're considering me for that they haven't even told my parents about. What if I missed my chance to be in it because I was too busy with Yashir?"

My spine began to tingle. "When you say you keep hearing Yashir and the others thinking these things, you don't mean literally, do you?"

Hennie dropped her forehead to her knees. "No," she said, her voice muffled. "It's just a figure of speech. You know how I can guess what people are thinking. It's just, lately it's been so obvious, sometimes I can practically hear their voices in my head. But I'm not crazy, I swear. I'm just overwhelmed. If I listen to music and focus on the songs, it goes away. I think I just need some space."

So they'd cracked Hennie, too. She had no idea that she truly *was* hearing voices in her head. Righteous anger welled up in me. It wasn't right to leave her tormented like this. There were probably techniques they could teach her to use to quiet the voices, but because of their insistence on watching, she wouldn't learn those for months.

"You definitely aren't crazy," I said. "But you are empathetic. Maybe too empathetic. You need to decide what you want—not what your parents want or what Yashir wants."

"I want to go out with him," Hennie said, "but my mom will be so disappointed, and when I spend too much time with him, I can't study as much, and—"

"Hennie!" Esther interrupted. "Did you even listen to what Dancia just said? We're talking about you, not your parents or your teachers."

"Right." Hennie's eyes shone with tears.

"Hey, I have a great idea," I said. "Why don't we forget all about boys for the next couple of weeks, or at least until we get back from the San Juans? My boyfriend just dumped me, Hennie needs some time away from it all, and Esther's had enough of boys to last a lifetime."

Esther nodded slowly. "You know, that's not such a bad idea. We're all going to be a mess anyway, because we can't shower while we're camping."

Hennie grabbed the pillow away from me and tossed it at Esther's head. "So you're agreeing to hang out with us because you're going to be smelly and unwashed? Thanks."

Esther giggled. "No, Dancia's right. We need some girl time. We're all on the verge of insanity, and when we get back from camping we're going to need to buckle down and study for exams. And then we'll be apart all summer. We might as well enjoy our time together while we have it."

Hennie leaned her head against my shoulder. "I don't know what I'd do without you guys."

"Me too," Esther said fervently.

I snuggled in and closed my eyes. "Me three."

Suddenly, things didn't look so bleak after all.

CHAPTER 27

PROJECT GIRL TIME got under way immediately. I think Esther was relieved to be back to her old self. She didn't have guys swarming around her, but she laughed a lot more, and she and I quickly fell back into our old routine of lounging on each other's bed during free time. I was pretty sure she still had a thing for Trevor—I caught her gazing at him longingly across the cafeteria, and when they bumped into each other in the halls, she could barely speak. But he was keeping a safe distance since I'd threatened him. He still stared at Esther a lot, but his watching was less noticeable now.

I don't think girl time was as fun for Hennie. She still looked sad and walked around with her earbuds in a lot when she wasn't with us. Yashir was always watching her with worried eyes. She hadn't broken up with him, but she had taken a page from Cam's book and told him she needed a break. I didn't know what to do for her. I just hoped the voices in her head were a little quieter now that she'd put some distance between herself and Yashir.

Then, at nine on Friday morning, hell froze over.

Catherine and I were studying in our room. Suddenly, she stomped over to my desk and put a form on top of my physics book. "I could probably request a single, but I figured you might not have anyone, if Esther and Hennie are rooming together."

The top of the form read, ROOMMATE REQUEST. We'd gotten them from our advisers earlier that week, but I'd shoved mine into my backpack without looking at it. Thinking about the following year still made me shiver.

"Seriously?" I asked. Catherine had the look on her face she usually reserved for telling me I'd left a sock on her side of the closet. "You *want* to room with me again?"

I guess it shouldn't have been a complete surprise. As far as I could tell, Catherine still believed I was well beneath her in terms of intelligence and overall value to society. But we had discovered we made decent roommates. We both liked to keep the room tidy, neither of us liked loud music, and we preferred to shower early and get to breakfast ahead of the crowds. We also discovered we liked talking to each other. She had a way of cutting through all the nonsense and emotion to strike right at the heart of an issue. And I gave her something she'd never really had before: sympathy and attention.

"Yeah, well, if you have other plans, it's fine." She snatched the paper back. "I'll get more done in a single anyway."

"No, wait," I responded. She looked oddly fragile in her white button-down shirt and navy skirt, gripping the sheet of paper so hard it wrinkled up at the edges. Somehow in the past few weeks, Catherine's veneer of toughness had worn away; at least it seemed that way to me. "I'd love to room together. As long as you quit messing up my desk and taking all my good pens."

I grinned. She stared at me for a moment and then slowly smiled back.

* * *

253

And as the days passed, with Hennie and Esther and Catherine beside me, I went from feeling like I was completely alone to finding myself surrounded by friends. I spent time running with Allie and hanging out after dinner with Hector and Alessandro. They couldn't solve all my problems, of course. I still had to resign myself to life without Cam. That hurt, but deep down I knew that breaking up—or taking a break, or whatever we were doing—was necessary. As long as we stayed together, my thoughts about Delcroix would always be colored by my fear of being disloyal to Cam. Being apart let me see things more clearly. There was something rotten in the Program. The Irin might have been dangerous, but if Jack were telling the truth, someone wanted to make them seem even worse—someone who became more powerful every time the Irin struck out against the Program and the Governing Council voted to increase the size of the Watcher army.

And I had a good idea who it was.

Grandma drove me to school on Monday morning. She didn't look well—her eyes were more watery than usual, and she had to keep dabbing them with a tissue. She hadn't bothered to put on her makeup and matching tracksuit, but she still insisted, as always, on getting out of the car to give me a hug good-bye.

"Is something wrong?" I asked, worried. "You aren't sick, are you?"

"No." She held my face between her hands and peered intently into my eyes. Then she hugged me tightly. "You're strong," she said against my chest. "You can handle this."

I drew back slightly. "Grandma, what on earth are you talking about? Of course I can handle this. It's a kayaking trip, not an expedition up Mount Everest."

She laughed and wiped her cheek. "I'm proud of you," she said. "Don't forget that."

Esther yelled to me from across the parking lot. I looked at her and then back at Grandma. "Are you sick? If there's something going on, I'll stay home. It's not a big deal."

Grandma pushed me away. "Of course I'm sick—I'm seventy-eight years old. But I'm not dying this week, and don't think you can get away with something just because I'm getting maudlin in my old age. Now, get on that bus."

She waddled back to the car in her sturdy orthopedic shoes and pulled out of the lot. I watched until her car disappeared. With a strange sense of foreboding, I threw my backpack over my shoulder and headed across the parking lot.

We took two buses out to Anacortes—the Silver Bullet and another yellow one they must have rented for the event. Hennie, Esther, and I sat in the back and amused ourselves by singing annoying songs like "Ninety-nine Bottles of Beer on the Wall," and throwing crackers at Hector and Alessandro. We were all dressed for camping. Esther had tied a bandanna over her hair, Hennie wore a pair of neatly pressed khaki shorts, and I had locked my curls down in a pair of pigtails. Catherine sat one row ahead, and to my amazement, occasionally joined in our obnoxiousness. Cam was on the other bus with Anna and Trevor. He'd nodded in acknowledgment when he saw me that morning, but that was it. I figured that was all I could hope for at this point.

At Anacortes they drove the buses onto the ferry that went to Lopez Island. The ferry looked like a cruise ship, or at least it did to me—tall, white, with big windows and decks wrapping around the sides. But unlike a cruise ship, the boat had a big open section where they packed the vehicles in bumper to bumper, and steep metal staircases connecting its four floors to the various observation decks. We couldn't see much of the takeoff, because they made us stay in the buses, but I felt a jolt and heard the boat's horn blast. After we were under way, we spilled out as quickly as we could. The first two decks were enclosed; most of our group went there. I climbed all the way up. It was drizzling and cold, but I'd never been so far from home before, and I wasn't going to miss it by sitting inside.

I hauled myself up the last few steps and took a deep breath of salty air when I got to the top. The water stretched flat and gray around us, islands rising like huge green turtles in the distance. I spent a few minutes trying to figure out where Mount Baker would have been visible if there weren't any clouds, and then started looking for whales. If Tara had been there, she could have sent a message to a nearby orca and gotten it to shake a flipper at me. It was hard to believe that in just a few weeks she and Barrett and all the other seniors would be gone.

I zipped up my parka and relaxed as the ferry hummed beneath me. There wasn't much opportunity for solitude at school, and it felt good to be alone for once. We passed a few fishing boats. I saw another ferry in the distance, but other than that, everything was quiet and still. A soft rain fell from the sky; I pulled up my hood.

"Beautiful, isn't it?"

My coat partly obscured my peripheral vision, but I didn't have to turn to know it was Cam. A familiar warmth stole into my stomach. "I've never seen anything like it."

I guess he'd been busy or something, because he hadn't

gotten a haircut in a while, and hair curled around the tops of his ears and fell over his eyes. He rested his forearms against the railing, and we stared out at the horizon, side by side.

"I like it when it rains," he said. "Less traffic out on the water."

"How cold is it?"

He laughed. "The Sound? Very. Why? You thinking about going for a swim?"

I shook my head, not wanting to seem foolish. "No! But it would be nice to say that I'd done it."

"You've never swum in the ocean?" he asked, amazed. "But you only live a few hours away. How's that possible?"

"The opportunity never came up," I said lightly.

Cam frowned. "I guess I didn't think about it. Your grandma doesn't like to drive far, and how else would you get there?"

"It's not a big deal. I'm here now."

We stood in silence.

"I've missed you," he said finally.

I held my breath when he covered my hand with his.

"Me too," I said. I pushed back my hood so I could look at him. Misty raindrops began to cover my hair and face. His touch was somehow both familiar and painfully new.

"I've been thinking a lot about what happened. About you and Jack and—"

"You were right to be upset," I interrupted. "I should have told you I'd talked to him."

"Hang on," he said gently. "Let me finish."

I smiled reluctantly and nodded for him to continue.

"I knew you and Jack were close, and the truth is that I

was always a little jealous of him. I hate to admit it, but part of the reason I let him go was because I thought, with him gone, I'd have a clearer shot at you."

I leaned back, shocked. I'd imagined a lot of reasons for why Cam might have let Jack go, but that one had never crossed my mind.

"Jack and I were just friends," I said firmly. "He wanted more, but I didn't."

"I guess I'm just going to have to trust you on that," Cam said. "And I do. But it's not easy. You're pretty amazing. I never know where my competition will come from next. It isn't surprising that Jack is still hoping you'll change your mind about him."

I lowered my face in embarrassed pleasure. "What about all those things Anna said about me protecting him and working with the Irin? You don't think any of that is true, do you?"

"No," Cam said. "I never did. But I admit I was surprised to hear you'd been in contact with him. To be honest, I can't stop thinking about the things you said. I know I should tell Mr. Judan about it, but . . ."

"But what?" I prompted him.

"I'm worried," he admitted. "I don't know what he'd do if I told him."

"I don't know, either." I figured that was as much as I could say. The rest, Cam had to come to on his own.

He squinted at the horizon. "I should tell them, just in case there's any chance the information could help the Program. But if I told Mr. Judan and he thought you . . . If he told them you . . . Well, you know what I mean."

"I do." I twirled my watch, not wanting to meet his gaze. Part of me wanted to tell him everything I'd heard and thought about since we broke up, and part of me knew I had to keep this distance between us.

There was a heavy silence.

"If it makes you feel any better, I stopped talking to Jack after that paintball thing," I said. "I thought he'd come around if I waited long enough. But now I know that's not going to happen."

"I can't say I'm sorry."

"Yeah, I figured."

We shared a halfhearted smile.

Cam shifted his stance as the ferry hit some choppy waves. The wind got stronger as we moved farther into the channel, and the rain began to sting as it blew into my face. Cam laced his fingers through mine.

"Maybe we can forget about it for a little while," Cam said. "I know it doesn't solve anything, but for the next few days, can we pretend it didn't happen?"

"Pretend what didn't happen?" I asked softly. "Pretend I didn't call Jack? Or pretend I didn't question the Program?"

Cam looked out over the water, the muscles in his jaw working as he struggled with something deep inside. "I know we're different, and I know you don't always agree with what I do. But the way I feel about you—well, it's different than what I've felt for anyone before. I'm in love with you, Dancia. I can't let that go."

Heat surged through me, from my heart right down to the tips of my fingers. I closed my eyes and gripped him tightly with one hand. "But what do we do about all this?" I asked. "As much as I want to pretend nothing happened, it did. We can't make it go away."

"You're right. It's not perfect, and it's never going to be. But I'm not willing to let that destroy us." He touched my shoulders and turned me gently to face him. One finger found my chin, and he tipped my face up toward his. Rain touched my eyelids and rolled down my cheeks.

I felt the warmth of his breath and then his mouth touching mine. One kiss and I was lost.

"Hey, look at that," we heard someone shout a moment later from the deck below us. A group of people had gathered at the front of the boat, and they were staring and pointing at something a few hundred yards away.

We broke apart just in time to see a black fin slice through the choppy surf, and then we saw another. A white, misty spray shot into the water as the distinctive black-and-white bodies became visible. The orcas crested the water, dived deep, and then surfaced on the other side of the ferry. The crowd followed as a voice came over the ship's loudspeaker, announcing the sighting.

Cam pulled me back against him. "Now if that isn't a good omen, I don't know what is."

He bent to kiss me again, but I pushed him back and assumed a serious expression. "Wait. I have one final thing I need to tell you."

He poked me in the ribs. "Okay," he said, "but it better be quick."

I closed my eyes. After a dramatic pause I said, "I hate your music. It gives me a headache."

There was silence for a moment, and then Cam burst out laughing. "That's it? Sheesh, for a moment there you had me worried. I figured that out a couple of weeks ago. The last CD I gave you didn't burn right. When you didn't notice it only had two tracks on it, I figured you probably weren't loving the music."

"I was busted and I never knew it?" I smiled.

Cam tickled the side of my waist with his fingers. "Yeah. You're busted. And now you have some making up to do."

We stayed on the deck together until the ferry came within sight of the landing and they called us to get back on our buses. We shared a secret look and squeezed hands, and then Cam rejoined Trevor on his bus, and I walked down the aisle of mine to sit with Hennie and Esther.

Hennie, of course, figured it out immediately. "You're back together!" she squealed.

"*Shhh*," I said, putting my finger to my lips. "You don't have to announce it to everyone on the bus."

Catherine spun around in her seat. "Did you say Dancia and Cam got back together?" she asked Hennie.

I blushed. Hennie answered before I could stop her. "Of course. It was only a matter of time, you know."

Esther yanked me down onto the seat next to her. "Tell us," she commanded.

I was saved from responding by Mrs. Callias, who stood up at the front of the bus and began talking about logistics. Once we arrived at Odlin County Park, most of us would set up our tents, while a small group would go to meet the guys bringing us our kayaks. Mrs. Callias assigned several of the campsite groups to help make dinner; others were put on cleanup duty.

As soon as Mrs. Callias was finished, three pairs of eyes were trained expectantly on me. I shrugged. "We made up. What can I say?"

"Spare us the pretend nonchalance," Catherine drawled. "Let's hear the details. Did he apologize first, or did you?"

"It was mutual," I said.

"It's never perfectly mutual," Catherine said. "I bet it was Cam."

Hennie nodded. "She's right. He couldn't stand being away from you."

"Look, all I care about is that we're back together," I said.

"So . . . I guess that means no more Girl Time?" Esther asked mournfully.

"No, I'm still committed to Girl Time," I said.

"Don't be silly," Hennie said. "You'll want to spend time with Cam over the next four days."

"Okay," I admitted, "I will. But maybe we can do shifts? A little of both?"

Esther relaxed in her seat. "Whatever," she said. "Girl Time's overrated, anyway."

"No, it's not," Hennie said. "But it's okay, Dancia. You can spend time with all of us, even Cam."

"Just don't forget who your best friends are," Esther said, wagging a finger at me.

I grabbed both of their hands and giggled. "As if I could ever forget."

CHAPTER 28

I DISCOVERED the next morning that Cam was right—the water was cold. Very, very cold. I dipped my toes, half thinking I would go for a swim, but I changed my mind when they immediately turned red and tingly. I could say I'd waded in the Pacific. Surely that was good enough.

After breakfast we had a navigation and safety lesson. I found it all enormously confusing. The charts of the islands showed lots of different currents, and you had to plan your trip just right to ensure that you didn't end up stuck in a channel with a rip that would throw you against the rocks—or find yourself paddling against the tide in an exposed area.

Catherine loved it. It probably had something to do with her talent. She had the maps memorized in a matter of minutes and sat down with some of the juniors to plan the next day's trip to Jones Island.

They took us out for a paddle in the afternoon, and I instantly fell in love with kayaking. The movement was soothing and rhythmic, and the kayak slid through the water so gracefully I felt like I was flying. We didn't see any orcas, but we did come across a couple of harbor seals, who nodded their heads in greeting.

We had a campfire that evening, and though I longed to huddle close to Cam, I sat between Esther and Hennie while we sang stupid songs and were scared senseless by a couple of guys telling ghost stories. After that, Cam and I walked down the beach until we found a spot between some rocks where we could sit in relative privacy. We talked and laughed, watching the water lap up against the gray sand and the sun dip behind the islands off in the distance.

They blew a whistle at nine to signal that it was time for everyone to get into their tents. Reluctantly, we walked back to camp.

We packed everything up the next morning and kayaked over to Jones Island. They had planned on having us stay at Odlin for a second night, but the reservation had gotten mixed up and we wound up needing to move a day earlier. Mrs. Callias wandered around all morning muttering about incompetent people and how she'd have to change all of her plans because *someone* didn't do her job. We all found this enormously amusing.

Jones was small and uninhabited, with a network of trails that ran from our group site on the south side to a secluded harbor for larger boats on the north. Our campsite was up a steep bluff overlooking the water. We pulled our kayaks high above the waterline and hauled all our food up the hill so the marauding raccoons wouldn't get it. Mr. Judan had also rented a speedboat, which was moored to a buoy in the harbor in front of our camp. The boat was supposedly for emergencies, though I was pretty sure Mr. Judan rented it so he could stand on the deck and look dapper, rather than having to squeeze into a kayak.

In the afternoon, I took a hike with Catherine, Hennie,

and Esther, and looked at the handful of boats moored in the harbor on the south end. There were a few good-size sailboats, but Catherine said they were nothing compared to her dad's forty-five-footer. Unfortunately, he'd never taken her out in it; she'd just seen it in pictures.

I lay awake for an hour that night after everyone had gone to sleep. Cam and I had talked about my sneaking into his tent after lights-out, but I don't think either of us had been all that serious. Coed tenting had been specifically mentioned on the list of infractions that would get you sent home from the trip, and I had no desire to arouse Grandma's wrath.

Still, I couldn't resist what might have been my only opportunity to fall asleep in Cam's arms. I set my watch alarm for four thirty, so I could sneak back into my own tent before anyone woke up, then rolled my sleeping bag under my arm and tiptoed through the wet grass to his tent site. Cam had brought his own one-person backpacking tent, which he'd tucked under a tree at the far end of the camping area.

He was in his sleeping bag, breathing slowly and evenly, when I unzipped the door flap. Gray moonlight was alternately covered and revealed by fast-moving clouds, but I could see his face, relaxed and open, as beautiful as a picture. I cringed at the sound the zipper made, but no one seemed to hear, and I squeezed through as soon as the opening was wide enough.

Cam opened his eyes and blinked, and his lips curved into a slow smile as I lowered myself to the ground. "I can't believe you did it," he whispered.

I wasn't crazy enough to crawl into his sleeping bag— not only would I have been expelled if we'd been caught, but Grandma would have killed me if she'd ever found out.

Instead, I climbed into my own bag and spooned against him. "Remember, we're just sleeping," I said primly.

He laughed and pulled me closer. I rested my head on the side of his arm and sighed happily. Nothing had ever felt so right.

CHAPTER 29

EVEN THOUGH I had set the alarm, I slept fitfully, waking every half hour or so to glance at the time and make sure I wasn't about to be hauled out of the tent by my ear. It was just after four when I saw the tip of the knife sliding through the thin nylon sidewall of the tent.

I froze as I watched the silver blade rend the delicate fabric. Then, as the knife headed for the bottom of the tent, my brain and body sprang into action. With a gentle tug on the forces surrounding it, I took control of the knife, holding it in perfect stasis long enough to elbow Cam awake.

He blinked sleepily and opened his mouth in a huge yawn, then started to roll back over onto his side. Frantic, I kicked him and gestured toward the tent wall. He looked from my wild eyes to the spot at which I was pointing, and his face grew deadly serious. We pushed our way out of our sleeping bags just as a pair of hands pulled apart the tent and a familiar face peered inside.

I almost wished it had been Jack. At least then I'd have had some hope that the guy on the other side of that knife didn't want to slit my throat. But it was Thaddeus, the round-faced leader who had nearly beaten Cam to a pulp at Anna's Valentine's Day party.

He was wearing the same bandanna and the same contemptuous look. He moved to one side to reveal a small crowd outside the tent. Then his massive arms reached in, and I reacted the only way I knew how—by jerking him back with all the force I had. He flew out of the tent and disappeared into the darkness. Unfortunately, as I'd discovered when we were playing paintball, I couldn't control an object I couldn't see. He might have broken his neck falling through the trees, or landed unscathed. I had no way of knowing.

I had very little time to worry about it, though, because there were four of them waiting right behind him. I focused on the one closest to me. It was the girl who'd been spinning around like a crazed marionette at Anna's house. I squinted, ready to send her into space, but at the same moment, a different girl came flying at me, tackling me against the soft down of my sleeping bag.

It wasn't much of a fight. Despite my best intentions, I had never progressed much in my hand-to-hand fighting skills. Within seconds, the other girl had my face pressed into the ground and my body pinned between her legs. It was the ballerina, I realized. I'd have recognized her sharp elbows anywhere.

Cam and I had one advantage—the tent opening was narrow enough that only one of them could come at us at a time. So, before anyone else could enter the fight, Cam threw himself at the ballerina and they somersaulted over my head, spilling out of the tent. That was when I realized that there was an uncanny heaviness in the air, as if the noise around us had been flattened and suppressed. I tried to scream, but nothing came out. I felt the air moving through my mouth and lungs, but it was as if my voice had been swallowed before it could emerge.

I scrambled outside the tent, my neck aching from the angle at which I'd been pinned. It was strange to move and not hear anything: no rustling of the sleeping bag, no sound at all as we emerged from the tent. Even my breathing had been silenced.

Only the glow of the stars illuminated our remaining attackers. There might have been more hiding in the trees, but I could still see only four of them—the ballerina, the spinner, the acrobat who had broken Geneva's arm, and another guy I didn't recognize. Perhaps it was his talent that was keeping everything around us silent.

While Cam's attention was on the ballerina, the other three rushed toward me. I didn't flinch. Using every technique I had learned in the last few months, I pushed back against all of them. I imagined the earth sucking them down as if they weighed a thousand pounds, and they fell like dominoes, each one hard against the next.

I wanted to help Cam, but I had never tried to use my talent against someone who was so closely intertwined with another person. They kept embracing and separating, as if in a strange dance that alternately had one in the lead, then the other. The ballerina's elbows were flying, but she couldn't land a direct hit. Cam was too fast. But Cam hadn't managed to do any serious damage, either. I suppose it was a measure of his skill that he was even holding his own.

I kept up the pressure on the three I had knocked down. I thought I might have injured them when they fell, but I didn't want to take any chances. Yet I also couldn't ignore Cam. I wanted to believe he would prevail, but as far as I could tell, his opponent's talent had to do with fighting like hell but making it look graceful and beautiful. At Anna's house, she had broken Kari's ribs without sustaining any visible damage herself. Now I almost had the impression that she was holding back, waiting for the right moment to unload all her power on Cam.

I squared my shoulders and prepared for my next attack. I cleared my mind of every distraction, holding the three others tied to the ground as I concentrated on the ballerina. Perhaps if I was careful and pulled on her head or arm, that would distract her long enough for Cam to strike.

It seemed like a good plan, but before I could execute it, my body was thrown down hard, the wind knocked out of me. It was Thaddeus, his round cheeks and baby face twisted in a look of grim pleasure. Somehow, he had returned from wherever I had sent him.

And he'd brought friends.

Five more figures hulked in the dusk behind us. Hot fear made it impossible for me to catch my breath. I lost control of the threads with which I'd been holding the three bodies tied down.

It's all mental. . . . I could hear Mr. Fritz's voice. But what could I do against ten of them? I had learned to control my power, could even manipulate two or three objects at once, but I hadn't been prepared for this.

The first group of them ran at Cam, subduing him with their combined attack, though I think he did some damage in return. I struck at the outer circle of Irin, sending objects and bodies soaring. But there were too many for me to direct all of them, and they turned haphazardly, first rising, then falling abruptly to the ground. The silence around us broke, and it occurred to me that I must have gotten the one with the talent for quiet. But out of nowhere, a foot connected with my stomach, and pain ricocheted through me.

Across from me, I saw Cam's face explode in fury. He

struggled to get to me, knocking two bodies out of the way. Suddenly a hand tangled in my hair. Cam froze as Thaddeus yanked me to my feet.

"I suppose you don't want to see her hurt?" My captor spoke softly, with obvious pleasure.

Three more people descended on Cam. One of them twisted his arms behind his back. But this time he didn't fight. He just stood there, chest heaving.

"Let her go," he snarled.

"No. I think I'd like to keep her."

Cam's body jerked hard at the arms holding him in place. It was clear we'd both be in enormous trouble if I didn't do something fast. If I'd used my power on Thaddeus or his guards, we'd both have ended up getting seriously hurt, so as soon as I could clear my mind I did something new— something that had always terrified me. I propelled myself up into the air.

I must have startled Thaddeus as much as I'd startled myself, because he loosened his grip on my hair just long enough for me to rise beyond his reach. My stomach was already roiling from the blow I'd received, but the nausea intensified a hundredfold as I flew above the ground. Thaddeus watched me for just a few seconds before pointing to the guys holding Cam. "It only takes one order for your boyfriend to die," he said to me. "I'd *prefer* to kill him, in fact."

I flinched, and one of the guys holding Cam hauled off and punched him in the face. Another followed with a punch to the ribs. Cam slumped forward, limp.

"What do you want from me?" I cried.

"Just stay away from us. You interfere again, and he pays the price."

With that, Thaddeus picked up Cam and threw him over

271

his shoulder and started to run. He headed into the woods.

I waited until Thaddeus and his group turned on to the path to the harbor, and the only Irin combatants left in the clearing were not moving. Then I dropped from my spot ten feet in the air, jarring my back and twisting an ankle.

I stopped for a moment to catch my breath and shake out my foot, praying I'd be able to run on it. But I couldn't escape the panicked thoughts that had bombarded me the second I touched down.

They had Cam.

What would they do with him?

A dark figure emerged from behind a tree. I almost sobbed with relief when I saw him. Some part of me still believed that he could somehow make this right. "Jack? Jack, is that you?"

The bandanna across his forehead held the hair back from his face, and his steel gray eyes glinted in the predawn light. He looked different from the way I remembered. He'd always reminded me of a wolf—coiled energy in every inch of his lanky frame—but before, this had been tempered by his youth. Now the sense of vulnerability was gone. In the short time since I'd seen him, his shoulders had gotten broader, his chest thicker, his face harder. Jack had turned into a man.

When he spoke, the ice in his voice made me shiver. "You should have come with me."

"What are they going to do with him?" I whispered.

"Hard to say. They plan on using him for leverage. But you heard Thaddeus. He's pretty pissed. Cam killed one of his best friends, you know."

An image of a face I'd seen on TV flashed before me. The one that could make sounds and destroy eardrums. Charles Scholz.

I eased my weight onto my sore leg. It hurt, but seemed able to bear the pressure. "Cam didn't kill anyone," I said.

"He led them there. Just because he didn't pull the trigger doesn't mean he's not responsible."

"Is that why you messed with those paintballs? Because you were hoping he'd get killed?"

"It was a good way to do some damage without getting in the news."

I walked a few paces, subtly stretching my ankle. I had little hope of convincing Jack to help me, but I had to try. And I had to be prepared to run if I failed. "I could have *died*, Jack, if I hadn't had my goggles on. Alisha had serious internal injuries. Not to mention that you flipped our car over when you ran us off the road. It was only luck that kept you from killing someone. You don't have a problem with that?"

For a moment, the casual mask he'd been wearing slipped, and a shadow of regret passed over his features. "You weren't supposed to be there. They told me it was the juniors that did those games."

"I'm training with them. You have to know whatever you do can come back and hurt me. And even if it didn't, it's still wrong. You're playing with people's lives, Jack. Killing people. Innocent people."

He shrugged. "We're going to destroy the Program, one way or another. If we take out a few people along the way, so be it."

"That's it? All you're about now is hate?'

"I'm about getting even," Jack said. "I'm about getting my share. You talk about peace and doing good, but it's only for some people. Not me. It's never been for me."

I felt sick. The boy I knew had become something twisted and evil. Or maybe it had always been inside him, waiting for the right time to emerge. "You're going to have to kill me, then."

Jack reached toward me. "It doesn't have to be like this. You can still come with me. You'll be safe, I swear."

"I'm safe now. At least I should be." The cold and damp of the ground seeped into my bare feet, and I shivered.

Jack dropped his arm, his expression hardening. "None of you are safe. Your own people aren't even loyal. How do you think we knew where to find you?"

I gaped at him, scarcely able to process what he was saying. "What do you mean? You followed us here. It isn't like we were hiding."

He laughed. "Come on, Danny. You haven't figured it out yet? How we know when you're having a party or playing a stupid paintball game?"

My whole body quivered when I realized exactly what he meant. "Someone's been giving you information. Someone inside Delcroix." I thought I might fall to my knees with the weight of it.

"Apparently." Jack shrugged and smiled that little smile I suddenly hated with all my being. "We know better than to trust our informer. Half the time we're being set up, the other half we're given the keys to the castle. It's all a game. But it's a game we're determined to win."

"They let you in? During Initiation?"

"Let's just say the guard wasn't at his post."

"I'll kill him," I whispered. I pictured black hair with wings of white, and blue eyes that made you think of the sea. "I'll kill him myself."

"It's not worth it," Jack said. "There's probably a hundred more behind him. You can't trust them. Any of them."

"No."

"Come with me." Jack's voice was low, seductive. "They're moving me up, Danny. I'm going to meet with Gregori after we pull this off. He wants me to train with his people in D.C. He just needed me to prove that I'm ready."

Gregori. The D.C. cell. The last few pieces fell into place, and I knew Jack was lost.

Meanwhile, every minute we talked, Cam was being forcibly moved farther away.

"I'm sorry, Jack, but I am not coming with you. I'm with the Program. Forever."

I had a strange feeling Grandma was watching me, nodding calmly. I was ready to fight. It all seemed so simple now. *They* weren't the Program—not Mr. Judan, nor the Watchers, nor the Governing Council. *I* was the Program. Me, and Esther and Hennie, Cam and Trevor, Barrett and his dad. We were the Program, and I wasn't going to let some cancer inside it take over, any more than I was going to let the Irin and its hatred decide what the world would become.

Jack didn't hide his disappointment. "Then we're on opposite sides. I can't be responsible for what happens next."

"Jack, don't let them hurt Cam." I almost reached out to touch him, but his eyes were so dark with hatred I pulled back. "He let you go. He saved your life. Don't you remember?"

"Thad would have been happy killing him right from the start. I convinced him that Cam's worth more alive than dead. Consider that my repayment."

"You're better than this." I shook off the fear that washed over me at hearing his casual statement. "I know you are."

He shrugged. "Judan made me. It's time for him to live with the consequences."

He turned and ran after the rest of the Irin.

CHAPTER 30

IT TOOK me a moment to clear my head. Then I started after him. Jack must have been working out. He'd never been much of a runner before, but now he easily outpaced me. I struggled to stay close enough to hear him moving through the woods. I wished I could have kept flying, but the few seconds in the air had left me exhausted. Pushing someone else into space was hard enough; launching myself seemed to require twice that amount of energy. If I wanted to use my power to help save Cam, I couldn't waste any more strength trying to fly.

Luckily, the whole trail wasn't much more than half a mile long. It wound around the side of the island through madrona trees and stunted pines, then turned north and cut across to the harbor on the other side.

Pine needles and sticks poked the soles of my feet, but the short run sent welcome heat into my body. I stopped running when the trail allowed the first full view of the harbor. The sky had begun to lighten, and bands of pink clouds spread across the horizon. The trail was on top of a steep bluff, giving a bird's-eye view of the water below. I caught my breath when I saw four people step onto a dock that stretched into the sheltered cove. I couldn't see their faces, but one of them was carrying someone's limp body over his shoulder. They headed straight for a speedboat tied to the dock.

From my vantage point, I wasn't able to see the rest of the group, but I figured they'd been left on the shore. All I could think was that if Cam got on that boat, I'd never get him back.

Reaching out with my mind, I pushed on the back of the boat with all my strength. It tipped slightly, but not as much as I'd hoped. I had spent all my time practicing on people and branches; moving a boat was an entirely different kind of task.

I tried again, and this time water sloshed over the back deck. I heard one of the figures swear, and then Thaddeus's voice rang out. "She's going to swamp the engine. Find her and keep her away. Do whatever you have to do."

I threw all my power at the back end of that boat and watched it lurch like a toy in a bathtub. A foot of water rolled over the deck, and one of the lines holding the boat grew taut, then snapped. The boat rocked violently, and the wake sent a foot-high wave over the dock, knocking one of the Irin off his feet.

There were grunts and panting as people ran up the hill from the harbor. I didn't know what "do whatever you have to do" meant, but I didn't want to stick around long enough to find out. Praying I'd done enough damage to their boat at least to slow their progress, I headed back to camp.

The voices behind me faded as I ran. It was only a couple of minutes more before the path opened up into the clearing where we'd made camp. I stopped for a moment, realizing I had no idea whom to turn to next. I didn't trust any of the teachers—I knew they were all scared of Mr. Judan, and I no longer had any idea whether he'd want to save Cam or not.

There was only one person who I believed would be absolutely loyal to Cam. I headed for Trevor's tent, shaking it by the poles until I heard a muffled exclamation.

"Get up," I whispered intently. "It's the Irin. Jack's with them. They've got Cam."

The tent was unzipped a moment later, and Trevor's face emerged, with no hint that he'd been awakened from a deep sleep. "When? Where?"

"Just now. They have a boat on the other side of the island, in the harbor. Some of them may be following me."

"You left them in their boat?"

"I swamped it as best I could. I don't know if it's out of commission, but they'll at least have to bail it out a little."

Trevor nodded sharply. "How many of them are there?"

"There were four on the dock," I said. "But there were more than that at Cam's tent. Maybe ten all together. I knocked out a few, but they may have recovered—"

Trevor was out of the tent and moving before I finished my sentence. We approached Mr. Judan's large gray tent, but before we could reach it, the ground underneath us shifted. I stumbled and tried to regain my balance, but fell to my knees when the earth moved again.

There was a loud rumble, like thunder, but deeper and farther away, almost like a groan coming from below the earth. Everything was still, and then the groan came again, louder this time, and the ground beneath me jolted violently. I landed flat on my stomach, gripping handfuls of grass. Around me I heard trees crack and fall. Fissures appeared in the ground, spreading like tiny fingers through the soil.

Screams began as trees started falling, and the shaking continued. Was it thirty seconds? A minute? I had no idea, but as soon as it stopped, I lurched unsteadily to my feet.

278

Did the Irin have the power to cause an earthquake?

It seemed hard to believe, but then again, nothing seemed impossible anymore. I scanned the area and was horrified to see two trees lying across some of our tents. Though all I wanted to do was run back to Cam, I paused long enough to lift the trees off the tents and lay them down elsewhere. It would raise questions, but I couldn't imagine leaving people trapped underneath.

Mr. Judan was out of his tent by the time we got there. "What happened?" he demanded. "Did you do this?"

My eyes widened. "No way!" I paused to take a breath. I was shaking; adrenaline and terror ran through me in equal measure. "It might have been the Irin. There's a group of them on the island. We fought, but they took Cam."

"Is he alive?"

The matter-of-fact way he said this gave me pause. I'd known it before, really, but now it all came together: Mr. Alterir's strange comments; the Irin being set up in D.C.; Jack's warning. I couldn't escape it anymore. The truth was staring right at me.

I swallowed the bile that rose in my throat and tried to bury the hatred deep enough that he wouldn't see it. "They knocked him out, but Jack said they were planning to keep him alive—to use him as leverage. I don't know what for, though."

"The books," Mr. Judan said. "They want our libraries. They want our knowledge and training. It's the only way they can become strong enough to confront us directly."

All around us, people were exiting their tents, silhouetted against the rising sun. There were cries for help from some of the flattened tents.

"Find Callias," Mr. Judan said, letting his gaze fall

between me and Trevor, on the rest of the camp. "Tell her to call the Council."

"And then we go after Cam?" I asked.

Mr. Judan shook his head. "The Council will have to take care of it. You two need to stay here."

I gritted my teeth. He was letting them have Cam. Just like that. "With all due respect, I think—"

"This isn't a question," he said, his voice resonant. "I'm not risking them getting you, too." He gestured toward the field, where the chaotic situation had only intensified since we'd been talking. "I've got other emergencies to deal with. No more arguments."

I stole a look at Trevor. His stony expression, with those startling light blue eyes, revealed nothing of his emotions. But he ran his hand hard over his scalp, something I'd seen him do only when he was frustrated or upset. Surely he was as concerned as I—Cam was his best friend, after all. Were we going to turn our backs on him?

I opened my mouth to protest; as I did, Trevor subtly shifted his weight, placing his toe on my instep. It was a small movement, and I thought it likely that Mr. Judan hadn't noticed.

I got the idea and snapped my mouth shut.

"Of course," Trevor said smoothly. "We'll talk to Mrs. Callias."

Mr. Judan slipped on his shoes and jogged over to the small tarp we'd set up over the group's gear.

Trevor and I turned in the opposite direction. As soon as we were out of earshot, he whispered, "Never argue with Judan. You'll always lose. And you'll end up believing he was right in the first place."

He darted ahead, and I hurried to catch up with him.

"Trevor, there's something I've got to tell you," I began.

He shook his head. "First, we find Mrs. Callias. Then we talk," he said.

Mrs. Callias was herding students into small groups and shouting orders to a few juniors nearby. Crowds had formed near the tents on which the trees had fallen. Cries could still be heard from inside. Everyone was white-faced, milling around nervously.

"Get out the emergency radio," she said to Molly. Her face was creased and her eyes puffy; her hair, usually tied at the back of her head in a tight bun, fell in long, unruly waves down her back.

Molly nodded and ran off. Then Mrs. Callias yelled at David, "You go check on the injured. Start with Claire. I need to know their condition." After this, she turned to Trevor. "Good timing. You can start counting off to make sure we haven't lost anyone."

"Do you mind walking with us for a minute?" Trevor asked. "We need to share something in private."

Mrs. Callias took note of his serious expression. "Must that happen right now?" she asked carefully.

Trevor nodded.

Mrs. Callias hugged a clipboard against her narrow chest and followed him to a spot a few feet away.

"You need to call the Council," I blurted out before Trevor could speak. "The Irin kidnapped Cam. They may be the ones who set off the earthquake, too. They're getting away right now!"

She stared at me blankly. "Kidnapped Cam?"

"Call the Council," I said impatiently. "About ten of them, maybe more, took Cam. They're in a boat headed out from

281

the harbor on the south side of the island. At least, I think they're headed out. I might have damaged their engine. I'm not sure."

"Does Mr. Judan know?"

"Yes. He said for you to call the Council."

She nodded, the fog slowly lifting from her. "Right. My cell doesn't work here. We'll have to use the emergency radio as soon as Molly comes back." She pinned us with a fierce look. "Don't you dare take off after him."

I didn't pause to wonder how she'd guessed our intentions. "But—"

"Look around," she said sternly. "We need you here. Not to mention that there could be a tidal wave headed our way. The last thing we want is for you to be following anyone out to sea."

Trevor applied his toe to my instep once again, and I tightened my jaw. This was not the way things were supposed to go.

"Mrs. Callias, can you tell me if anyone's seen Anna?" Trevor asked.

"One of the trees caught Claire in the head. Anna's with her."

Trevor stiffened. "Is it serious?"

"She's conscious. I sent David over to help."

"Dancia!"

I spun around to find Esther, Hennie, and Catherine running toward me. As much as their hair and figures were distinct from one another's, their faces were a remarkably similar mix of exhaustion and panic. "Thank goodness," I exclaimed. "You're all okay? No one hurt?"

They nodded, and we shared a brief hug.

Esther shot Trevor a quick sideways glance.

Hennie eyed me with concern, taking in the line of dirt around the hem of my pajama pants, and my flushed cheeks. "What about you? You don't seem right."

"Nope, not hurt. I'm fine," I assured her.

Someone yelled to Mrs. Callias. She tapped meaningfully on the back of the clipboard as she stared at Trevor and me, then hurried away.

I looked around the circle, wishing there were some way to ditch Trevor. But he remained there, looming next to me and gazing at the clearing with that wicked stare of his. I thought of what he'd said about Mr. Judan and took a deep breath. He wanted to save Cam, too. And we couldn't do it alone.

I mentally filed away my conclusion that Mr. Judan was working with the Irin, and turned to face my friends. "We need your help. It's an emergency."

Trevor's eyes widened and his jaw dropped. It was the first time I'd ever seen him register such a strong emotion. "Dancia, you aren't going to . . ."

I ignored him. "It might be dangerous."

"Of course. We'd do anything for you," Esther said.

Trevor gave me a warning look that any reasonable person would have heeded.

But right now I was not reasonable.

"I have something I need to tell you," I said. "It's complicated, and I don't have much time to explain. You'll just have to trust me."

"Dancia, *no*," Trevor commanded.

"It's the only way, Trevor. If you and I try to take off, they'll know. We're going to need the keys to the motorboat, and Mrs. Callias and Mr. Judan will be watching us like hawks."

"Of course it's going to be complicated," Trevor said, "but that doesn't mean you tell them."

"I'm telling them," I said stubbornly. "We need their help. You know it as well as I do."

Catherine cleared her throat. "Excuse me, but tell us *what*?"

"The truth about Delcroix."

That statement brought a round of confused and surprised looks. Hennie grabbed my arm, and our eyes met. Instantly, I found myself remembering that day in the forest when I made the branches rain down around Barrett and Mr. Anderson, and then I saw our fight with the Irin, and pictured myself sending people flying into space. Finally, in my mind's eye, I watched Thaddeus carry Cam away.

Hennie blanched. "I can't believe I didn't see it before," she whispered.

Trevor put a hand on her shoulder. "Hennie, don't jump to conclusions."

"Conclusions about what?" Esther demanded. "What are you talking about? Is Hennie hearing those voices in her head again?"

At any other time that remark might have been considered a joke, but this time, no one laughed.

"Wait!" Catherine turned to listen to a distinct tone blasting from the emergency radio.

It was a sound we'd all heard from a radio before: three short blasts of sound followed by one long note. Then came a tinny voice, a recording from the National Weather Service. We knew what was coming before they said it.

Tsunami.

CHAPTER 31

THEY ESTIMATED twenty minutes before the wave hit. The quake had occurred along the Tacoma Fault, just north of the city of Tacoma, and had a magnitude of 7.1. It wasn't the "big one" they always worried about along the Cascadia fault, but the wave could be ten feet high or more, which would be devastating to the low-lying areas on some of the islands.

Obviously, we couldn't evacuate. Our campsites were already on a bluff about thirty feet above the waterline, so the chances of a wave reaching the group were slim. But the island was small, and depending on the size of the wave, anything might happen. Our path was clear—we were to head for the highest point on the island, as quickly as possible.

"Trevor, we've got to do this now," I said, "before the teachers start sending us away. Claire's out of commission, at least until David gets to her, and they'll need Kari and Geneva to help the injured people. We're the only ones left."

Though the sun was up now, the air was still cold. I rubbed the goose bumps that marched along the pale skin of my forearms.

Esther gazed directly at Trevor. She was one hundred percent Esther again: frizzy hair, dark brown eyes, round face. "Please, let us help."

He caught her glance, and for just a minute, I thought I saw something in his eyes, some flash of emotion that he quickly disguised. "Go ahead, Dancia," he sighed. "But make it quick."

"You have to promise you'll never tell another soul," I said, remembering Cam's warning to me last semester.

Esther nodded first. "I'm in."

"You might as well tell me, too," Catherine said. "It isn't like I've got anything better to do."

I boiled the story down to a few lines. I told them Delcroix had a special program for students with extraordinary powers—and they were all candidates. I told Esther she had the power to shape-shift, Hennie had the power to read minds, and Catherine had some higher-level math power I couldn't even begin to understand.

I didn't mention Jack or try to explain about the Irin—that would have taken too long. I did tell them there were some bad guys who had kidnapped Cam. And we needed help to rescue him.

At first, this unbelievable story elicited only a few blinks, and then some nods of acceptance around the circle. Hennie grabbed Esther's hand and squeezed it. Esther began to cry. Catherine's jaw tightened. She wrapped her arms around her body and looked out at the horizon. They knew, deep in their hearts, that I was telling them the truth. They had always suspected they were different. Now they were sure.

I outlined my plan. It was clearly risky, since it involved having each of them use a Level Three Talent before any training, but I figured that this was essential to rescuing Cam.

First step: I needed Esther to shape-shift into *me*. That was how I would fool Mr. Judan and the other teachers into thinking I hadn't run off to find Cam. She'd have to stay toward the back of the crowd, but if she could even copy my hairstyle, I thought it would work. She'd have to imitate Trevor, too, if anyone looked for him, and maybe Anna, if we brought her with us.

Esther's eyes got bigger and bigger as I spoke. "I don't know," she said. "Maybe I can imitate you, but not Trevor."

I brushed aside her doubts. "You play guy teachers all the time. There's no reason you can't be Trevor."

"Esther, you're stronger and more powerful than you can imagine," Trevor said. "I know. I've been watching you. You just have to trust yourself."

There was a strange emotion in his voice. I looked at him with amazement. Was it possible that he *liked* Esther? I had always assumed he watched her because he had to—it had never occurred to me that he might actually have fallen for her.

They locked eyes.

Trevor grabbed her hand. "You can do it."

"I'll try." She closed her eyes. A moment later, her hair began to change, growing lighter and lighter, curling into a mass of blond ringlets around her head. Her features stayed pretty much the same, but her eyes widened, and her mouth curved slightly to mimic mine.

I gaped at her, hardly able to believe how closely she now resembled me.

"Wow. That's really—er—creepy," Catherine said. "Dancia's hair on Esther's body."

"You'll have to put on some baggy clothes and stay close to Hennie," Trevor said. "They'll be able to tell what's going on if they get a direct look. But that's pretty amazing."

Esther blushed at the praise. I realized her skin tone

had lightened, and her neck even sprouted a few blotches as we continued to stare at her, just like mine did when I got nervous.

Buoyed by our first success, I continued on. "Hennie, you've got to try to make contact with Cam, just like you did with me a few minutes ago. We need you to figure out where they're taking him."

"Picture him in your mind," Trevor instructed her. "Close your eyes if you need to. Remember everything you can about him. Dancia, what was he wearing?"

I thought for a moment. "Dark blue T-shirt and boxers."

We trained our stares on Hennie. Her face turned pink under the scrutiny, but she closed her eyes and took a deep breath. There was a long pause, and then she jumped. When she opened her eyes they looked dazed. "I never thought . . . Oh, my goodness!"

"What?" I demanded. "What is it?"

"It worked."

"Of course it worked," I said impatiently. "You've been doing it for months. You were just trying to pretend it wasn't happening. Now, tell us what you saw."

"He's watching them. They're still in the harbor. Something happened to the engine, and they had to fix it. But it's running now. They're getting ready to leave."

"They probably got water in the engine when Dancia swamped the boat," Trevor said. "At least we've got a chance of catching them."

"Is he okay?" I asked Hennie.

She shook her head. "I'm sorry. That's all I got. But he's conscious. That's got to be a good thing."

"They must be headed for Orcas," Trevor said. "It's less than a mile away and has an airport."

"Are you crazy?" Catherine asked. "There's a tsunami headed in our direction. A *tsunami*. Nobody's going anywhere."

"There's sixty of us and ten of them. They know they'll be dead if they stay here," Trevor said.

"They still won't go to Orcas," Catherine said. She planted herself in the middle of us, completely comfortable taking over the group. "People will be in a panic. The roads will be jammed and the airport even worse. If the quake cracked the runway, it will be unusable. I bet they head for open water. That way, the wave will pass under them."

"How do you know that?" I asked her.

"I read some geology books while I was home over spring break," she said. "This whole area is riddled with faults, so I thought I'd do a little research before our trip. It's quite interesting, on a mathematical level, how tidal waves work."

I rolled my eyes. I knew it was Catherine's talent, but still, it was hard to imagine getting excited about math.

"They got it started," Hennie suddenly exclaimed. "They're leaving the harbor."

"Can you tell which way they're going?" Trevor asked.

"The sun's on Cam's right side, and he's looking at the front of the boat," Hennie said. "So, I guess they're going north."

"If they're headed for open water, then we're following them," Trevor declared.

"There's something weird, though," Hennie said. "The water. It's receding. All along the coast."

"What?" We ran openmouthed to the edge of the bluff. Just as Hennie had said, water was slowly pulling away from the shore—it looked like a giant bathtub being drained—leaving behind dark brown sand littered with debris, giant rocks, and huge clumps of seaweed. Our boat, moored a good forty feet offshore, was still floating, but not by much.

"It's the wave," Catherine said softly. "It's coming."

"At least we won't have to swim far," Trevor said. "I'll go find Molly. She can get us the keys." I noticed that Trevor was still holding Esther's hand, and a pink blush had colored her cheeks. It was definitely disturbing to see him touching someone that looked surprisingly like me. "We'll meet down at the shore. Or rather, where the shore used to be."

I nodded, feeling a fresh wave of panic. Trevor stopped and pulled Esther close, whispering something in her ear, then let her go, disappearing into the crowd. Esther just stood there, blinking.

"How sweet," Hennie breathed.

I grimaced. Not that I didn't want Esther to be happy, but did it have to be with Trevor? I turned to Catherine, blocking the thought of the two of them together from my mind. "You're telling me we can't follow them because of the wave, but what would you do? Leave Cam out there to die?"

"Of course not," she said. Her eyes sparkled with intensity, and her usually dour face was so animated she actually looked pretty. I had the sudden realization that for someone as isolated as Catherine, life must not have a lot of moments like this, where she was part of a group with everyone working together. Of course she'd created a lot of her own problems by being so difficult, but that didn't mean I couldn't feel a little sorry for her. Or be happy that, for once, she was truly part of the team.

"Just stop and think a minute before you rush out after him," she continued. "They're starting to call everyone together, and you've got a clone standing next to you, so we'd better split up. Esther and Hennie, you head for the back of the group. Dancia, come with me. I've got charts in my tent."

Hennie and Esther and I gripped one another in a quick hug. I swallowed convulsively as it occurred to me that I might be saying good-bye to them for the last time.

Then I ran with Catherine to her tent, even as Mr. Judan and Mrs. Callias began herding a line of people into the woods away from shore. One injured girl rode piggyback on somebody's shoulders. Another limped, with help on either side.

A distant voice yelled, "No one goes back to their tents!"

Catherine ignored it. She pushed aside the fabric opening and knelt on the tent floor, rummaging around under her sleeping bag and withdrawing a heavy plastic bag that held a number of charts. "Your best hope is to go like hell toward British Columbia. Head north and a few degrees west, and shoot between Flattop and Waldron islands. If they're smart, they'll do the same. And avoid the spring passage. The currents will be unusually strong from the receding water. Keep to the west side of Jones."

I nodded gratefully. "Thanks, Catherine."

She pushed me away. "Just make sure you come back. I don't want to have to train another roommate."

I exited the tent and crawled around the back, out of sight of the rest of the group. I heard Catherine's voice receding in the distance as she called, "Dancia, is that you?"

She must have been talking to Esther. Praying that our plan would work, I darted out and headed for the beach.

The water looked so quiet and peaceful it was hard to believe a tsunami was forming. I waded out across the rocky bay toward our emergency motorboat. The radio back at camp continued to play that horrible sound—the emergency alert—and I cringed every time I heard it. I wondered what kind of panic was taking place on Lopez, where the land was pretty flat, and San Juan Island, where so many people lived near the beach. Surely they'd be okay. They had to be okay.

It couldn't have been more than two minutes later that Trevor and Anna appeared. Anna didn't look me in the eye. Her hair was a tangled mess, her gray T-shirt ripped at the hem. A dark streak ran across her arm. Blood, I assumed. Maybe Claire's.

Trevor flashed the keys. "Ready?" he asked.

"I always wanted to swim in the Pacific," I said.

Anna tore off her shoes and ran into the shallow water. Trevor and I flashed each other grim smiles and followed. The water was icy cold and sucked the breath from my lungs. I waded out until it reached my thighs, then swam awkwardly the rest of the way to the boat, holding the charts in one hand. We climbed on board, racked with shivers, panting as if we'd just run a mile. Trevor's T-shirt clung to his impressive six-pack, while Anna's slight form was outlined by her wet T-shirt. For once, I didn't waste time being jealous of her figure; all I cared about was the steely determination in her doelike eyes. If I wanted anyone by my side during a fight, it would be Anna.

Trevor started the boat. It had a pointy front and a small deck in back, with room for three or four people. An open bay beside the steering wheel must have led into a cabin below the front deck. I held out the bag with the maps to Trevor. "Catherine suggested we stay on the west side and shoot north."

"Sounds good," Trevor grunted.

He went slow until we entered deeper water, then slammed the boat up to top speed. I sat down on a cushioned seat in back and watched the shore, shocked to see so much ground exposed. I imagined the water being pulled in like a slingshot. How in the world would we survive when it came shooting back into the inlet?

In the quiet that followed, I found my head spinning. Thaddeus's kick to my stomach had left me badly bruised, and the sustained use of my talent had exhausted me to the core. I focused on my breathing and tried to collect my thoughts. I had to tell them. I had to tell everyone. But how? Who was going to be branded a traitor? The only evidence I had against him was Jack's word, and the deep conviction that I was right.

Anna went below and rummaged around. She came back on deck holding a wicked-looking knife. "At least we've got a weapon."

My eyes opened wide. Even Trevor looked nervous when Anna started tossing the knife lightly from one hand to the other.

"How's Claire?" I asked, needing to break the silence.

"She'll be okay. David's with her."

"She took a nasty bump on the head," Trevor added. "We're lucky David's around."

Anna sat in the seat next to Trevor and ran her finger lightly over the blade. "So, what exactly happened with the Irin?" she asked, meeting my eyes for the first time.

I described exactly how the fight had gone down, and Jack's appearance.

"Do you still care about him?" Anna asked quietly.

"The Jack I knew is gone," I said, defeated. "I don't know who killed him, but he's gone."

Anna stared over the edge of the boat, the wind ruffling her hair. "We've all lost friends along the way."

I stared at her, confused by the almost sympathetic tone.

We sat in silence, watching the water retreat and listening to the sirens wail from the island. Standing at the wheel, Trevor wore his usual frown, but beneath that stern look, I now knew, there was another side to him; I'd seen it myself when he caught my best friend in an unexpected embrace. Somehow, this gave me the strength to speak up.

"Have you two ever noticed that the Irin get stronger every time we increase the number of Watchers?"

"I think it's the other way around," Trevor said. "We increase the number of Watchers when the Irin get stronger."

I chose my words carefully. "What if someone inside the Program stood to benefit from the Irin getting stronger? What if that person got more powerful every time the Irin struck out against us?"

Anna turned sharply. "What are you saying, Dancia?"

Trevor frowned as he steered the boat, but didn't take his eyes off the water.

"We all know the truth about them, right?" I continued. "They're former Program students, or at least they've been associated with the Program in some way. That association makes them hate us, but then we do these things to make it worse. We pick off their people. We break up their cells. We refuse to let them study or build schools."

"Of course we do," Trevor said. "We can't let them get stronger."

"And I'm not saying we should." I bit my lip, trying to force my thoughts into coherence while the world around me kept spinning. "But what if it turned out they hadn't done some of the things we accused them of doing. Like going after the president. What if the Irin had nothing to do with it?"

Anna pushed her hair behind her ears. "Dancia, I'm too

tired to deal with mysteries right now. Just come out and say whatever it is you want to say."

I took a deep breath and then closed my eyes and spoke quickly. "I think there's a traitor on the Governing Council. I think he's trying to make the Irin worse, because then he gets more power, maybe enough to take over the whole Council someday. And I think he's sending the Irin information so they can attack us. I think he's working both sides."

When I opened my eyes, Anna and Trevor were staring at me, openmouthed.

"I can explain," I said weakly.

"It will have to wait," Trevor snapped, looking toward the horizon. "There's a boat up ahead. And some people on board I think we know."

CHAPTER 32

THEY WEREN'T MOVING. A cloud of grayish smoke hung over the back of their boat. Thaddeus stood by the wheel, swearing, while a girl crouched beside him, presumably working on the engine. Another figure was silhouetted against the light. I shuddered when I recognized the slender figure—it was the girl with the electric hands.

A person with broad shoulders and dark brown hair was barely visible at the back of the boat. Though I couldn't see the face, I knew it was Cam.

Trevor did a quick scan of the boat. "There's someone below. Three on top. Two have guns."

It took a second for them to hear us approaching, but when they did, Thaddeus called out a warning that brought the girl beside him—the ballerina—to her feet. He coolly turned to us, brandishing his gun. Anna and I hit the deck. Trevor dropped to his knees, but not fast enough to avoid a spray of plastic exploding from the windscreen.

I popped up just long enough to send Thaddeus's gun spinning into space. But at the same time, Jack's head emerged from the cabin below, and our boat came to a sudden stop. There was a crunching sound from the front; we were all thrown forward, then back. Anna's head smacked against the dashboard, while I grabbed frantically at a railing to keep myself from falling into the cabin below.

"What happened?" Anna asked when the boat came to rest. She had a long white mark on her forehead, which I imagined would be a healthy bruise in a few hours.

"Don't know," Trevor grunted. He rubbed his stomach where it had slammed into the wheel. Tiny red spots marred his forehead, which had been hit by flying bits of plastic. Carefully staying below the line of the deck, he revved the engine. "It was like we hit something."

Another series of shots came over our bow. I jumped up when I heard a pause and sent the ballerina's gun into the water. "It's Jack," I panted, dropping back down. "He must have made a wall of air."

Anna cursed. "How are we supposed to get through that? We can't very well swim to them."

"Remember, he hasn't been trained," Trevor said. "He won't have the skill to hold the wall very long."

I thought about all the exercises Barrett and Mr. Fritz had forced me to do, and how far I'd come in one semester. I hoped Trevor was right.

"You got rid of their guns," Anna said. "That helps."

"Dancia, when I count to three, you do whatever you can to distract Jack," Trevor said. "When his concentration breaks I'll move our boat next to theirs."

I took a deep breath. "Okay." The last time I'd used my talent this much I'd been unable to get out of bed for a week. And that had been without a kick to the stomach.

"I'll be ready to board," Anna said.

Trevor nodded. "Quickly, now. One . . . two . . . three!"

I didn't want Jack out in the air where he could see us, so I popped up, got a quick look at where he stood, and pushed him down, hearing a thud when his body hit the floor of the cabin below the deck. A second later, our boat shot forward. Anna climbed the silver rail that ran around the deck of the boat and balanced herself on top, the knife gripped firmly in her teeth. She launched herself across the water at Thaddeus and the ballerina as soon as Trevor cut the engine. Electricity Girl hung back a ways, her hands raised like a boxer's. I had no doubt what she was preparing to do.

Anna landed lightly on her feet. Thaddeus flew at her, seemingly unfazed when she sliced at his side with the knife. He drew back for only a second when her knife cut through his shirt, then lunged again to grab her wrist with one meaty hand. A line of red appeared across his ribs. Electricity Girl danced around Anna's back, trying to catch the edge of her shirt or arm.

Trevor leaped across the water just as the ballerina started swinging. There was little room for her to dance, which was probably a good thing, because Trevor was immediately able to land an uppercut to her chin, but then fell back when she caught him with a high kick to the head.

Once Thaddeus had Anna's wrist, he yanked her forward, smiling when she stumbled and almost fell into his arms. "Get her, Reva," he called to Electricity Girl.

The tiny black-haired girl didn't hesitate; she laid her hands on Anna's arm and squeezed. Knowing we had only five seconds, I focused on Reva, ignoring her screams as I lifted her into the air. But in doing so, I came to a painful realization. My stores of energy were wearing down. As a result, Reva bounced unevenly in the air. I pushed her over the edge of the boat and dropped her into the icy water, then swayed dizzily.

I'd have to start conserving my energy.

I shook my head and blinked to clear my vision. When I was steady again on my feet, I made my way to the deck rail, shrinking at what I saw there. Blood covered the white deck—hopefully Thaddeus's, though I couldn't be sure, because Anna's shirt and the side of her face were also spattered with red. The two were locked in battle: Anna on top, Thaddeus underneath, holding her wrists tight.

Trevor was in front of the hole leading to the lower cabin, trading punishing kicks with the ballerina. Red drops were smeared across his forehead, too, while a steady stream of blood dripped from the ballerina's nose. There was no sign of Jack; I assumed Trevor had knocked him back below deck, or that I'd injured him when I brought him down to the floor of the cabin.

My eyes landed on the broad-shouldered figure I'd been desperate to see.

Cam. His face was bruised, and one eye was swollen shut. A piece of silver tape covered his mouth, and his arms were tied to the railing behind his back. I balanced nervously on top of the silver railing for a second and then jumped across, managing to land directly between the fighting couples.

I wanted desperately to throw Thaddeus into the air, but he was holding on to Anna, and I had a feeling he'd have liked nothing more than to take her with him into the sea. Besides, I needed to save my strength. So I pinned his body to the ground, forcing him to lie still. From the corner of my eye I could see Trevor and the ballerina making their way on to the deck around the front of the boat, fighting at a steady pace.

Thaddeus didn't loosen his grip on Anna's wrists, but she must have felt it the instant his body became still, because she tucked in her body and landed a knee right in his groin.

His eyes grew wide and his face went white, and then his hands fell limply to the ground. Anna jerked free of his grasp and jumped lightly to her feet.

We looked at each other for one triumphant moment. "You get him over the side," Anna said. "I'll get Cam."

She took to the ropes with her knife, holding Cam while I nudged Thaddeus's body into the air above the deck. Moving up and down was the easiest step—side to side was much harder. I had him halfway over the edge when Jack reappeared, and suddenly Thaddeus's body wouldn't budge.

It took me a moment to figure out what had happened. It was as if I were running into a wall. I pulled him in every direction, but he seemed to be in a solid, invisible cage. I struggled to punch through it, but it moved like quicksilver, dissolving and re-forming as it went. Thaddeus bounced around inside, but never fell into the water. My energy was quickly depleted, and I finally let go, watching in amazement as he bumped down an invisible set of stairs, landing back on the deck with a thud.

"Clever, don't you think?" Jack said with satisfaction.

Behind me, I heard Cam jump up and down a few times as Anna freed him. I turned to look as he dived at Thaddeus, with a sound that could only be called a war cry.

Anna rushed at Jack, moving only a few feet forward before stumbling, as an invisible hand pushed her toward the edge of the boat. First, she lurched forward, and then she was thrust back, flailing with her arms. She landed on the seat where Cam had been, and began crawling up the back. I could hear her gasping for air, and realized that she was being squeezed to death.

"Let her go, Jack!" I cried.

"I'm sorry, Danny, but you're not in a position to demand that."

Beads of sweat popped up on my forehead as I used the last of my energy to pull Jack a few feet off the ground. "I'm not kidding. Let her go!"

Anna's hands clawed at the space on either side of her neck. Her lips were starting to turn blue.

"Or what?" Jack asked softly. "Will you kill me, too? Like Reva? Send me into the water and let me drown?"

I didn't want to consider the thought that I'd killed anyone, but I knew how cold the water was. Our kayak instructors had made a point of telling us that the waters of Puget Sound were about fifty degrees, so, if exposed, you only had ten minutes or so before hypothermia set in. Once it did, the chances of making it out alive were slim to none.

"Let us go," I said. "We'll get back on our boat, you can stay in yours." I gripped the deck railing tightly for support as I felt the energy draining from my muscles.

"I'm afraid I can't do that," Jack said. Anna moaned, her head lolling forward.

I looked at Jack with renewed fury. "This ends now, Jack." I was trembling with both anger and exhaustion. Carefully, I moved him out over the water, as far as I could.

Anna fell to the deck, and an invisible weight was dropped on my back. I collapsed onto the cool white fiberglass deck, the heavy weight immediately squeezing my lungs. I turned my head to one side and gasped for air. "Jack," I panted, "stop it."

"You should probably know that I can't swim," Jack called from the air above the water. "Are you sure you can live with yourself if you kill me?"

Blackness started to swirl around my eyes. I fought with myself for a few seconds, and then arrived at the only answer that made any sense. I closed my eyes and said a silent good-bye to the boy I'd once known.

Then I let him drop into the water with a splash.

It took Trevor and a recovering Anna working together to subdue the ballerina. Cam helped bind her to the deck rail, tying her hands and feet separately and taping her mouth shut. Thaddeus had sustained some serious head injuries from being slammed around by Jack and me and then facing Cam's wrath. He didn't need further restraints, but they tied him up anyway, just to be sure.

When the ship was finally quiet, Cam caught me in his arms, and we held each other in a long, trembling embrace. I shut out any thoughts of tsunamis, the Irin, and the boy I'd sent into the icy water, and pretended we were alone together somewhere beautiful, on a boat with blue skies above us and a sandy beach off in the distance.

"I thought they were going to kill you," he said hoarsely. "I didn't know what to do. I couldn't imagine . . ." He broke off, holding my head against his chest.

I sensed his slow, steady breathing and surrendered my whole being to that moment. I couldn't make my lips form words, but it didn't matter. I knew he understood exactly how I felt.

"I'll never let them hurt you again, do you hear?" Cam said fiercely. "Never again."

"She did a pretty good job defending herself," Trevor said drily. "Dancia, maybe you and I can partner up from here on out."

"No way. You've got Cam. She's my partner now," Anna

chimed in. "She set me up for an amazing shot to the crotch." She gestured toward Thaddeus. "That's something only a girl can do. You guys are too squeamish."

That set us all laughing. Everything hurt, so it was a painful sort of reaction, and it felt wrong to be doing it when the water that gently lapped at the sides of our boat had just swallowed up someone I knew. Someone I used to care about—maybe even loved. But we were all laughing together, so for a moment, I let the feeling of relief overwhelm me. When we paused for breath, Anna raised her hand. "Do you hear that?"

There was a sound of splashing a few feet in front of the boat. Anna peered over. "It's the girl you threw in the water, Dancia. Her electricity must be keeping her warm."

Cam shuddered. "What should we do with her?"

I hesitated for only a moment before I spoke. "We get her on the boat," I said firmly. "We can't leave her in the water."

"But the wave," Anna said. "It will be here soon."

"Then we have to move fast," I said. "I won't leave her in the water. Not if we've got a chance to save her."

Cam blinked. "What wave?"

I'd forgotten how much he had missed. "There was an earthquake," I said, unable to tear my eyes from the horizon. "You were unconscious. They predicted a tsunami. Which is why we're going to do this quickly," I said. "We'll throw Electricity Girl a rope and let her climb out."

No one mentioned the fact that there was no sign of Jack.

"And when we get back? What will we do with her then?" Anna asked.

"Mr. Judan will call the Governing Council," I said, "and he'll tell them we need someplace to put her—and her friends, too." Thaddeus lay sprawled on the deck, unconscious, and the ballerina was slumped on the floor, eyes half closed. "They aren't exactly shape-shifters or computer geniuses. There are prisons that can hold them."

I felt a powerful sense of certainty as I spoke. I wouldn't be party to more killing. I didn't care what Mr. Judan or anyone else in the Program thought. We would have to find a different way.

"It's worth a shot," Trevor said.

Cam rubbed his hand over his chin, the darkening shadow on it marking the time since we'd left Danville two days before. "You do tend to make up your own rules, don't you, Dancia?"

I wedged myself against his side, looking down so Cam and the others wouldn't see me blush.

All I wanted was to do something good. That's all. Maybe I did break the rules. Or maybe I just knew that I could make my own rules. In any case, I was finally realizing that that was just how it was going to be. I wasn't like everyone else. I never had been and never would be.

Trevor pulled a rescue buoy off the side of the boat. We watched him carefully lean over the edge preparing to throw it out. "If you try to shock us, we're throwing you back, understand?"

There was no response. Then came a weak "Just help me. I can't stay out here much longer."

Trevor threw the white float out as close to her as he could.

I stared at the horizon, unable to stop myself from searching for another head bobbing in the waves.

Suddenly, I noticed a line of white slowly approaching the boat.

I swallowed hard and pointed. "Is that . . . ?"

Anna ran to the side of the boat. "It's coming."

"Grab this." Trevor handed me the line to which Reva was now attached. She'd managed to grab the float and was looking at me with wide, terrified eyes. "I think I'd better go see if I can do anything about the engine," he said, and then he headed down.

From the distance there came a faint roar, sort of like the sound you'd hear if you put a big shell to your ear. The line of white was moving quickly, close enough for us to be able to see the sun glinting off the foaming water. It wasn't a pretty surfing wave. It was more like a little wall of water, formed from the dark, churning sea below.

Hurriedly, I pulled Reva's float toward us. When she was close to the side I reached over and grabbed her hand. It was ice cold, the flesh almost purple. Without hesitating, I pulled her up to the railing, and Anna and Cam helped her flop over it and onto the deck. None of us said much. We just stood staring at the approaching tide. The rushing sound was getting louder, the white wave less than a few miles away.

"Is there anything you can do?" Cam asked.

"I don't know," I said. "I don't think I have much left."

The wave didn't seem much taller than our boat. Maybe we could just ride over it, I thought.

Cam's arm came around my waist. I grabbed his hand and squeezed it. Reva sat on the deck, shivering. Something about her reminded me of Hennie. I didn't know why I couldn't hate her after all she'd done, but I just couldn't. It felt too important, somehow, to believe we could save her, maybe even bring her back to our side.

Anna was standing a few feet away. I poked Cam and

motioned toward her. He looked confused for a moment, but then nodded. Still holding me tight, he reached out a hand to Anna.

She took his hand with a small, grateful smile. "Thanks."

"Trevor," Cam called. "Forget that engine and get up here."

Trevor came up a few moments later. "It's no use," he said. "The engine's toast. Might as well face it head-on."

Anna grabbed his hand. "We're going down together, right?"

Trevor grinned and tugged us close together. "Of course. We're a team."

The wave smashed into the front of the boat like a solid moving mass. There was no pretty crest or arching backside to it. Just a churning, roaring mass of muddy water and white foam, flecked with dirt. The boat tipped up at a crazy angle. I felt us slipping and knew we would be pitched into that icy water if I didn't do something.

I felt Cam's hand on one side of me and Anna's on the other.

"You did the best you could," she said.

But I hadn't. Even as tears squeezed out of the corners of my eyes I realized I had more inside of me, and I wasn't ready to give up. Not when they were depending on me, counting on me to fight for them the way they'd fought for me. I pictured Anna throwing herself at Thaddeus, and Trevor fighting Ballerina Girl, and I knew I couldn't give up.

So I roused every last bit of energy I had. I imagined Mr. Fritz telling me that my exhaustion was all in my mind. And then I felt something inside me snap, and it was as if I'd unlocked a door I didn't know existed. I felt the power, red-hot, molten, spilling into me. The energy shot through me, and my whole body trembled. I focused my mind and lifted all of us—even the Irin—off the deck.

We floated there in the air for a few seconds. It felt like forever, but it was just long enough for the wave to pass under us and the boat to fall back into the water. It lurched to one side, then the other, barely remaining upright as water washed over the deck and out past the stern.

And then the wall of water was gone. As the boat shuddered and finally came to rest, I let go of every thread I'd been holding, and we collapsed onto the deck. Cam stood up first, untangling our limbs and gently lifting me to my feet. He then grabbed one side of me and Anna held the other. We stumbled to the back deck, where they lowered me onto a cushion.

"You did it," Anna said softly.

"Saved our lives," Trevor said.

"Your talent lit up the sky," Cam said, awe in his voice.

I watched as they scurried around the deck and went down to the cabin, gathering blankets, looking for food and water, and setting up the emergency radio. By the time we tuned in, the wave had already hit the surrounding islands. We were told later that it was a fifteen-foot surge. That was enough to cause some serious damage, but only to the low-lying areas.

Cam sat on the deck next to me and held my hand. I wanted to close my eyes and give in to unconsciousness, but there was one more thing I had to do.

"There's something I need to tell you," I croaked. "Something important."

CHAPTER 33

THEY MOVED the prisoners down into the cabin so they couldn't hear us talking. Anna and Trevor helped fill in the missing pieces of my story. Apparently, they'd been thinking about it even as we fought the Irin. I had to tell the parts about Jack, and how he'd informed me the Irin hadn't ever intended to kill the president, and that there was a traitor at Delcroix. Anna said this part made the most sense—she'd never understood how they got through the security at Initiation. Trevor said he hadn't understood why they'd wanted to go after the president.

No one seemed particularly surprised about Ethan Hannigan.

I told them how my conversation with Barrett's dad had changed everything for me. It was then that I had realized that Mr. Judan had enormous power as the head of the Watchers, and that the more dangerous the Irin became, the more his power grew. I still wondered if Mr. Alterir knew what Mr. Judan was doing, or if there were others, maybe at other schools or even on the Governing Council, who suspected. I didn't think Mr. Judan had created the Irin; they'd been around a lot longer than he had. But if I was right, he had used every tool at his disposal to make them stronger—to solidify their hatred and build up their organization, thereby cementing his own power.

There was no turning them back now. The Irin wanted the Program destroyed; Jack himself was evidence of that. But the black streak running through the Program, poisoning its true purpose, could be changed. That I believed.

Throughout it all, Cam stayed quiet. Our hands were connected. I watched the steady rise and fall of his chest as he breathed and wondered if he believed me.

"So, what does this mean?" he finally asked. "Are you through with the Program, Dancia? Is all this a lead-up to you telling me that you've had enough?"

I slid off the seat to sit next to him, a silver emergency blanket draped around my shoulders, and grabbed his other hand. "No," I said firmly. "Never. Don't you see? We're going to do something about it—you and me and Trevor and Anna . . ." I looked around for corroboration, noting with relief that they were both nodding in agreement. ". . . And everyone else we can find."

"But we'll have to be smart about it," Trevor said. "We aren't sure who else knows about this, and it would be way too easy for us to 'disappear' just like old Ethan Hannigan."

That was a sobering thought. I looked back at Cam. His battered and swollen face made his expression hard to read. "Are you"—I gulped—"are you with us?"

"He gave me a home," Cam said. "I can't forget that. But I'm not stupid. He said he needed someone he could trust, but in the end, he just wanted someone he could manipulate." Cam's deep brown eyes, so familiar and beloved, were filled with pain. I wished I could heal him with just my touch. "The problem is, I'm with him so much that I sometimes lose sight of what *I* believe, and what he's planted in my head."

He turned to face me. "That was the worst part about D.C. Something about it felt wrong, but this voice in my head kept telling me it was right.

"That's why I needed you so much when I got back, Dancia. You're my compass. When I'm with you, I can clear away his voice and see through to *my* heart." He sighed. "You're right about this. I hate to believe it, but I know you're right."

I laid my head against his shoulder. "We're going to come up with a plan to stop him," I said fiercely.

"And when he figures out what we're doing?" Cam asked. "What then?"

"We cross that bridge when we come to it," Anna said crisply, her voice eerily reminiscent of her mother's. With her T-shirt stained with blood, face sporting several impressive injuries—including a lengthy bruise across her forehead—and a determined set to her jaw, Anna looked like a true warrior. "Now, I, for one, want to know what happened to the rest of our friends on land. Can we put this conversation on hold while we call them?"

"Yes," I said firmly. Cam nodded, and Trevor fiddled with the dials on the radio. It crackled for a moment, and then we heard a voice on the other end.

"Who's there?" It was Mrs. Callias. She sounded exhausted, her voice hoarse.

Cam spoke into the receiver. "This is Cam, Mrs. Callias. And I've got Anna, Trevor, and Dancia with me."

"Cam?" For a moment there was silence. Then Mrs. Callias said softly, "So she managed to do it. Thank God." I heard a whoop go up in the background. I wasn't sure how Esther maneuvered herself to be by the radio, but I thought the cheer sounded like it came from her.

"Report your status, Cam." The voice on the other end turned smooth and deep. We all shuddered. It was Mr. Judan. "Is everyone all right? Remember, this line is not secure."

"Minor injuries," Cam said. "Potential hypothermia. We will need assistance when we come in."

"Assistance?" Mr. Judan repeated.

"We have some guests," Cam said, turning his back to us as if he didn't want us to witness some internal struggle buffeting him as he spoke to his mentor. I squeezed his arm, hoping he could feel my support.

"Are you in any danger?" Mr. Judan asked.

I met Anna's eyes, and from the tight positioning of her mouth, I knew I wasn't the only one who worried that the answer to that question was *yes*.

"No. They are incapacitated."

"All of them?"

Cam hesitated, glancing at me. "One will not be returning."

In all the excitement, I'd forgotten about Jack. I looked at the water now moving calmly around us and felt a deep sense of regret. Not for what I'd done, but for the way the Irin had changed him.

"I see," Mr. Judan said slowly.

"Can you tell us if everyone there is okay?" Anna asked. "Claire? Molly? David? What happened with the wave?"

"The wave passed well below us. Everyone here is safe. Reports are just coming in, but so far the damage is limited. No deaths, as of the last report we heard." The four of us shared a smile of relief. "But there may be more wave activity. Stay on the water until you get the signal that it's safe to return," Mr. Judan continued.

"We'll be waiting," Cam said.

"Excellent."

We hung up a few minutes later. Anna and Trevor managed to fix the boat's engine with some help from Reva. I lay resting on the cushions, with my head leaning against Cam. Everyone was quiet. I think we all feared what would happen when we got back on land, but I felt an odd sort of peace. From here on out, I would fight for the Program. It was part of me, and I was part of it.

Grandma had always said she wanted me to stand up for what I believed in. Well, I'd done it. And even though I could never tell her exactly what had happened, I could feel her smiling all the way from Danville, and I knew she was proud.

ACKNOWLEDGMENTS

I HAVE been lucky to work with a number of incredibly talented, hardworking people who deserve their own name on the cover of a book. Special thanks to Ari Lewin for her stewardship of this story and dedication to making Dancia shine; to Abby Ranger for stepping in and watching over Delcroix; to Laura Schreiber for supernaturally good editing; and to Hallie Patterson for her tireless work in getting me where I needed to be and making it all look easy. To Emily Sylvan Kim: I couldn't ask for a better agent and friend—you are my rock in this crazy world of publishing. To all the schools that have hosted me and trusted me to teach your students, I question your judgment, but I appreciate your support! Of course, the greatest hugs go to all the readers who e-mailed, Tweeted, texted, Facebooked, and, most astonishingly, came out to meet me—I adore you. Each and every one of you.

I am always indebted to Susan Seyfarth, who has never let me languish in the POD for long (though it is fun down there sometimes); and to my darling husband and resident knight in shining armor, who reads everything and makes my books so much better. Thanks also go to Nate Wood, tsunami expert from the USGS, who taught me about faults, tsunamis, and mudslides and can't wait for me to write about the Pacific Northwest's next natural disaster. I took some liberty with science, Nate, but the mistakes are all my own.

And finally, to Daphne—the first and best reader and fan. Thanks.